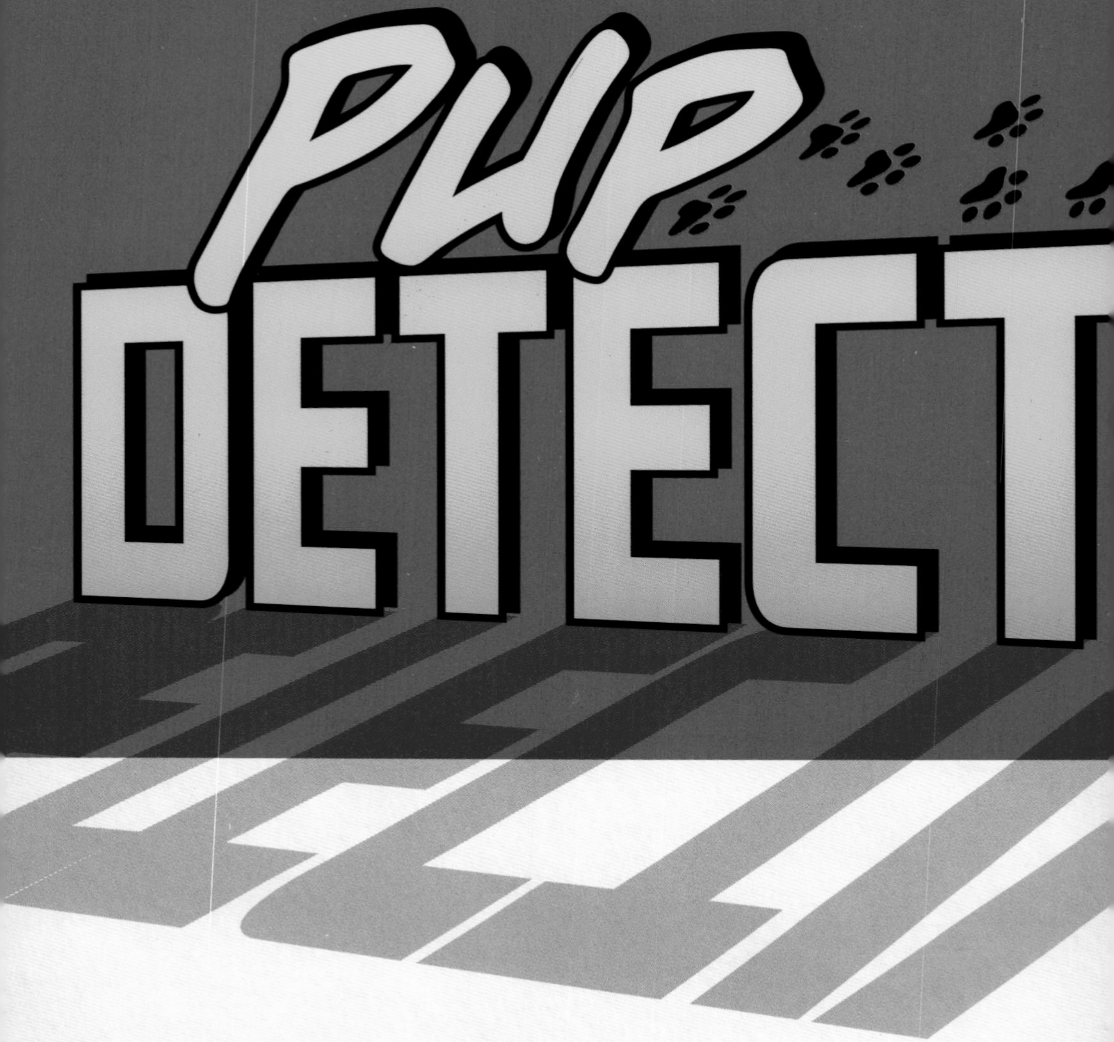
PUP
DETECT

IVES

THE FIRST CASE

Written by FELIX GUMPAW
Illustrated by WALMIR ARCHANJO
at GLASS HOUSE GRAPHICS

LITTLE SIMON
NEW YORK   LONDON   TORONTO   SYDNEY   NEW DELHI

LITTLE SIMON
AN IMPRINT OF SIMON & SCHUSTER CHILDREN'S PUBLISHING DIVISION
1230 AVENUE OF THE AMERICAS, NEW YORK, NEW YORK 10020
FIRST LITTLE SIMON EDITION FEBRUARY 2021
COPYRIGHT © 2021 BY SIMON & SCHUSTER, INC.
ALL RIGHTS RESERVED, INCLUDING THE RIGHT OF REPRODUCTION IN WHOLE OR IN PART IN ANY FORM. LITTLE SIMON IS A REGISTERED TRADEMARK OF SIMON & SCHUSTER, INC., AND ASSOCIATED COLOPHON IS A TRADEMARK OF SIMON & SCHUSTER, INC. FOR INFORMATION ABOUT SPECIAL DISCOUNTS FOR BULK PURCHASES, PLEASE CONTACT SIMON & SCHUSTER SPECIAL SALES AT 1-866-506-1949 OR BUSINESS@SIMONANDSCHUSTER.COM. ART AND COLOR BY WALMIR ARCHANJO, RAPHAEL KIRSCHNER, HUGO CARVALHO & JOÃO ZOD • COLORS BY WALMIR ARCHANJO & JOÃO ZOD • LETTERING BY MARCOS MASSAO INOUE • ART SERVICES BY GLASS HOUSE GRAPHICS • THE SIMON & SCHUSTER SPEAKERS BUREAU CAN BRING AUTHORS TO YOUR LIVE EVENT. FOR MORE INFORMATION OR TO BOOK AN EVENT CONTACT THE SIMON & SCHUSTER SPEAKERS BUREAU AT 1-866-248-3049 OR VISIT OUR WEBSITE AT WWW.SIMONSPEAKERS.COM.
DESIGNED BY NICHOLAS SCIACCA
MANUFACTURED IN CHINA 1120 SCP
10 9 8 7 6 5 4 3 2 1
LIBRARY OF CONGRESS CATALOGING-IN-PUBLICATION DATA
NAMES: GUMPAW, FELIX, AUTHOR. I GLASS HOUSE GRAPHICS, ILLUSTRATOR.
TITLE: THE FIRST CASE / BY FELIX GUMPAW ; ILLUSTRATED BY GLASS HOUSE GRAPHICS.
DESCRIPTION: FIRST LITTLE SIMON PAPERBACK EDITION. I NEW YORK : LITTLE SIMON, 2021. I SERIES: PUP DETECTIVES ; BOOK 1 I AUDIENCE: AGES 5-9 I AUDIENCE: GRADES 2-3 I SUMMARY: RIDER WOOFSON AND THE OTHER PUPPY DETECTIVES AT SCHOOL SET OUT TO NAB A CAFETERIA BANDIT. IDENTIFIERS: LCCN 2020024868 (PRINT) I LCCN 2020024869 (EBOOK) I ISBN 9781534474949 (PAPERBACK) I ISBN 9781534474956 (HARDCOVER) I ISBN 9781534474963 (EBOOK) SUBJECTS: LCSH: GRAPHIC NOVELS. I CYAC: GRAPHIC NOVELS. I MYSTERY AND DETECTIVE STORIES. I DOGS–FICTION. CLASSIFICATION: LCC PZ7.7.G858 FI 2021 (PRINT) I LCC PZ7.7.G858 (EBOOK) I DDC 741.5/973–DC23
LC RECORD AVAILABLE AT HTTPS://LCCN.LOC.GOV/2020024868
LC EBOOK RECORD AVAILABLE AT HTTPS://LCCN.LOC.GOV/2020024869

CONTENTS

CHAPTER 1
THIS IS PAWSTON ELEMENTARY SCHOOL 06

CHAPTER 2
LITTLE DID WE KNOW... 27

CHAPTER 3
OUR FIRST MYSTERY 38

CHAPTER 4
THE NEXT DAY... 52

CHAPTER 5
TO SOLVE THIS CASE 62

CHAPTER 6
IT'S BANANA FEVER! 75

CHAPTER 7
HE ESCAPED! 86

CHAPTER 8
THE LUNCHTIME BANDIT! 106

CHAPTER 9
ARE YOU GOING RIGHT TOWARD THEM? 118

CHAPTER 10
I KNEW THIS WOULD COME IN HANDY AGAIN! . . . 130

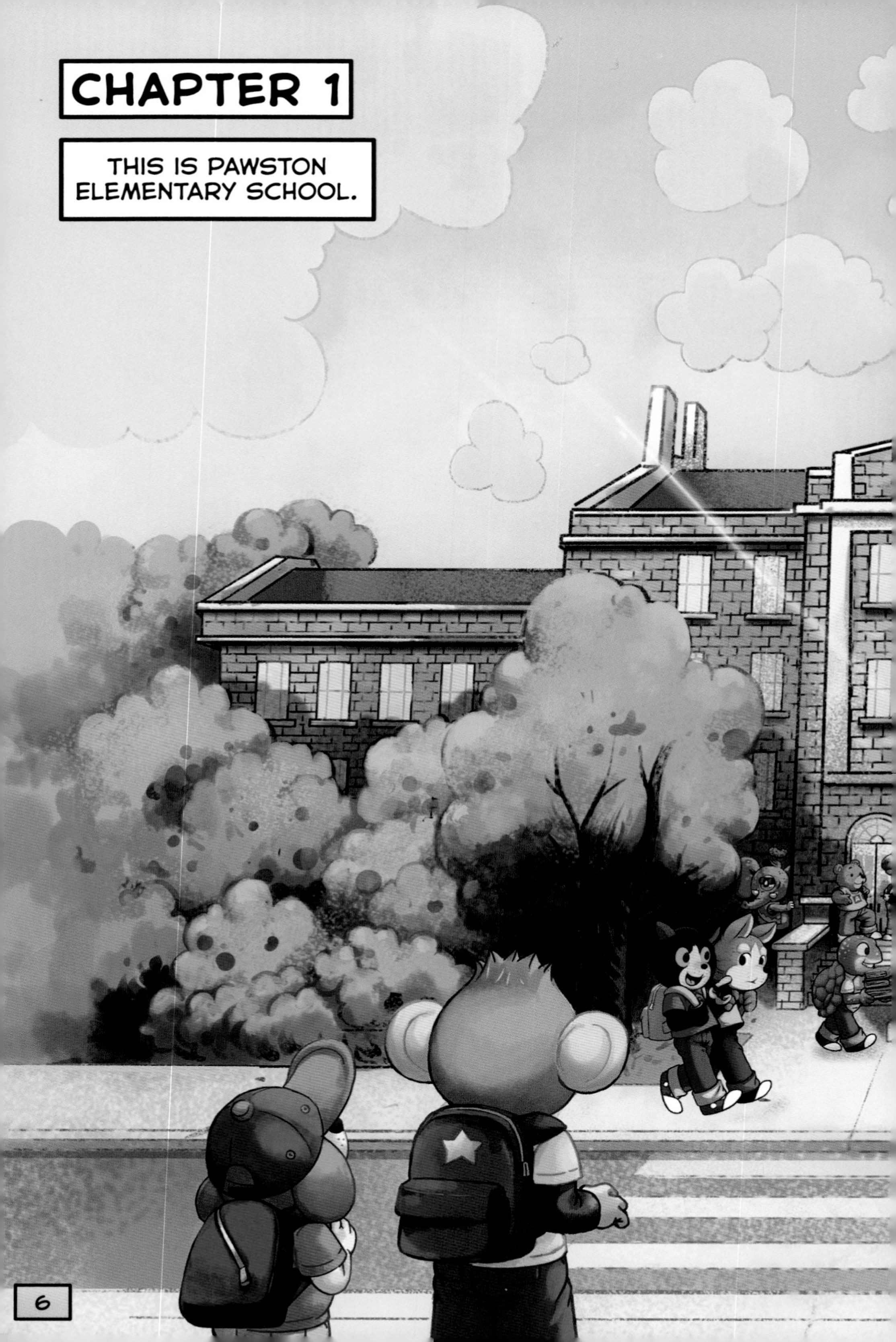
CHAPTER 1
THIS IS PAWSTON ELEMENTARY SCHOOL.

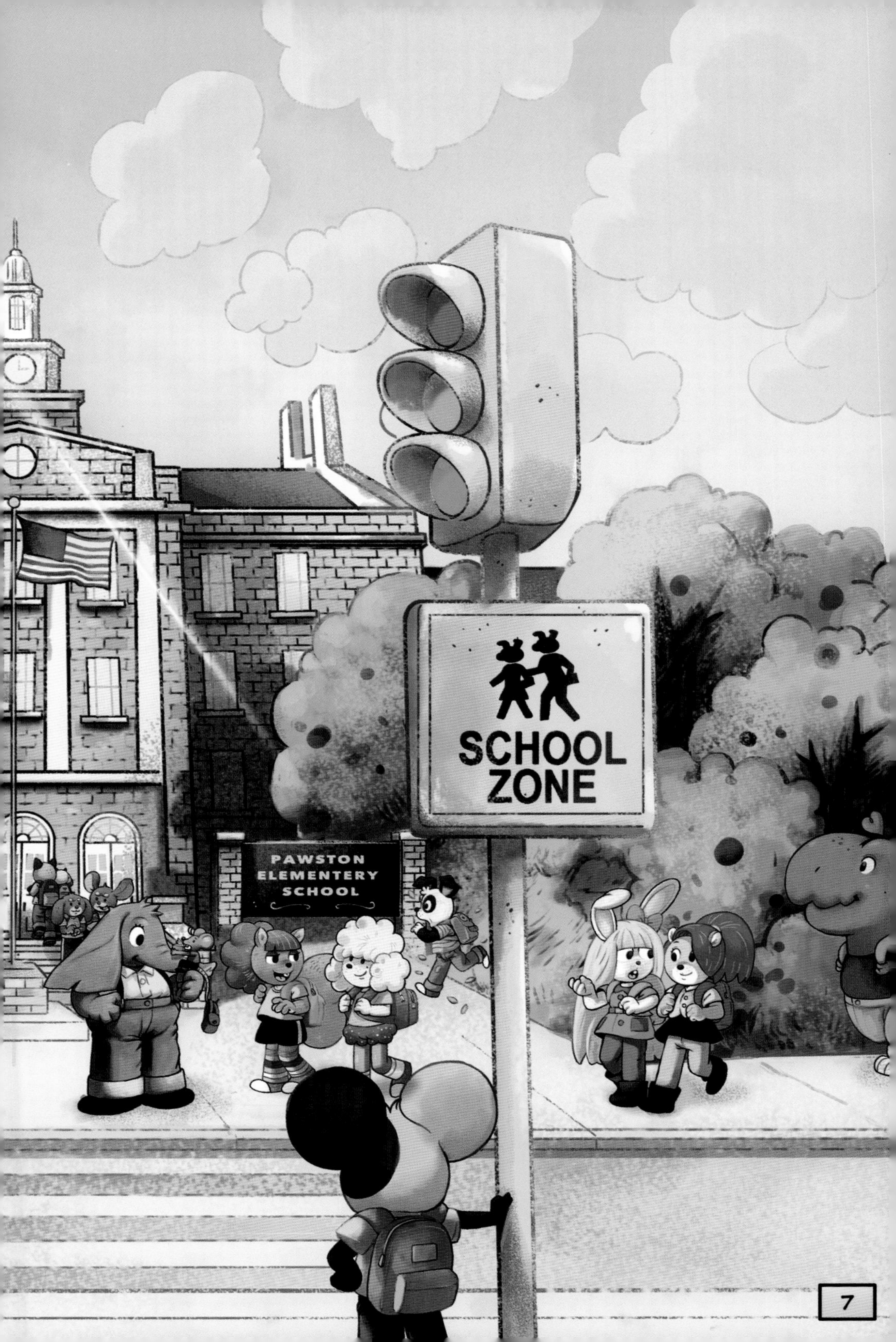
SCHOOL ZONE
PAWSTON ELEMENTERY SCHOOL

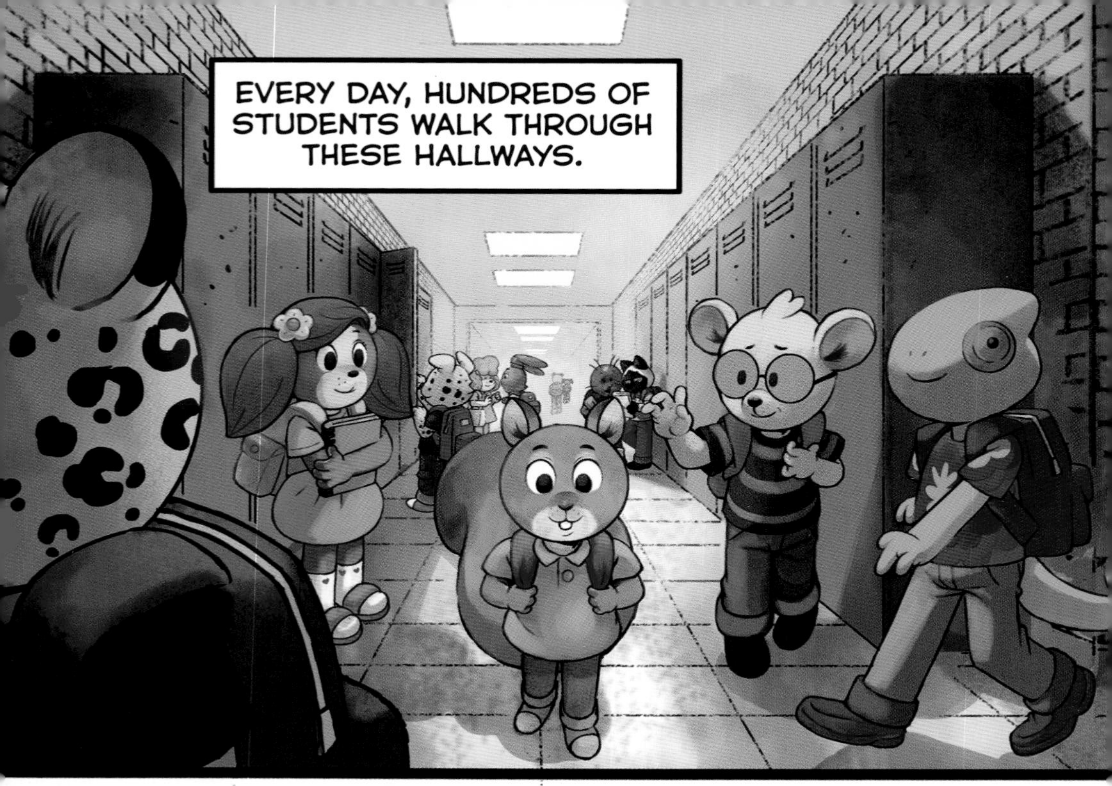
EVERY DAY, HUNDREDS OF STUDENTS WALK THROUGH THESE HALLWAYS.

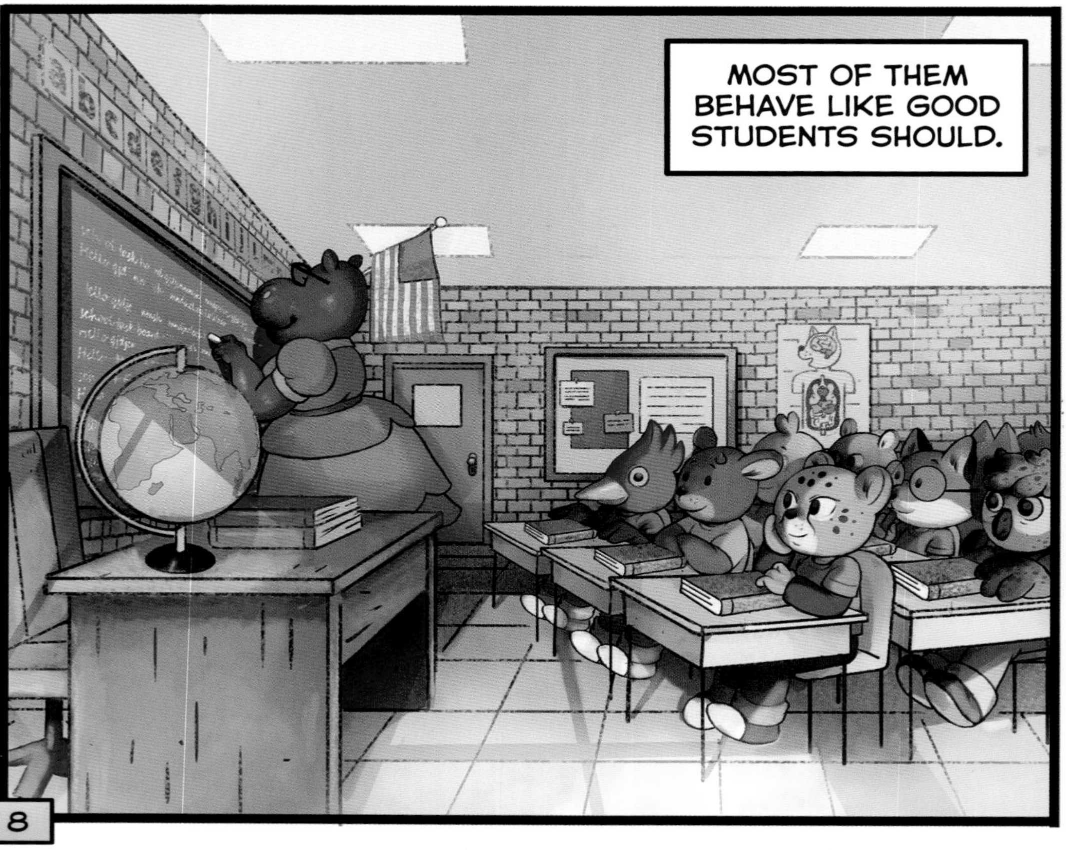
MOST OF THEM BEHAVE LIKE GOOD STUDENTS SHOULD.

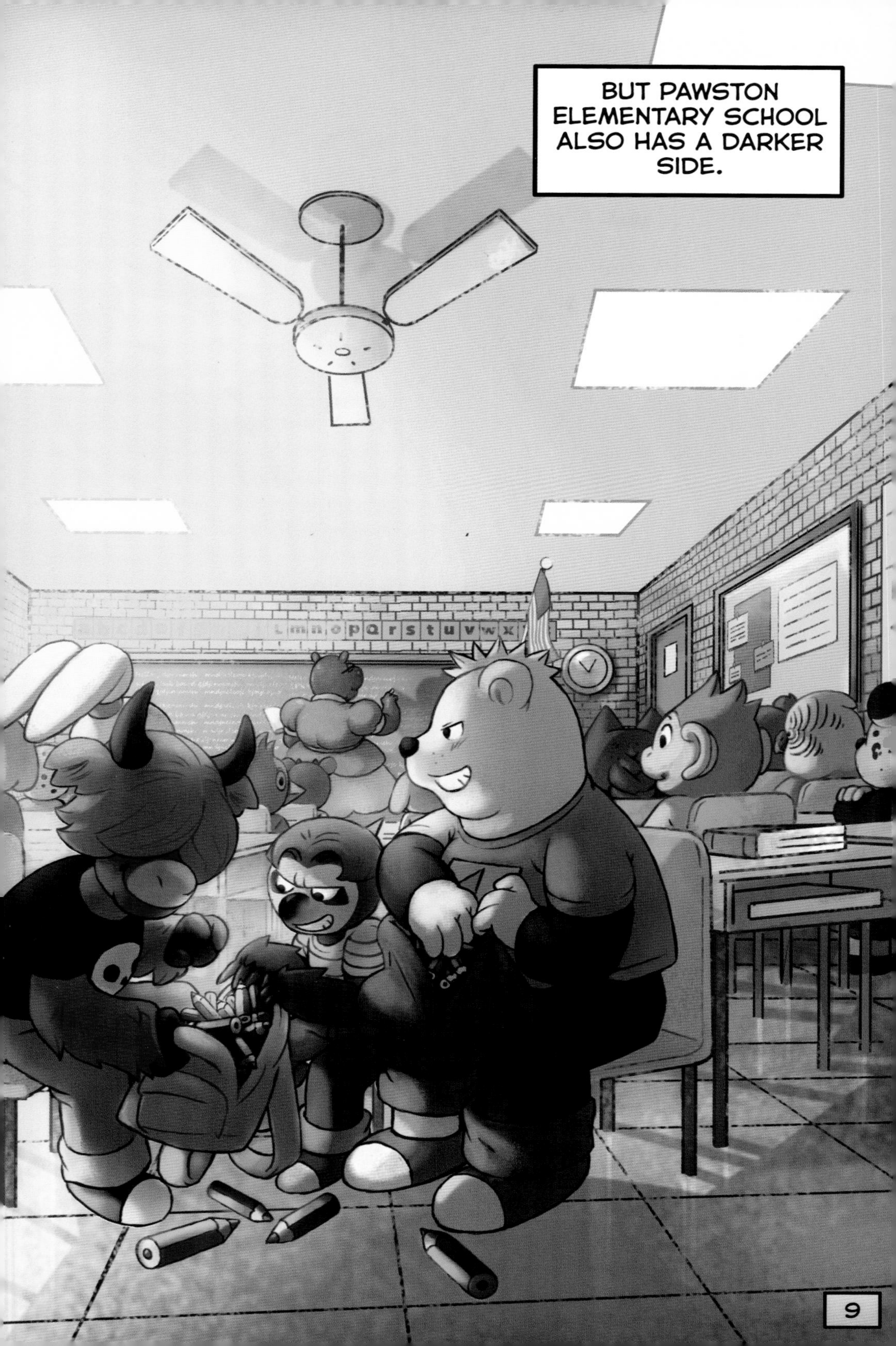
BUT PAWSTON ELEMENTARY SCHOOL ALSO HAS A DARKER SIDE.

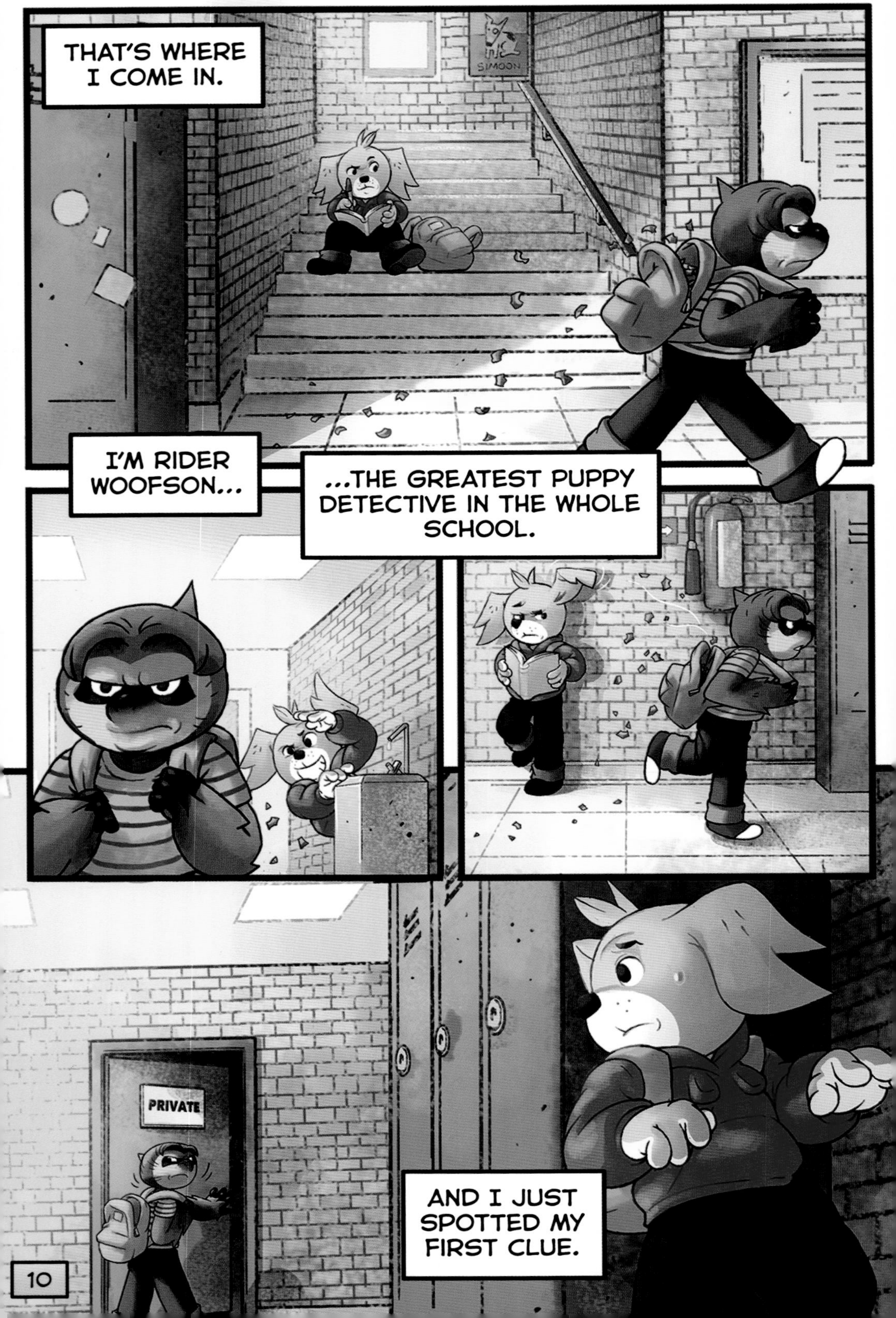
THAT'S WHERE I COME IN.
SIMOON
I'M RIDER WOOFSON...
...THE GREATEST PUPPY DETECTIVE IN THE WHOLE SCHOOL.
PRIVATE
AND I JUST SPOTTED MY FIRST CLUE.

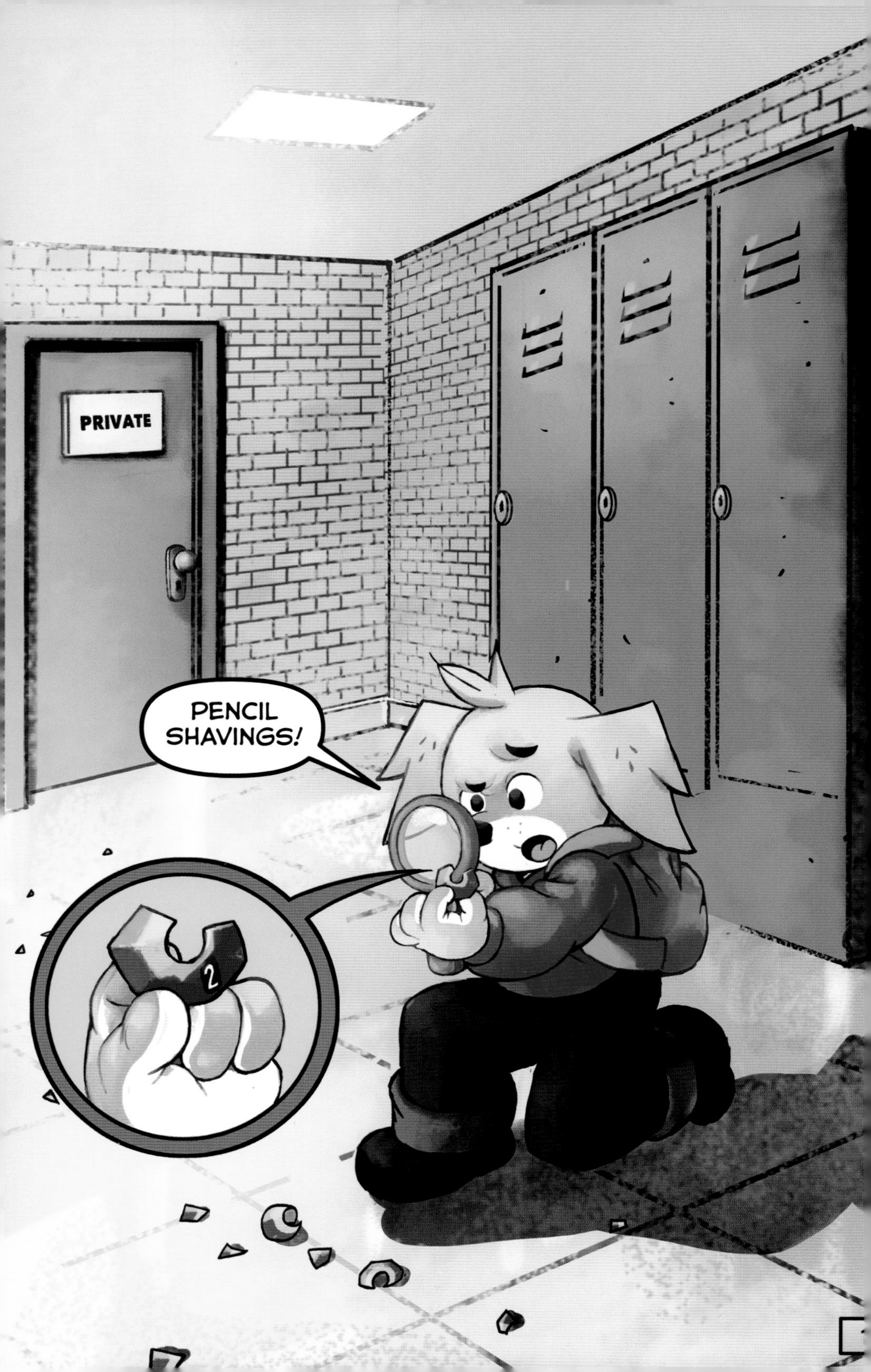
PRIVATE
PENCIL SHAVINGS!

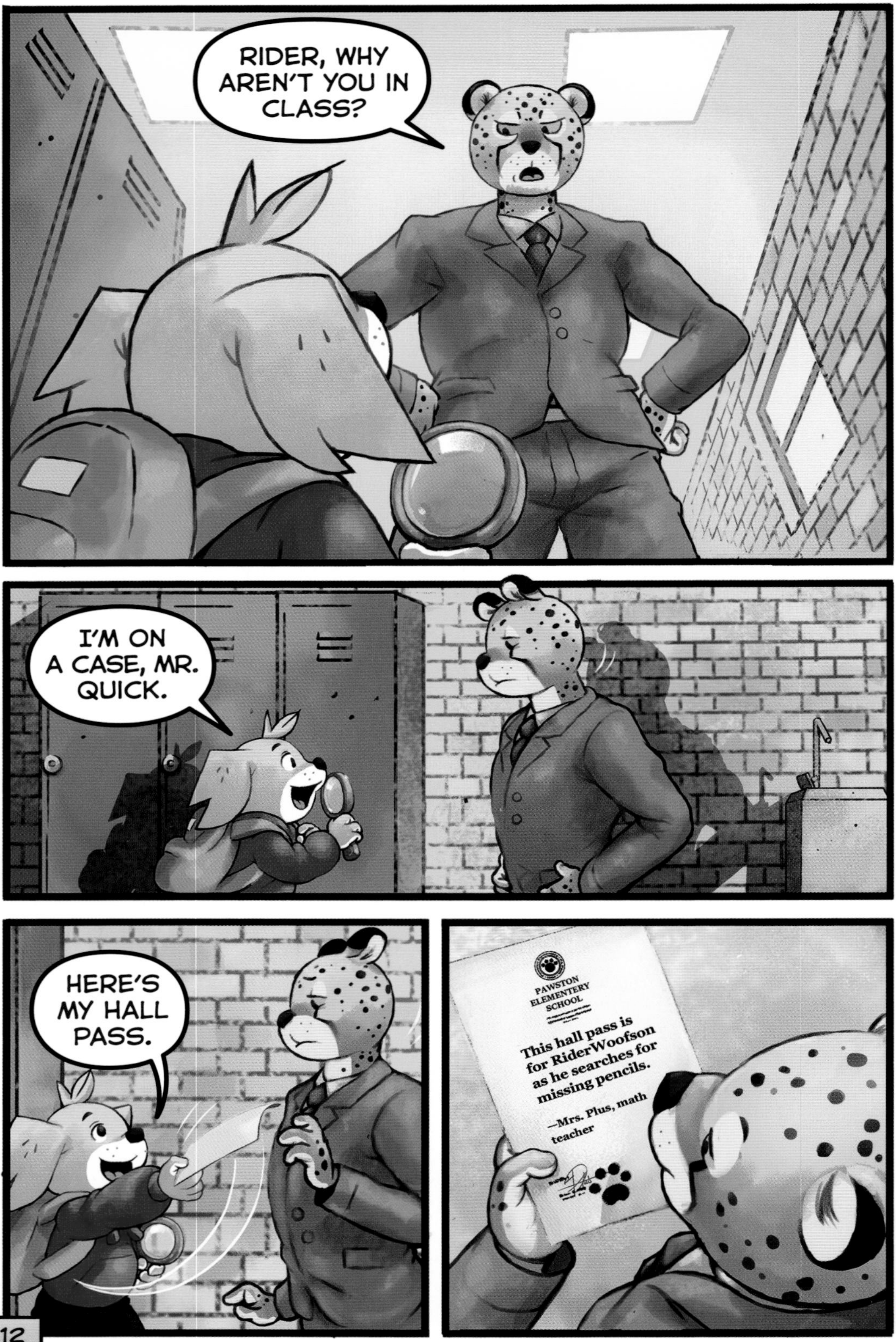
RIDER, WHY AREN'T YOU IN CLASS?
I'M ON A CASE, MR. QUICK.
HERE'S MY HALL PASS.
PAWSTON ELEMENTERY SCHOOL
This hall pass is for RiderWoofson as he searches for missing pencils.
—Mrs. Plus, math teacher

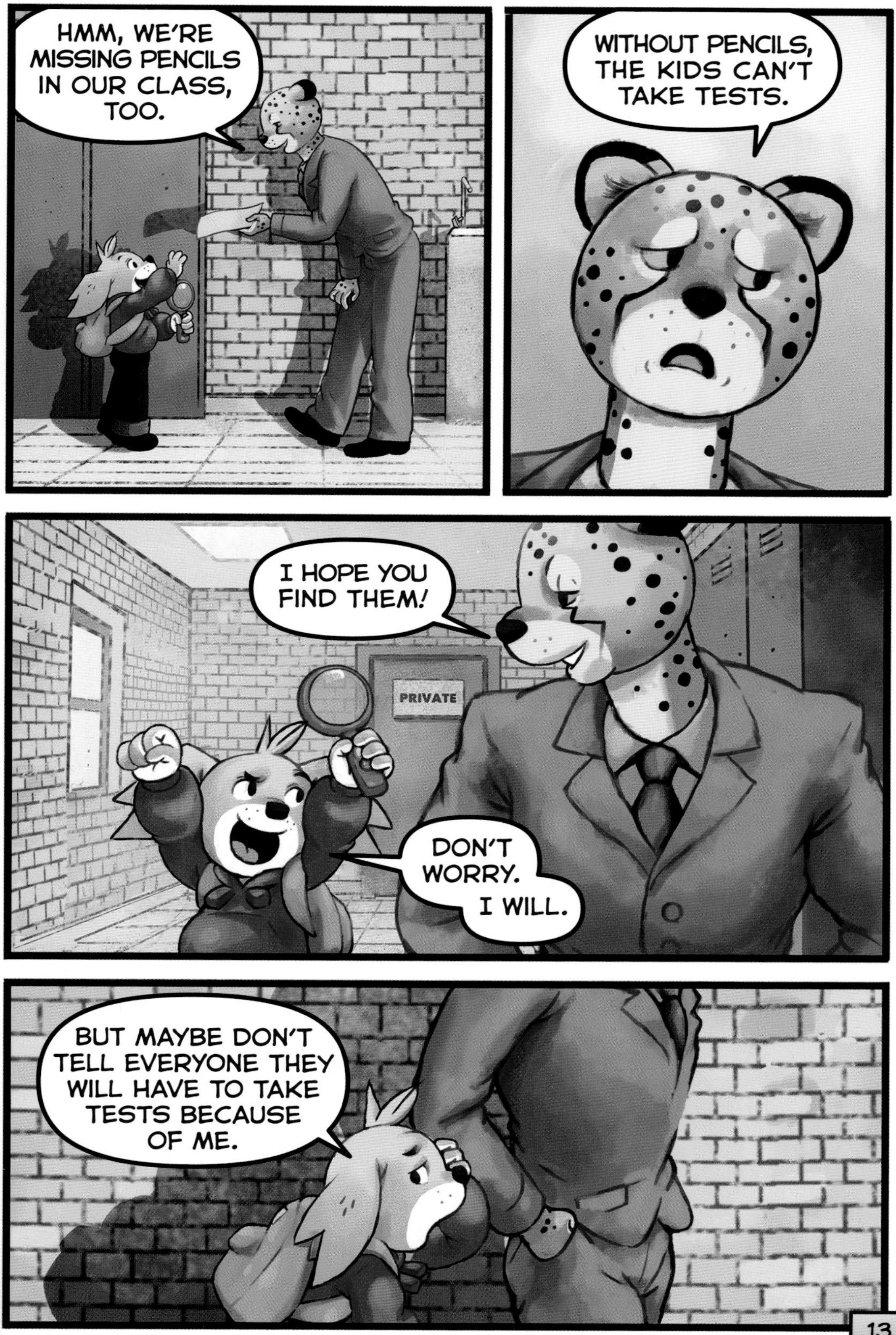
HMM, WE'RE MISSING PENCILS IN OUR CLASS, TOO.
WITHOUT PENCILS, THE KIDS CAN'T TAKE TESTS.
I HOPE YOU FIND THEM!
PRIVATE
DON'T WORRY.
I WILL.
BUT MAYBE DON'T TELL EVERYONE THEY WILL HAVE TO TAKE TESTS BECAUSE OF ME.

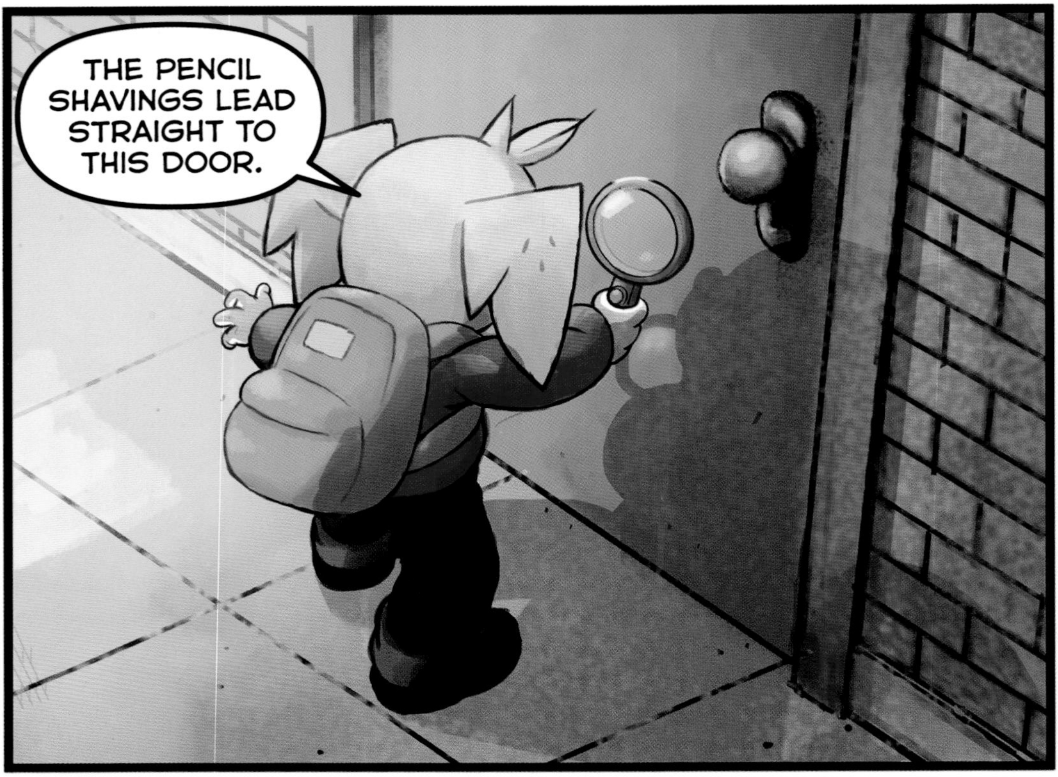
THE PENCIL SHAVINGS LEAD STRAIGHT TO THIS DOOR.

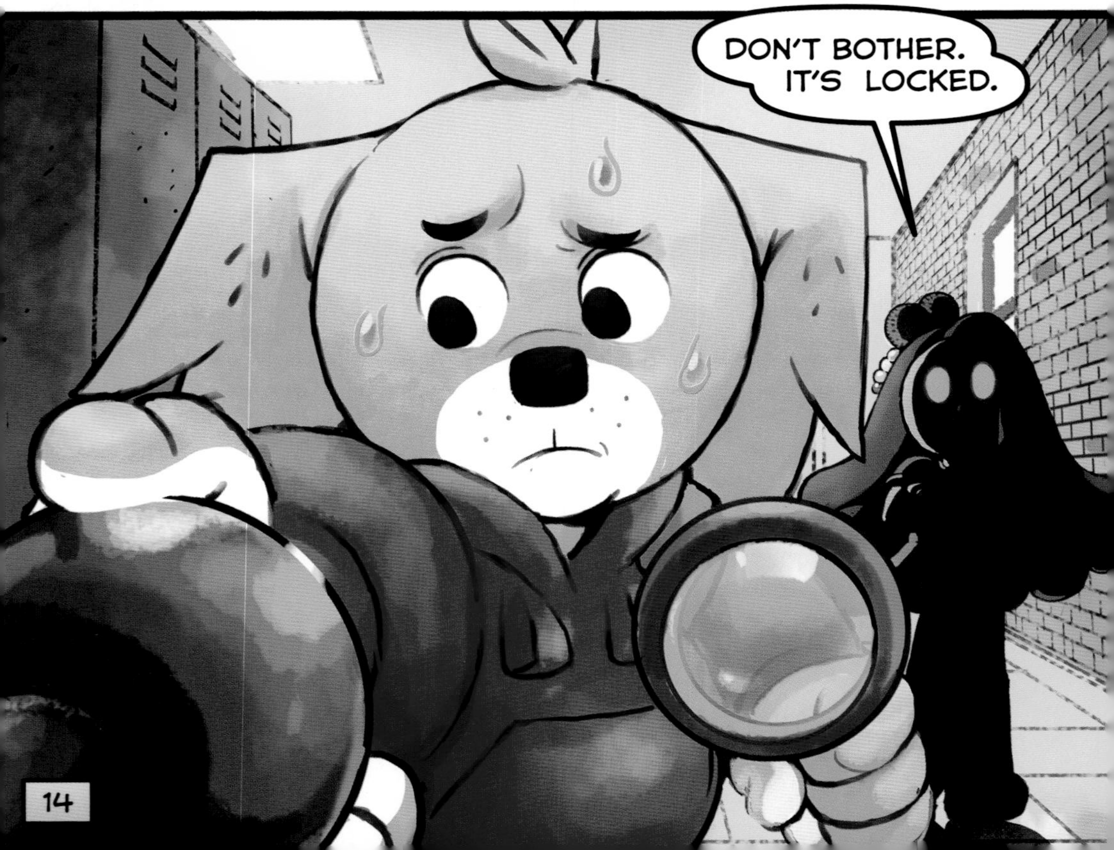
DON'T BOTHER. IT'S LOCKED.

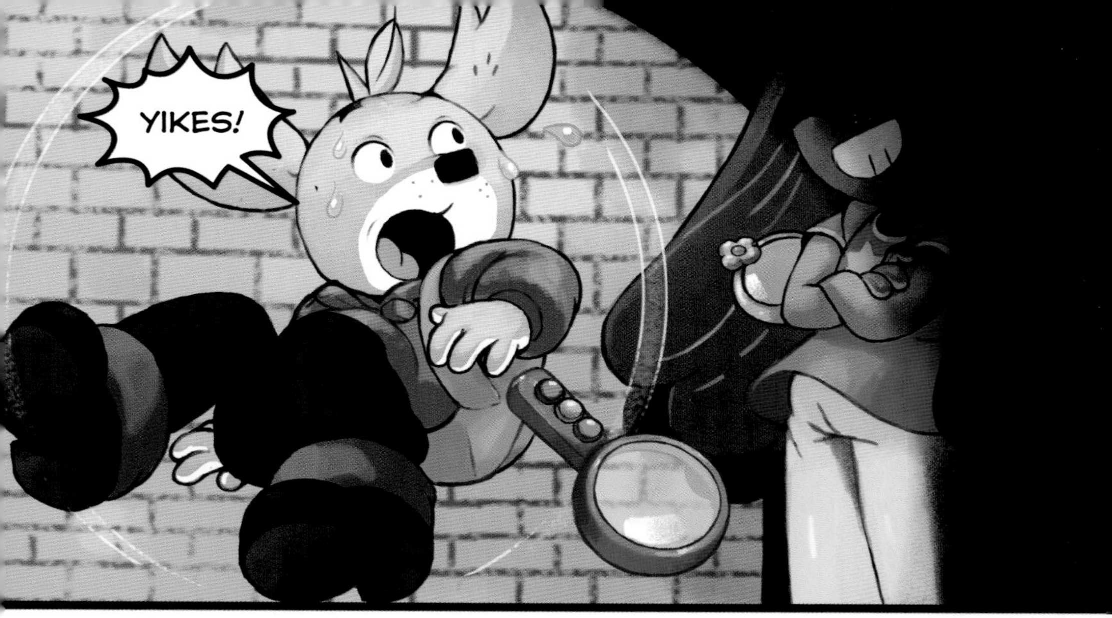
YIKES!

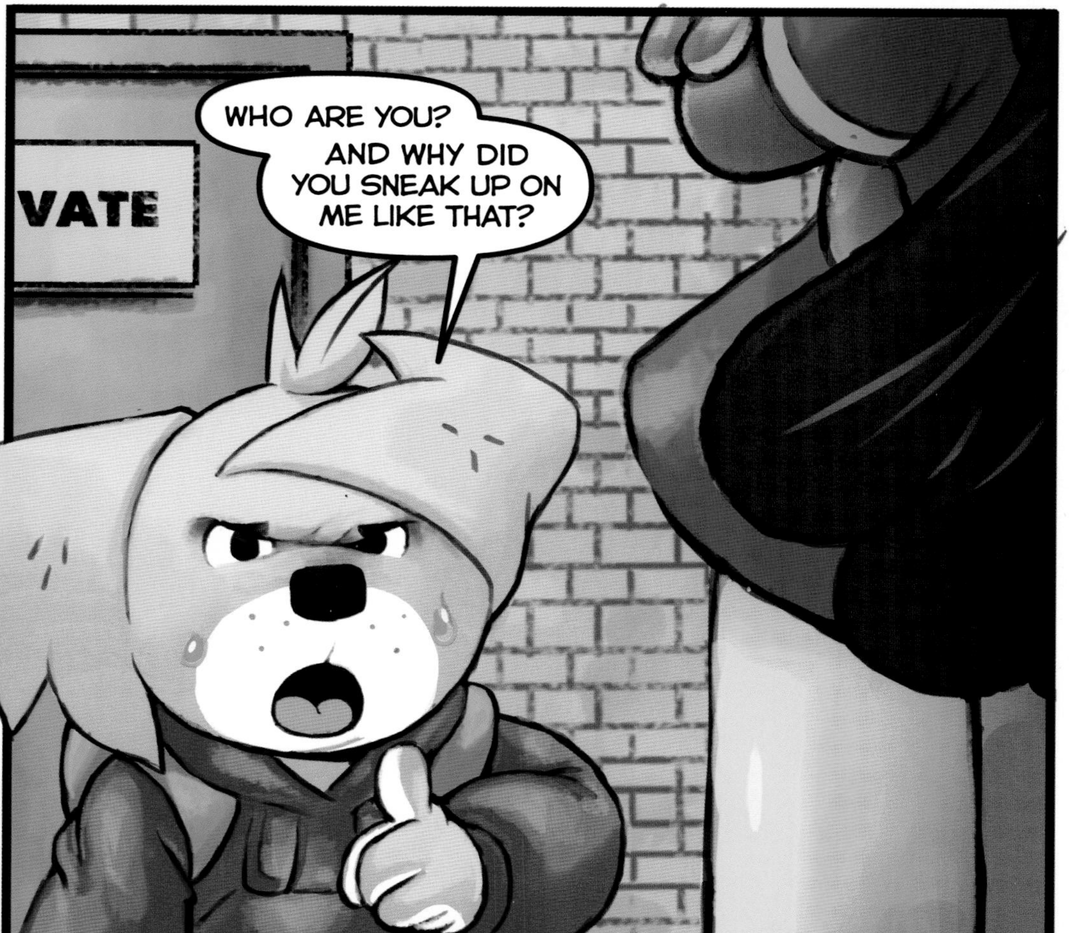
VATE
WHO ARE YOU? AND WHY DID YOU SNEAK UP ON ME LIKE THAT?

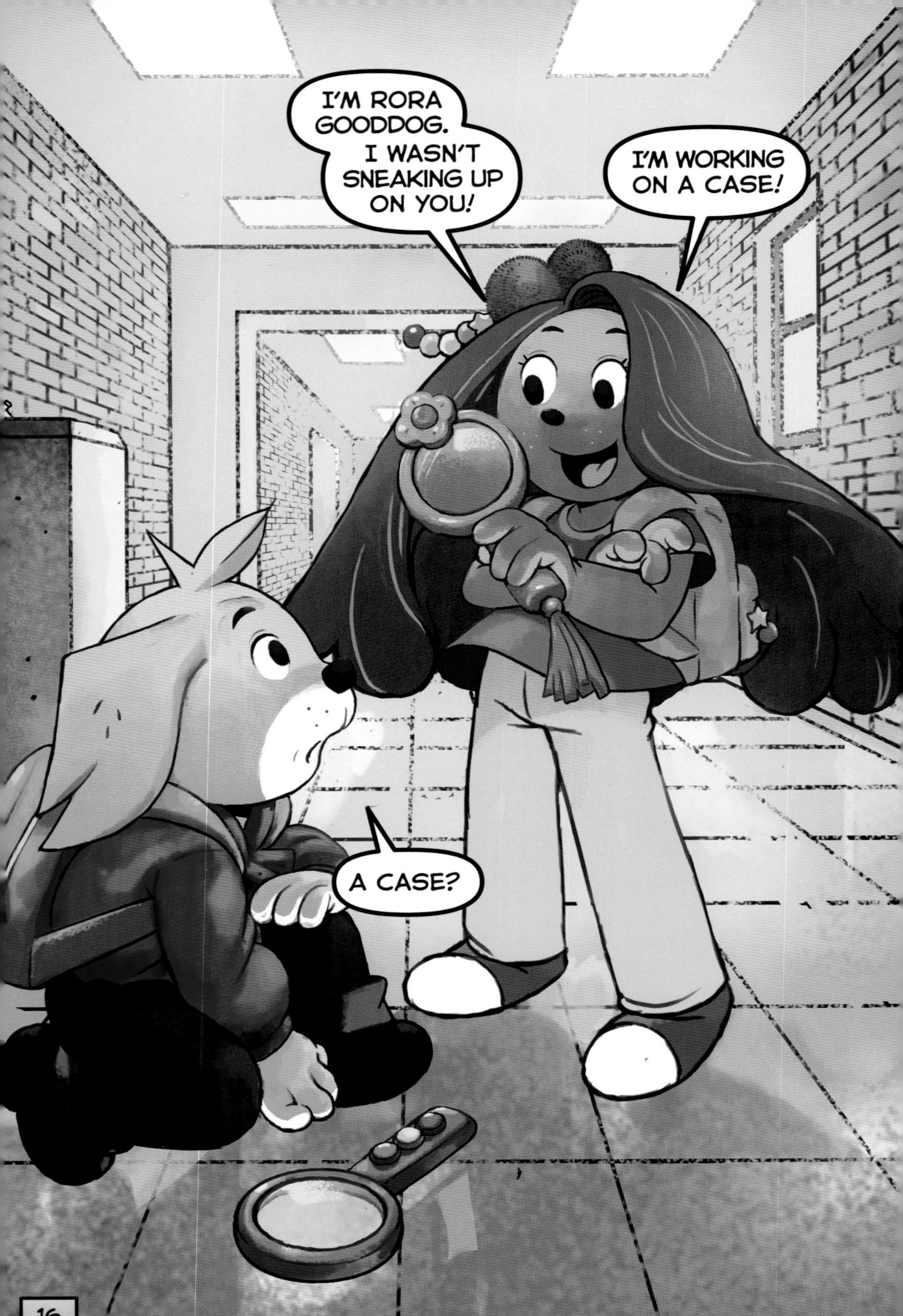
I'M RORA GOODDOG. I WASN'T SNEAKING UP ON YOU!
I'M WORKING ON A CASE!
A CASE?

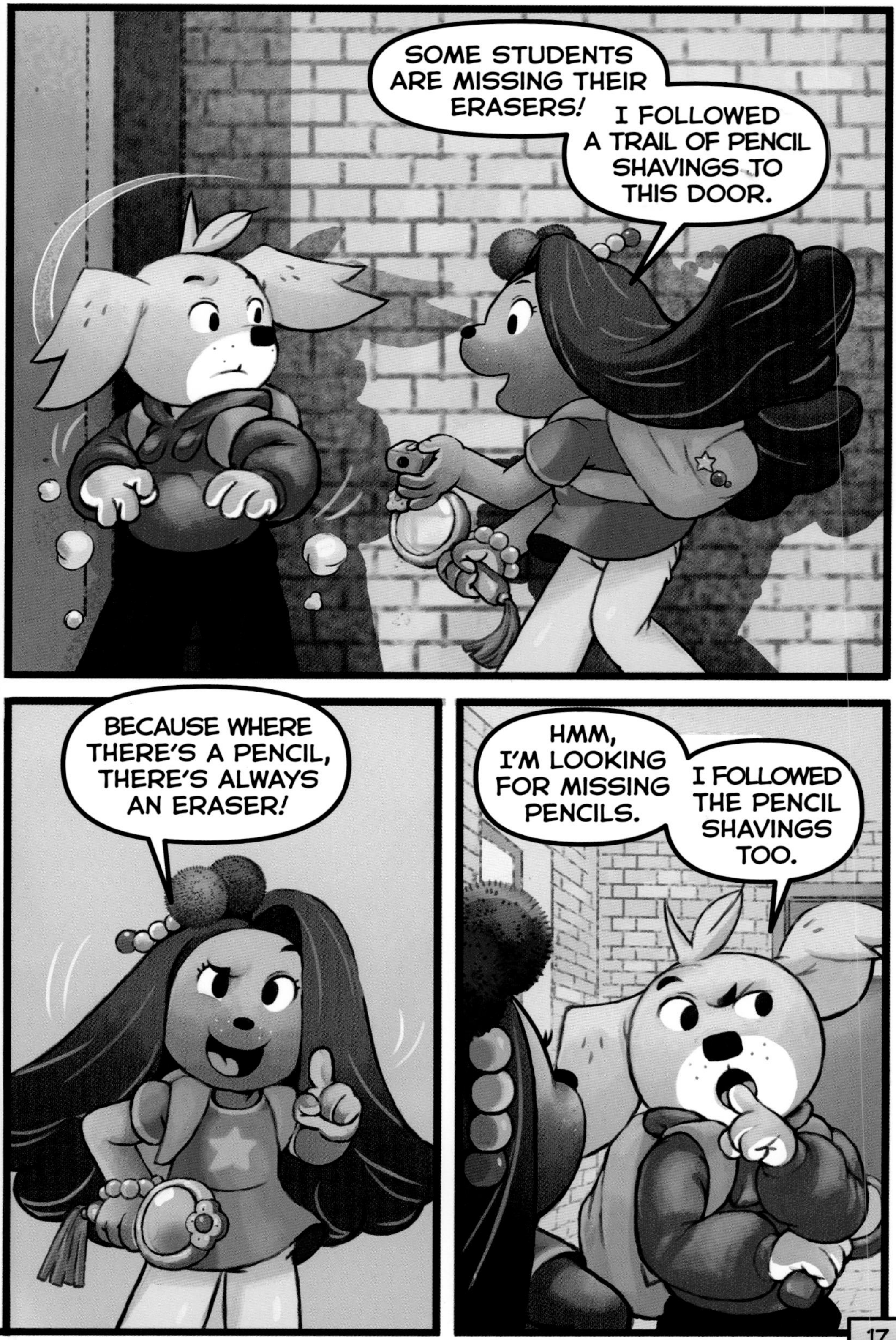
SOME STUDENTS ARE MISSING THEIR ERASERS!
I FOLLOWED A TRAIL OF PENCIL SHAVINGS TO THIS DOOR.
BECAUSE WHERE THERE'S A PENCIL, THERE'S ALWAYS AN ERASER!
HMM, I'M LOOKING FOR MISSING PENCILS.
I FOLLOWED THE PENCIL SHAVINGS TOO.

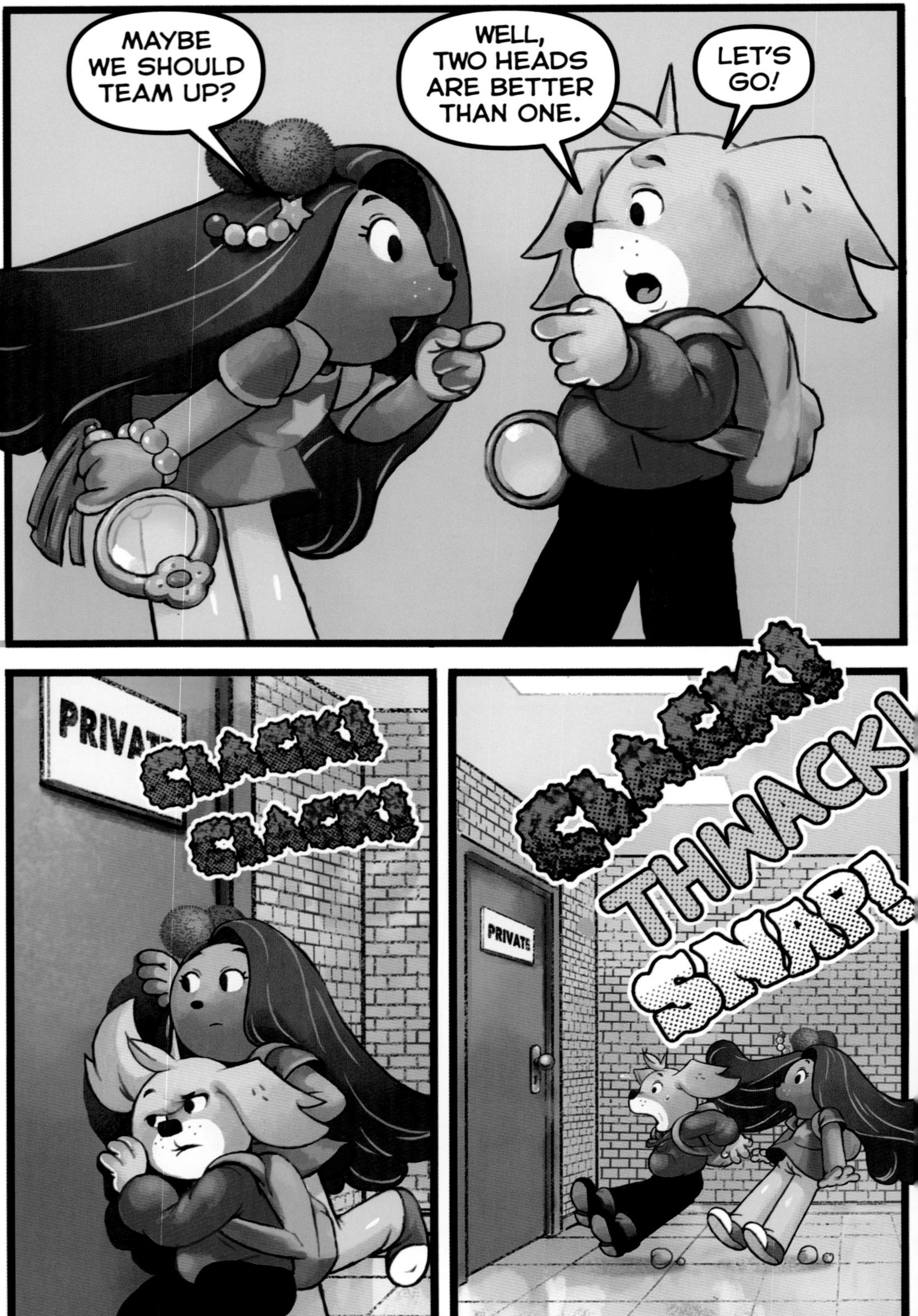
MAYBE WE SHOULD TEAM UP?
WELL, TWO HEADS ARE BETTER THAN ONE.
LET'S GO!
PRIVATE
PRIVATE
THWACK!

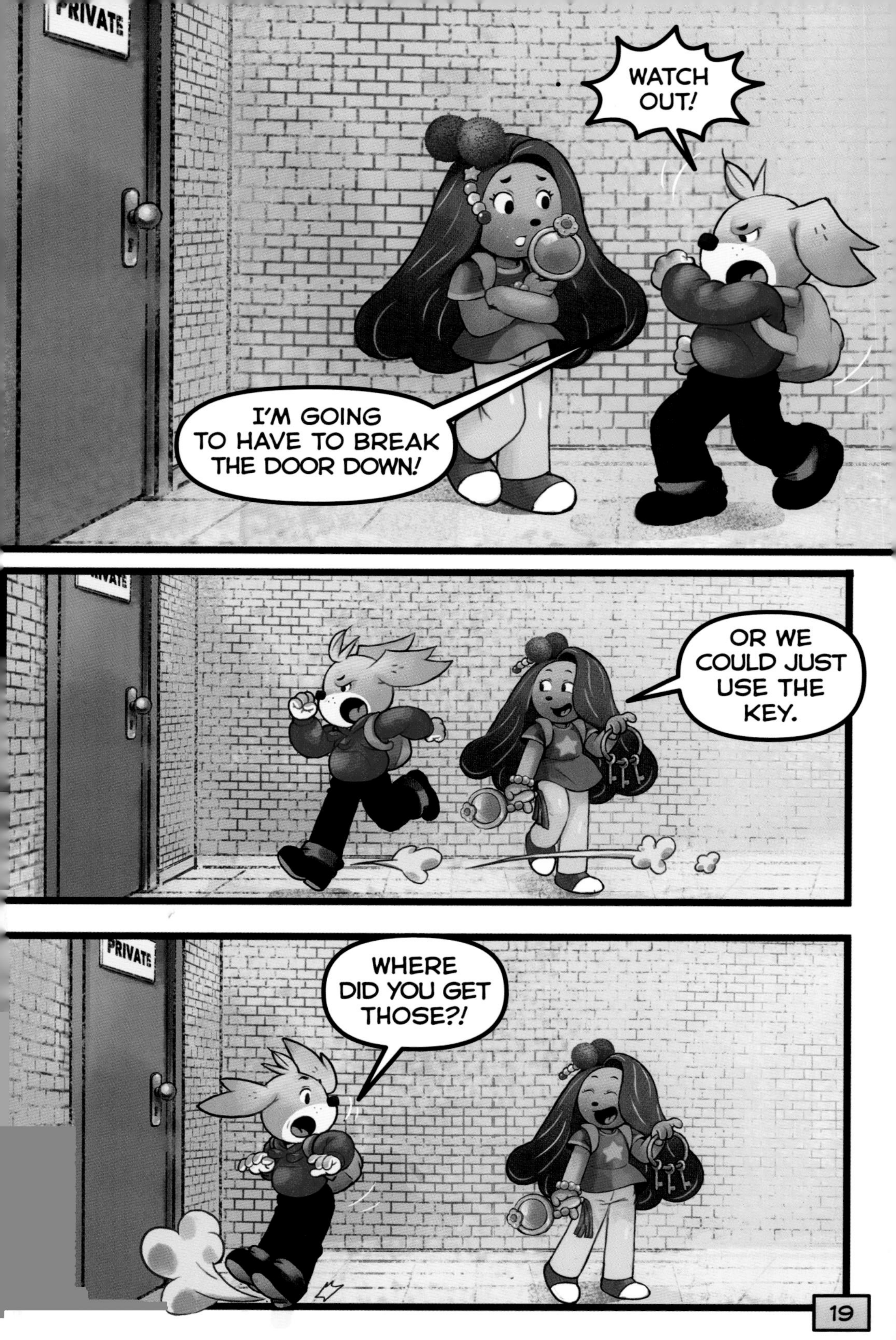
PRIVATE
WATCH OUT!
I'M GOING TO HAVE TO BREAK THE DOOR DOWN!
OR WE COULD JUST USE THE KEY.
PRIVATE
WHERE DID YOU GET THOSE?!

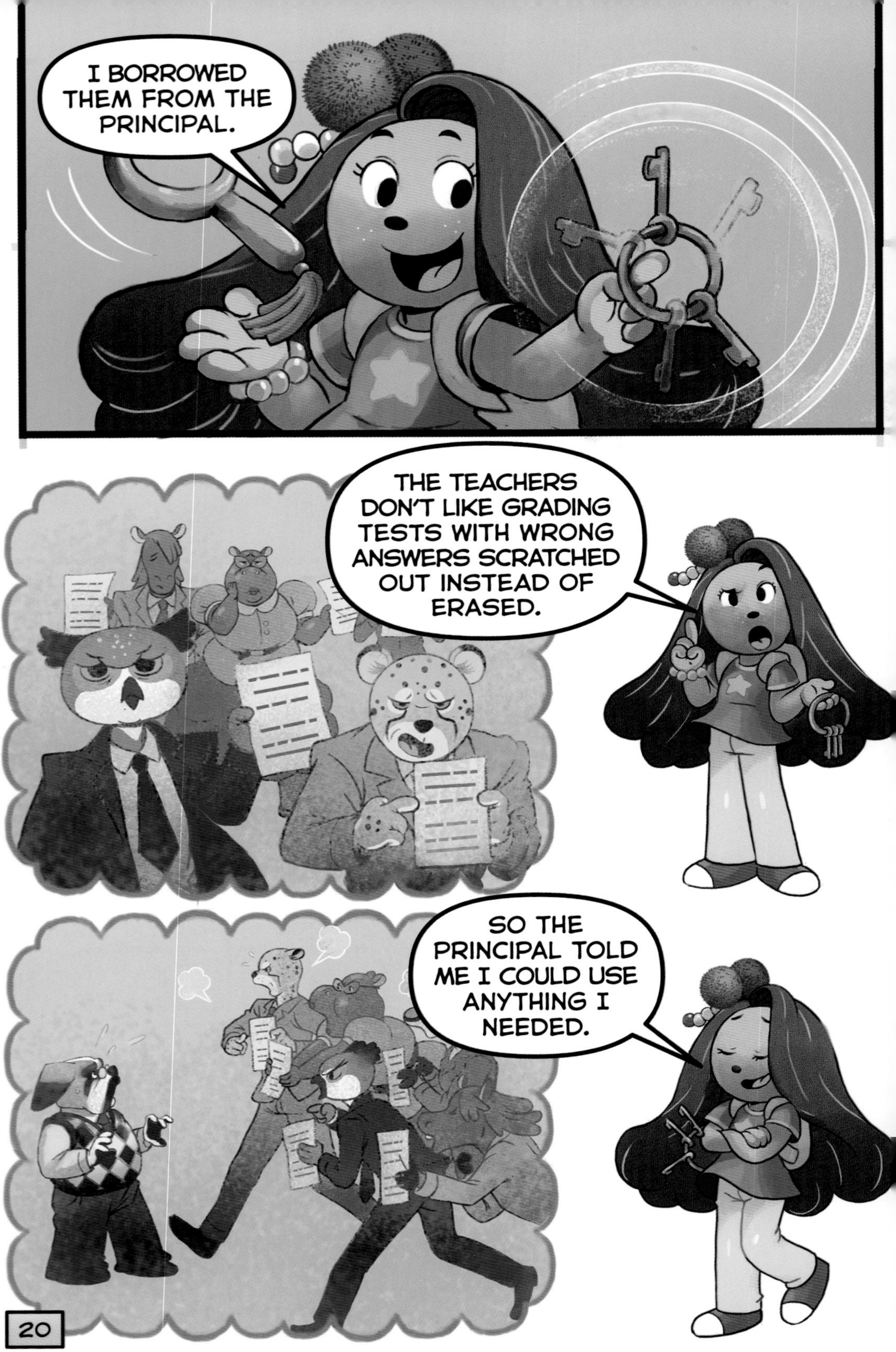
I BORROWED THEM FROM THE PRINCIPAL.
THE TEACHERS DON'T LIKE GRADING TESTS WITH WRONG ANSWERS SCRATCHED OUT INSTEAD OF ERASED.
SO THE PRINCIPAL TOLD ME I COULD USE ANYTHING I NEEDED.

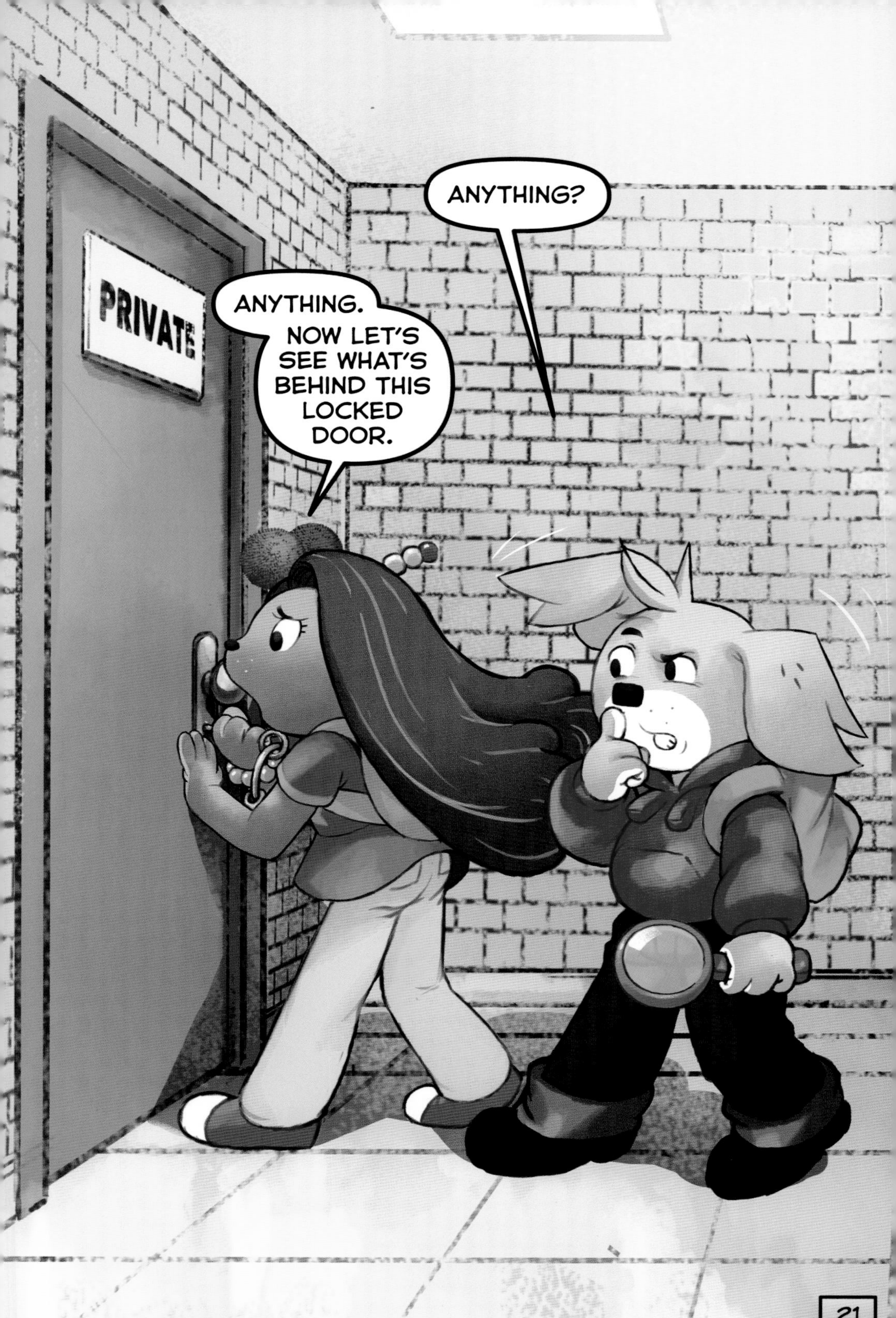
PRIVATE
ANYTHING. NOW LET'S SEE WHAT'S BEHIND THIS LOCKED DOOR.
ANYTHING?

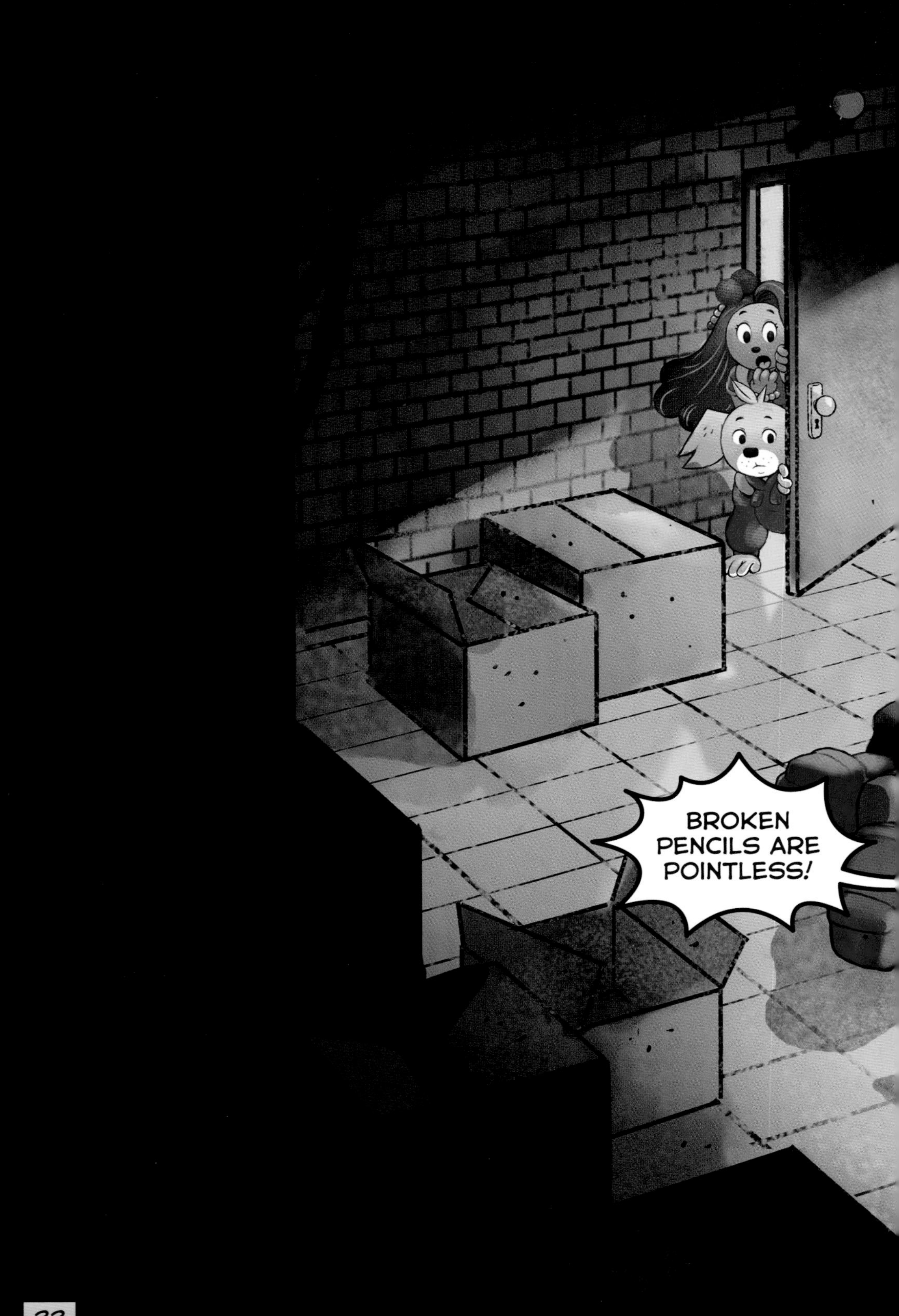
BROKEN
PENCILS ARE
POINTLESS!

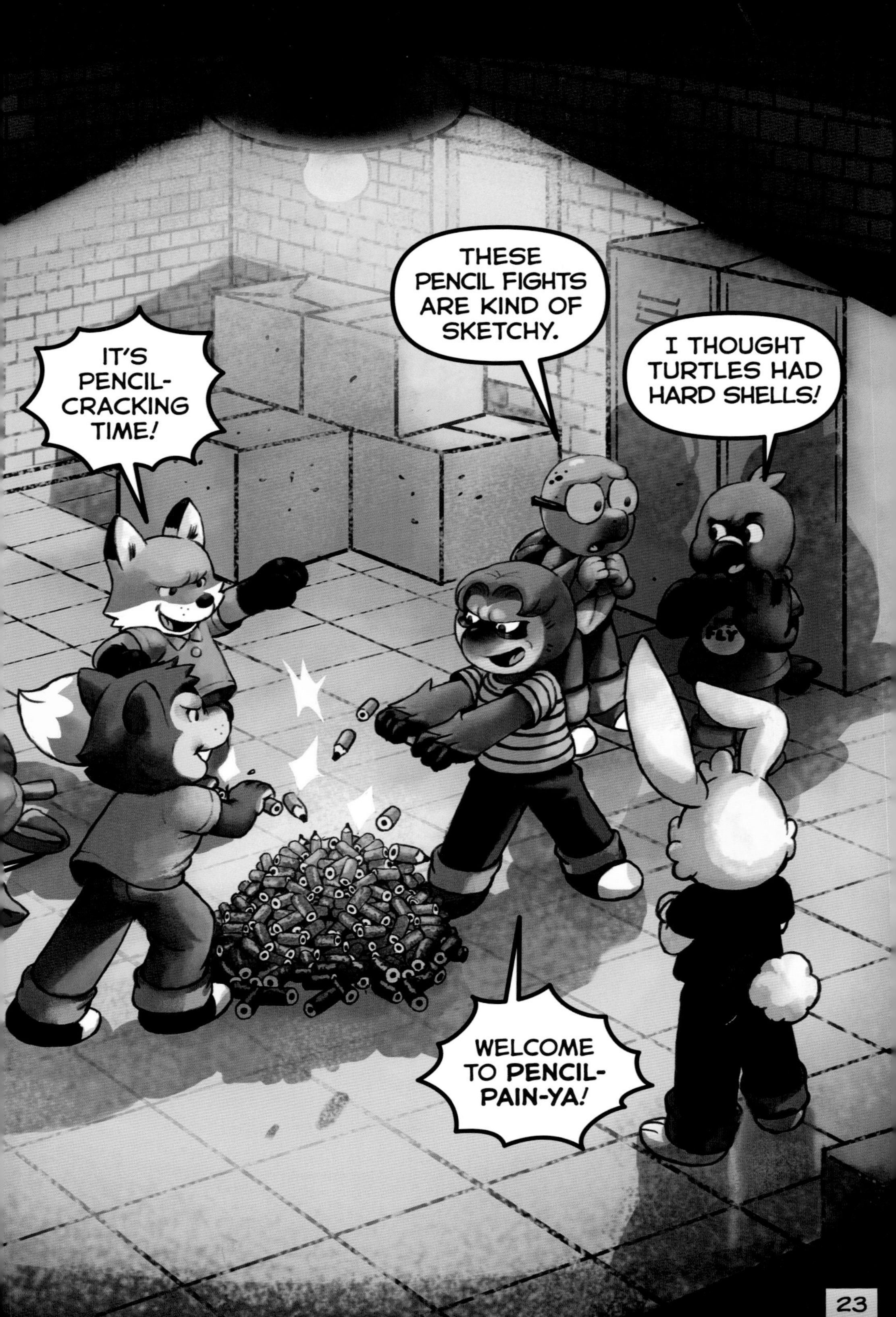
IT'S PENCIL-CRACKING TIME!
THESE PENCIL FIGHTS ARE KIND OF SKETCHY.
I THOUGHT TURTLES HAD HARD SHELLS!
FLY
WELCOME TO PENCIL-PAIN-YA!

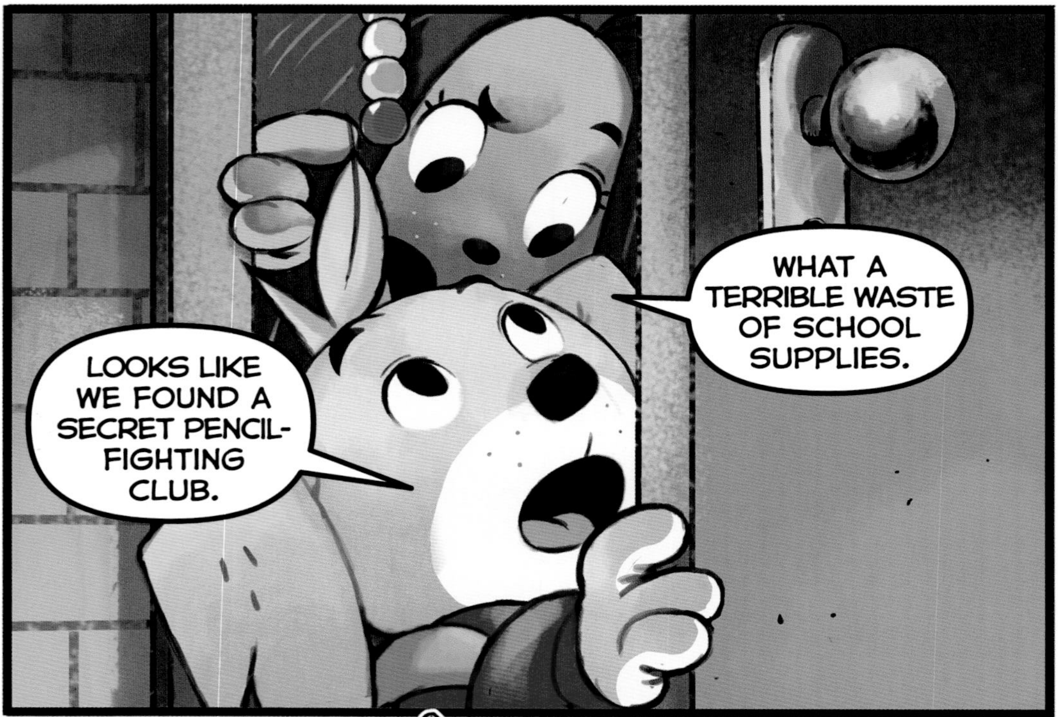
LOOKS LIKE WE FOUND A SECRET PENCIL-FIGHTING CLUB.
WHAT A TERRIBLE WASTE OF SCHOOL SUPPLIES.

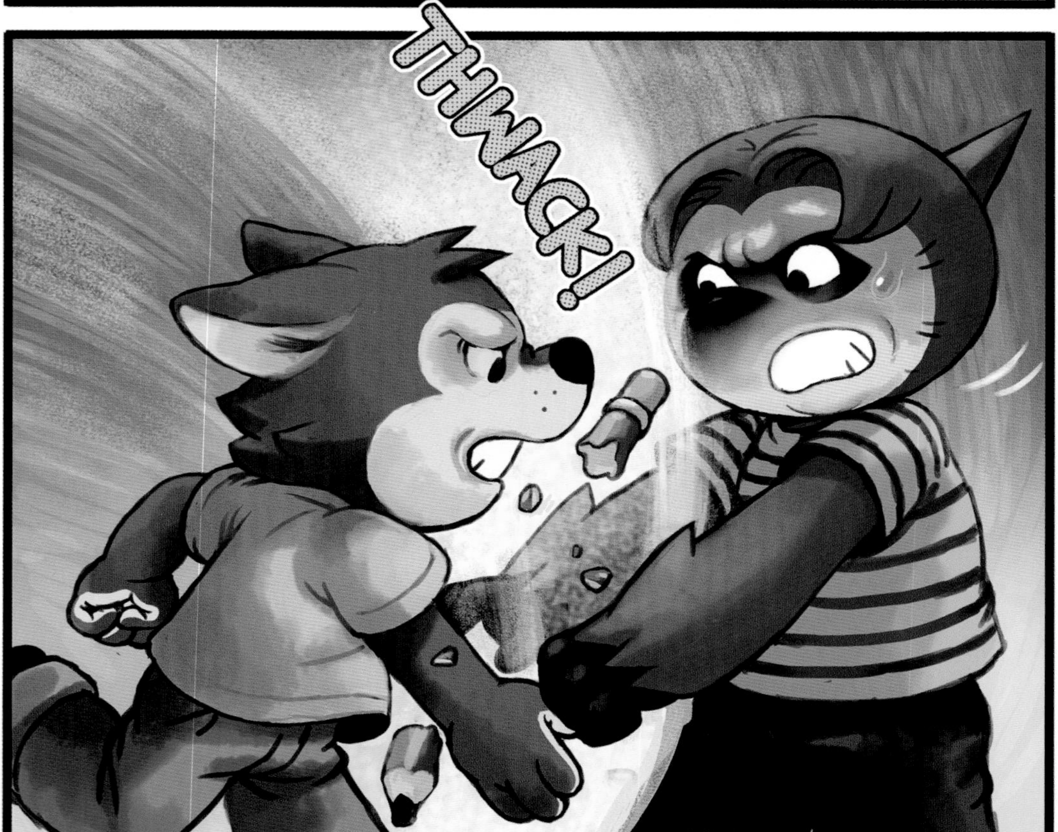
THWACK!

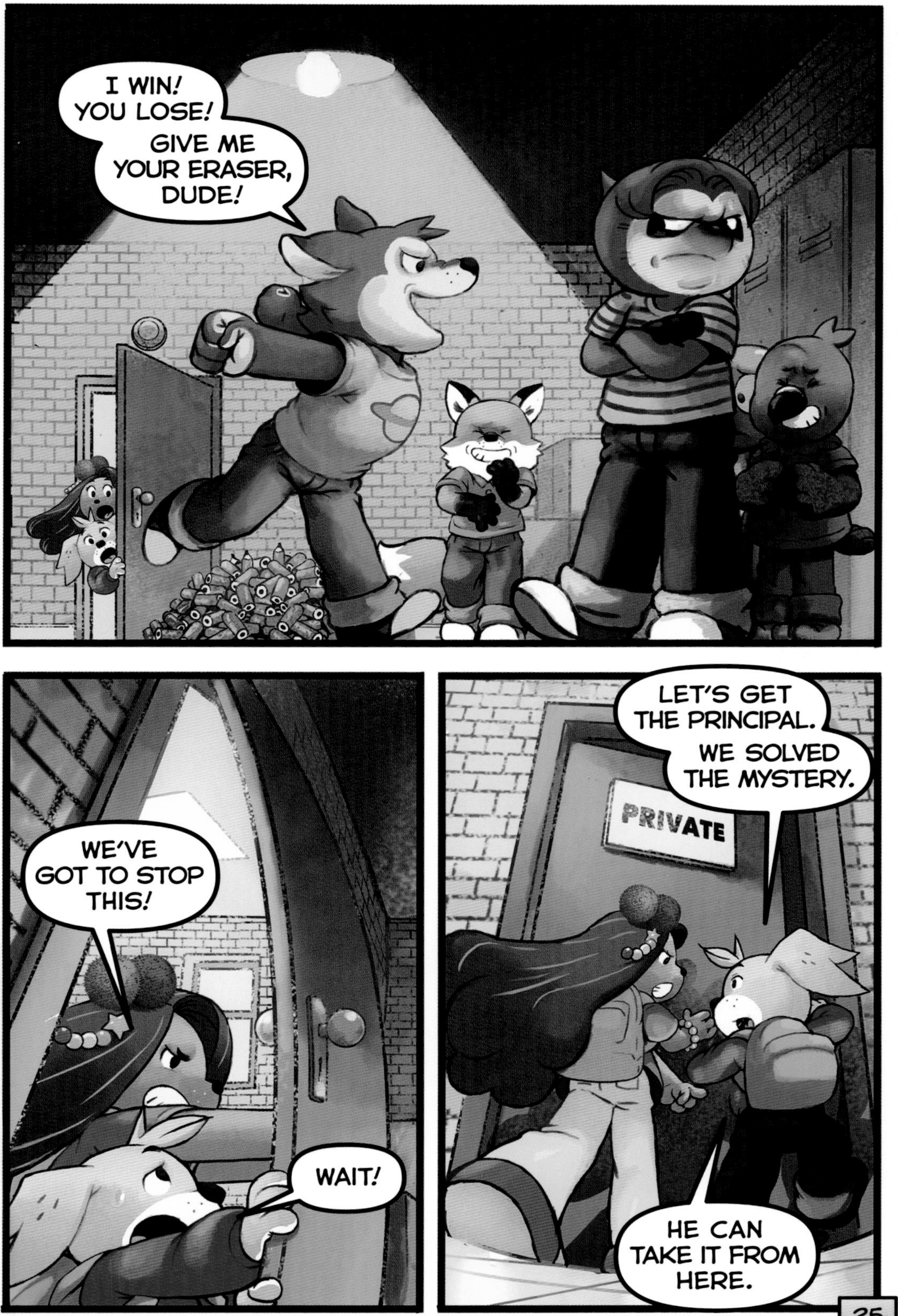
I WIN! YOU LOSE!
GIVE ME YOUR ERASER, DUDE!
WE'VE GOT TO STOP THIS!
WAIT!
LET'S GET THE PRINCIPAL.
WE SOLVED THE MYSTERY.
PRIVATE
HE CAN TAKE IT FROM HERE.

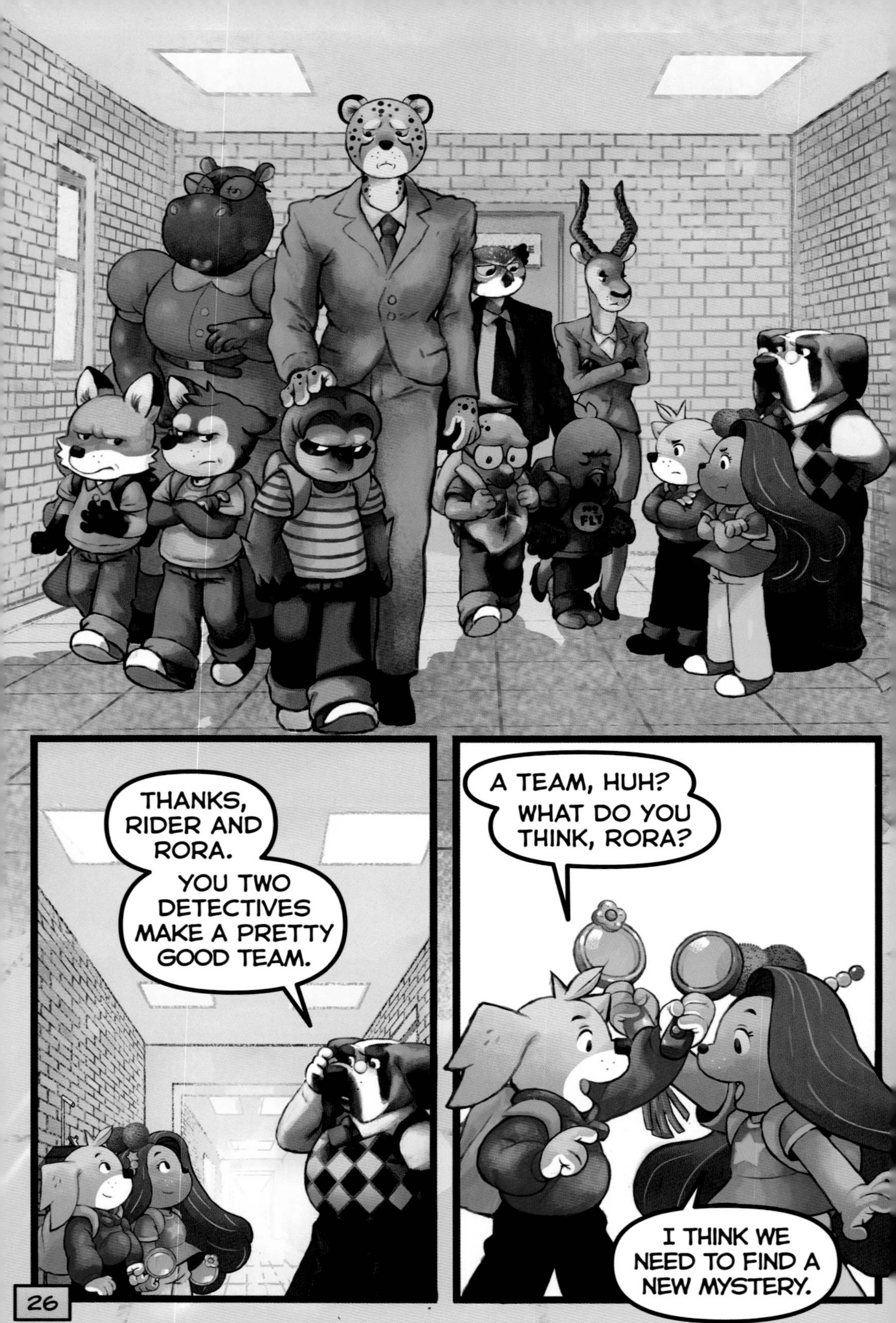
THANKS, RIDER AND RORA.
YOU TWO DETECTIVES MAKE A PRETTY GOOD TEAM.
A TEAM, HUH? WHAT DO YOU THINK, RORA?
I THINK WE NEED TO FIND A NEW MYSTERY.

CHAPTER 2

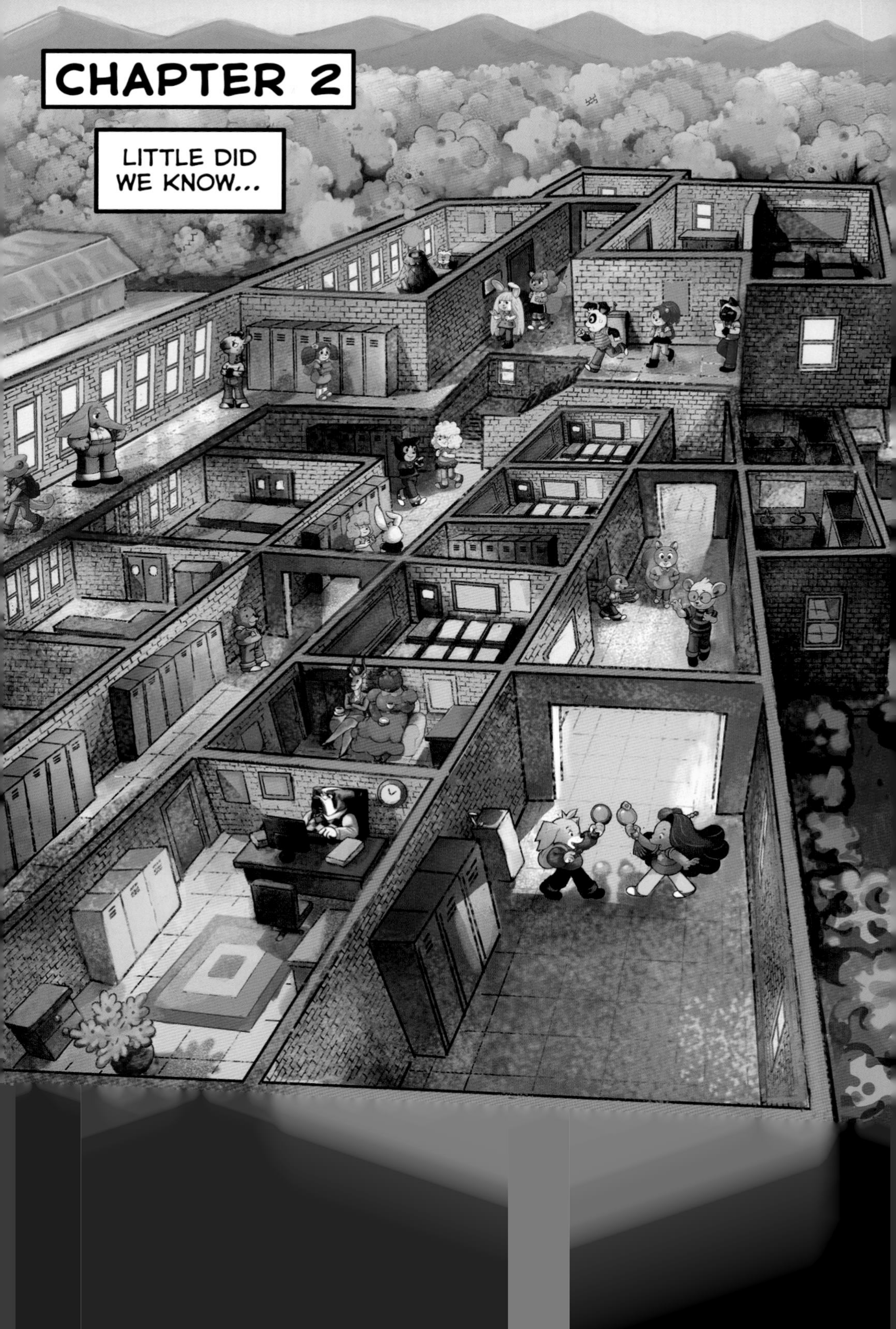
LITTLE DID WE KNOW...

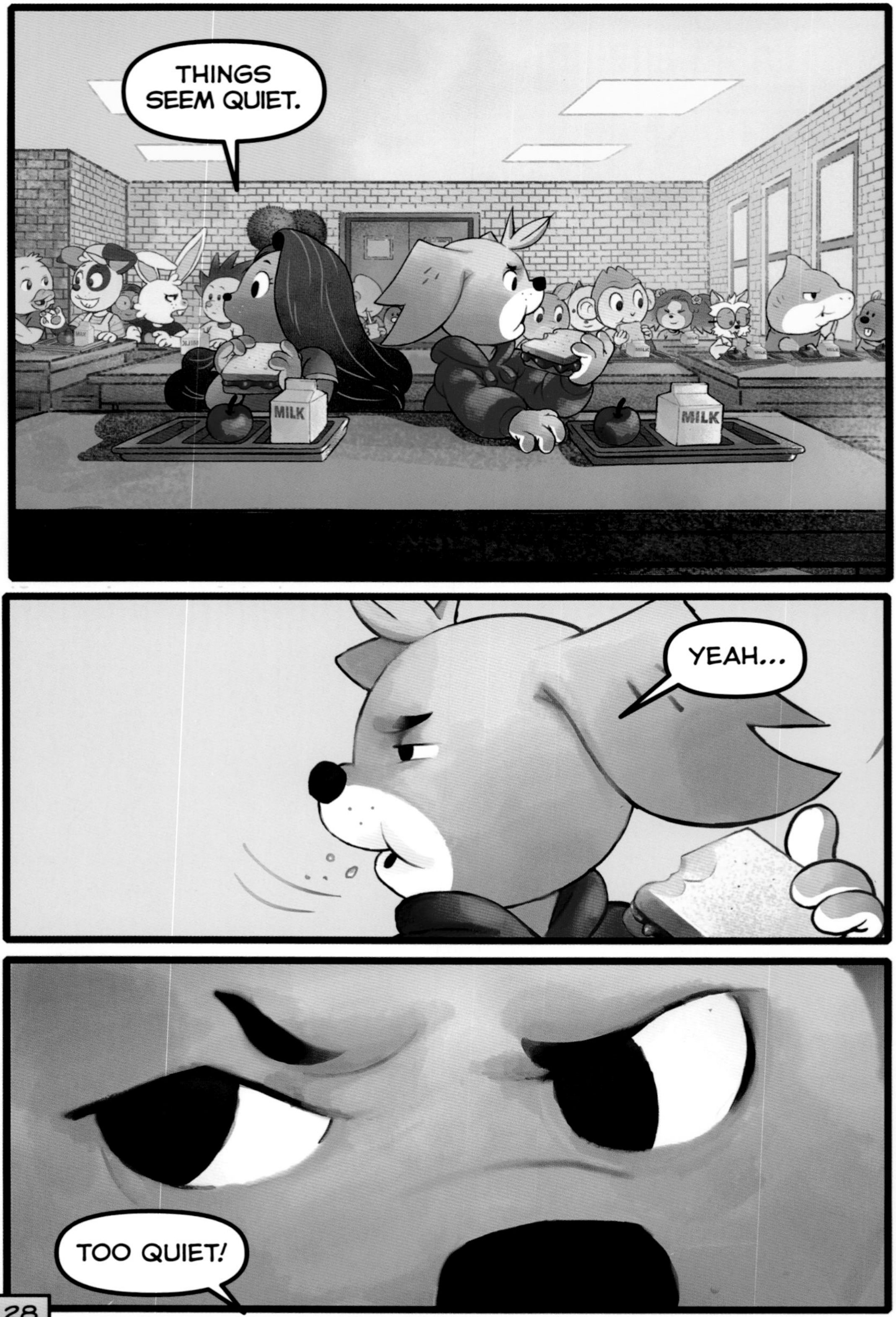
THINGS SEEM QUIET.
MILK
MILK
YEAH...
TOO QUIET!

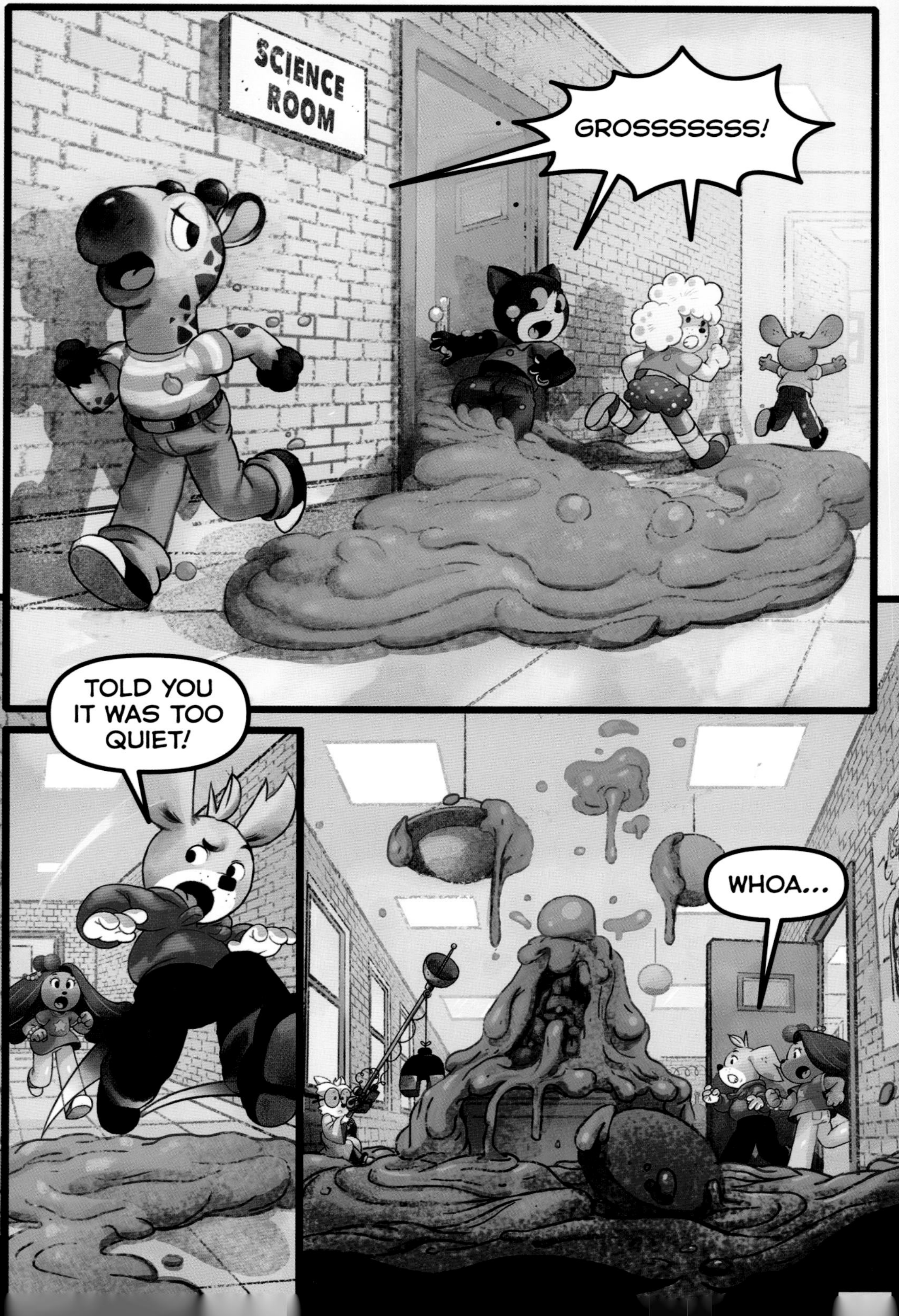
SCIENCE ROOM
GROSSSSSSS!
TOLD YOU IT WAS TOO QUIET!
WHOA...

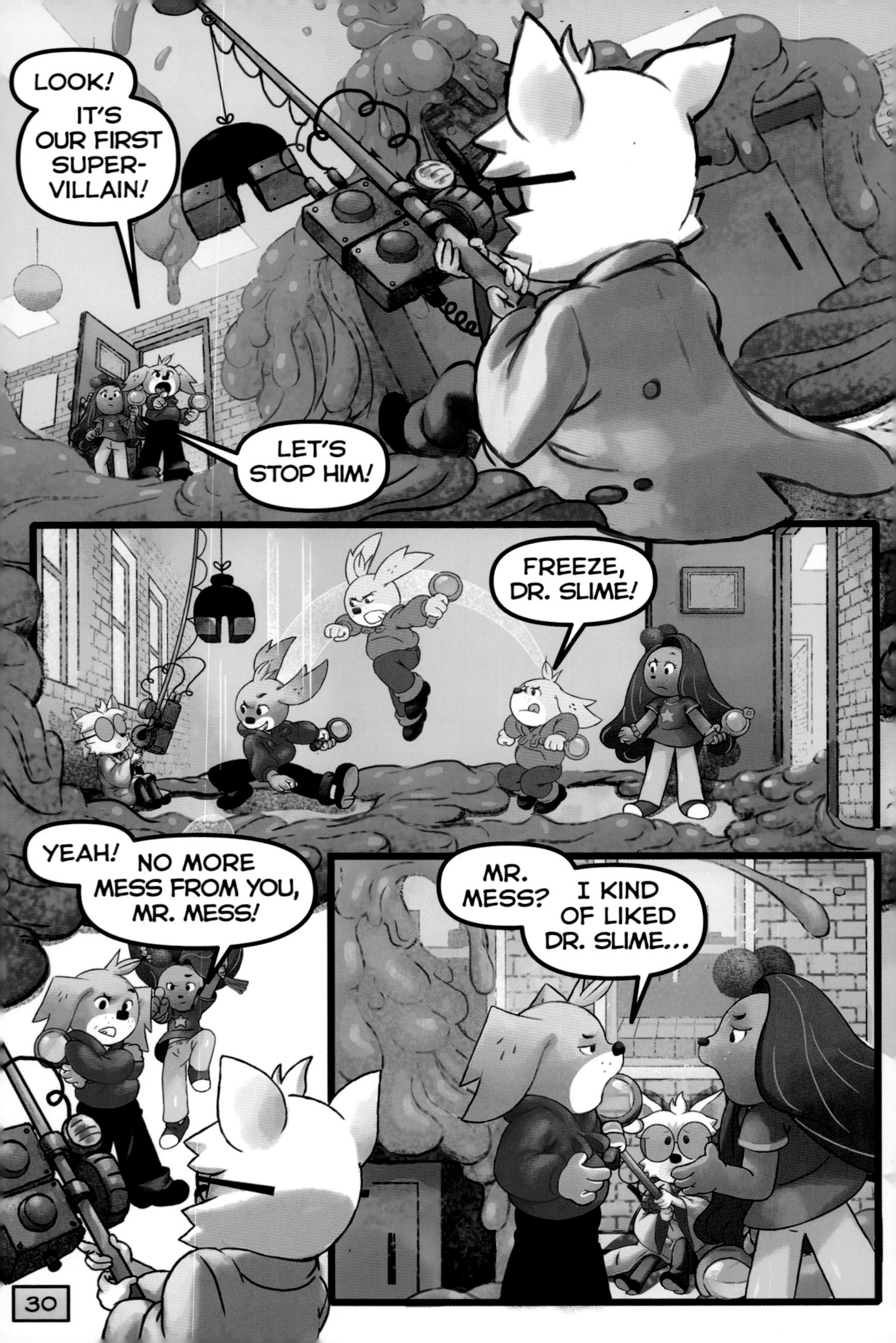

LOOK! IT'S OUR FIRST SUPER-VILLAIN!
LET'S STOP HIM!
FREEZE, DR. SLIME!
YEAH!
NO MORE MESS FROM YOU, MR. MESS!
MR. MESS?
I KIND OF LIKED DR. SLIME...

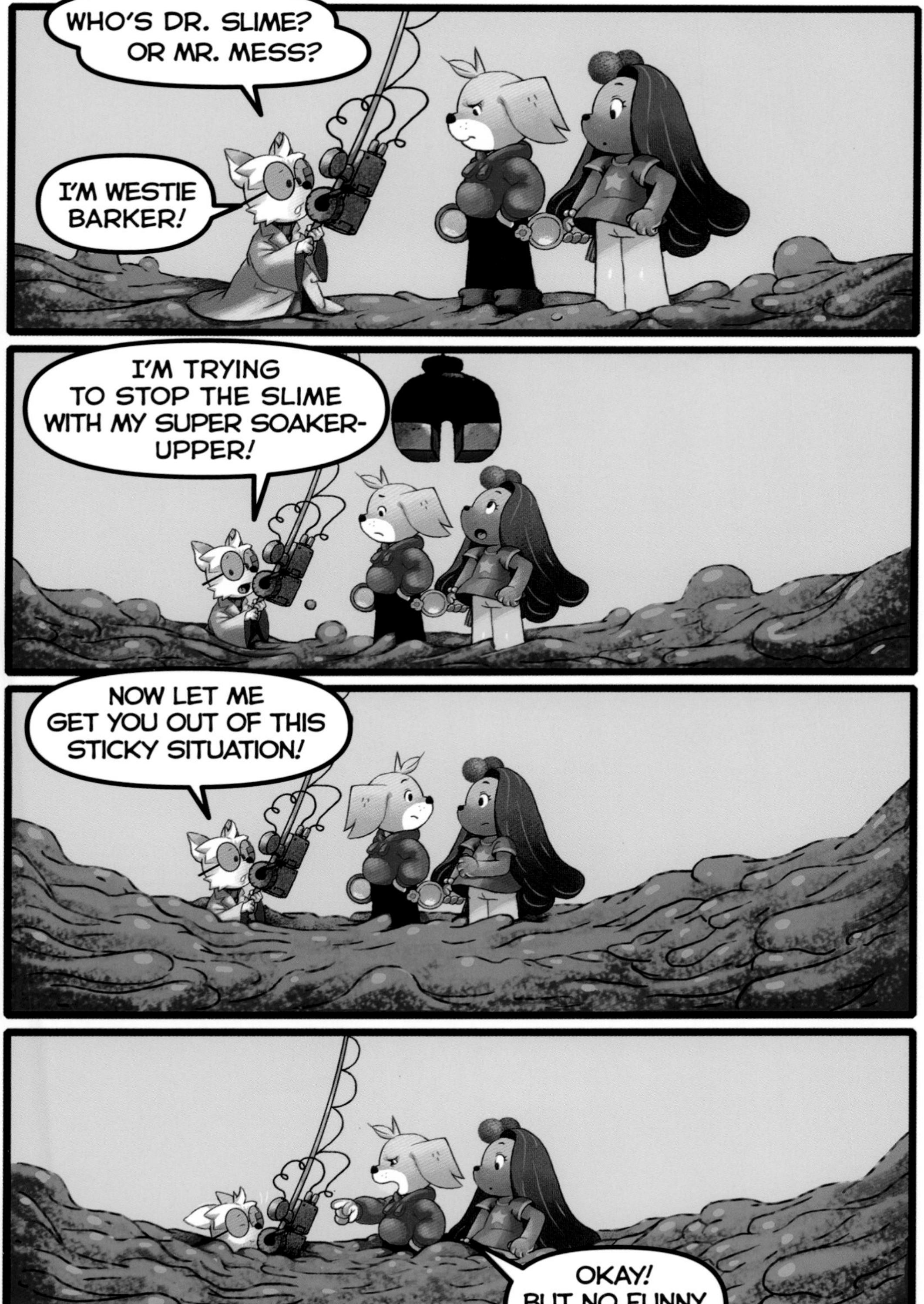
WHO'S DR. SLIME? OR MR. MESS?
I'M WESTIE BARKER!
I'M TRYING TO STOP THE SLIME WITH MY SUPER SOAKER-UPPER!
NOW LET ME GET YOU OUT OF THIS STICKY SITUATION!
OKAY! BUT NO FUNNY BUSINESS!

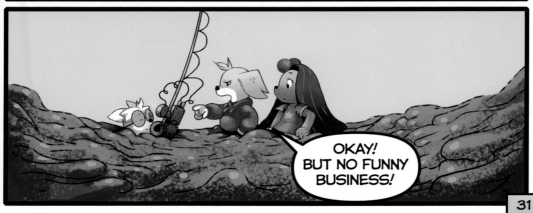

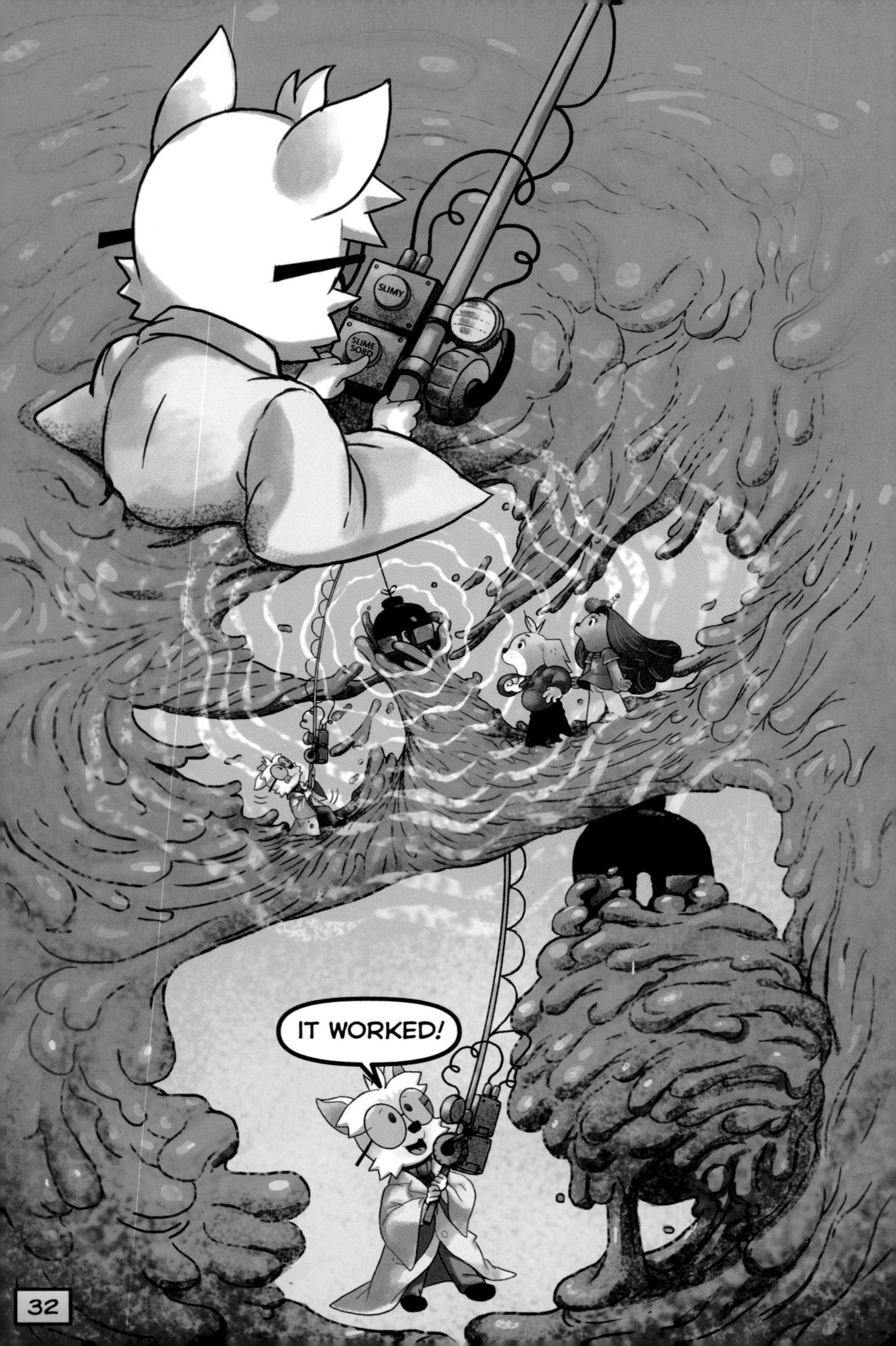
SLIMY
SLIME SORD
IT WORKED!

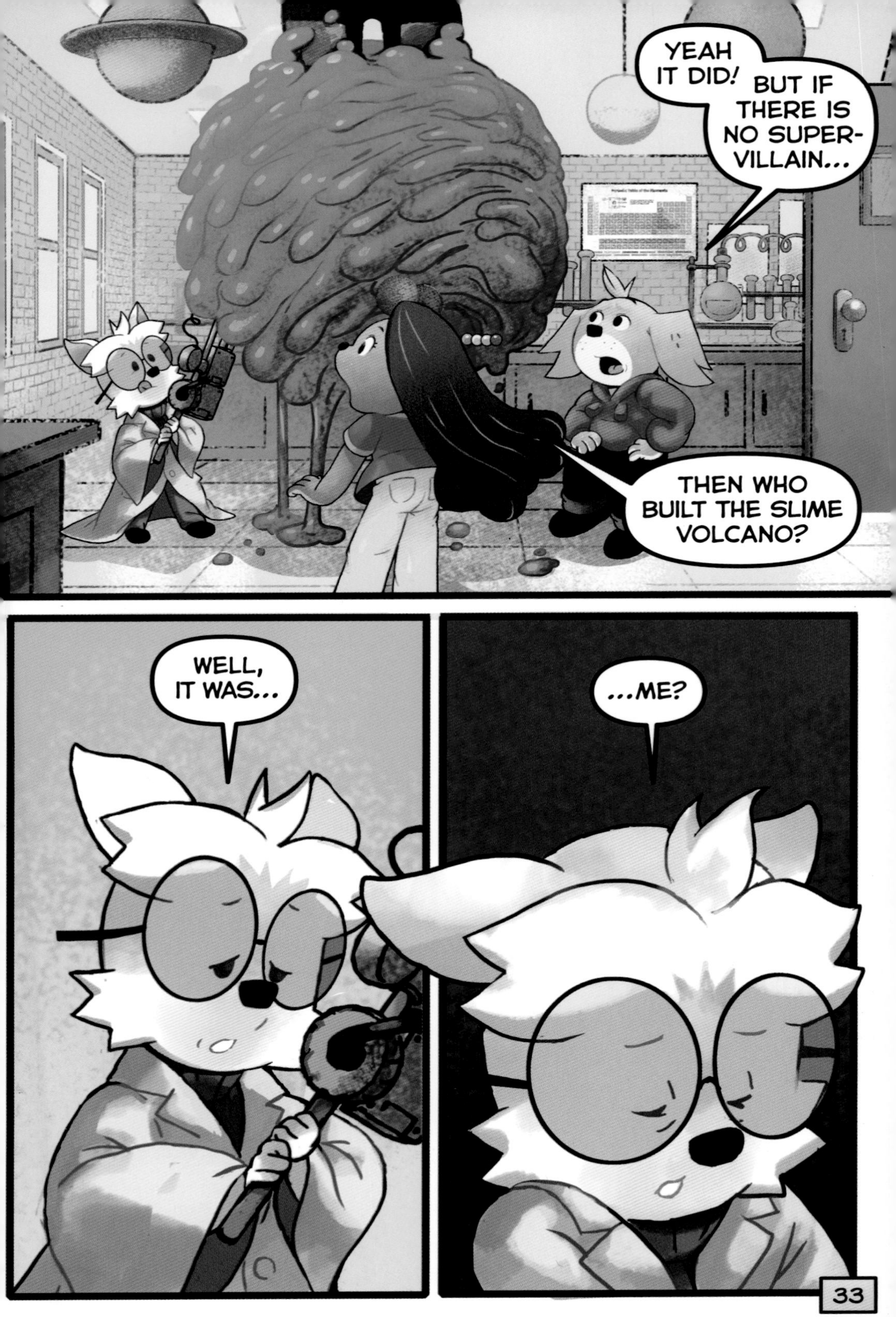
YEAH IT DID!
BUT IF THERE IS NO SUPER-VILLAIN...
THEN WHO BUILT THE SLIME VOLCANO?
WELL, IT WAS...
...ME?

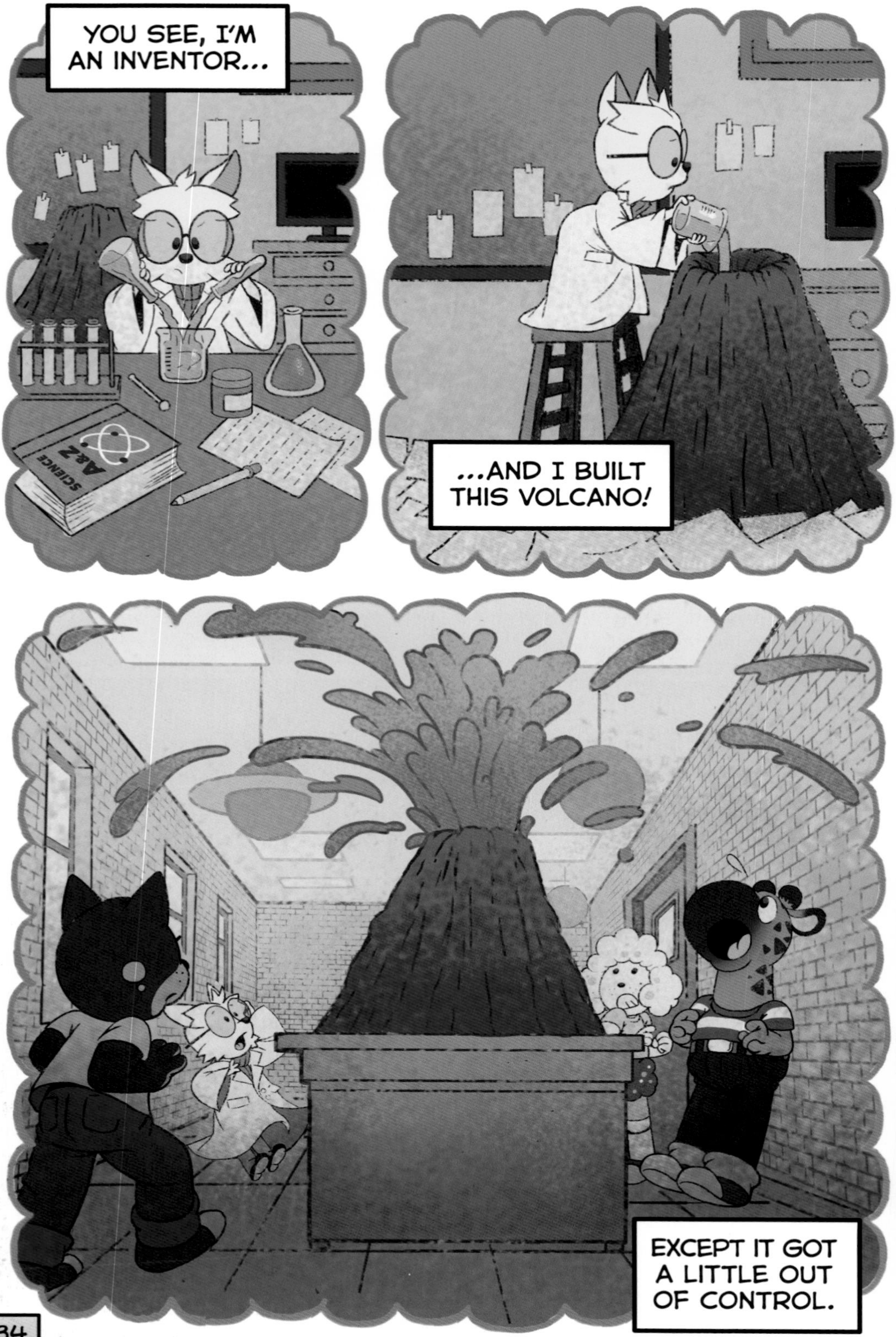
YOU SEE, I'M AN INVENTOR...
SCIENCE
A&Z
...AND I BUILT THIS VOLCANO!
EXCEPT IT GOT A LITTLE OUT OF CONTROL.

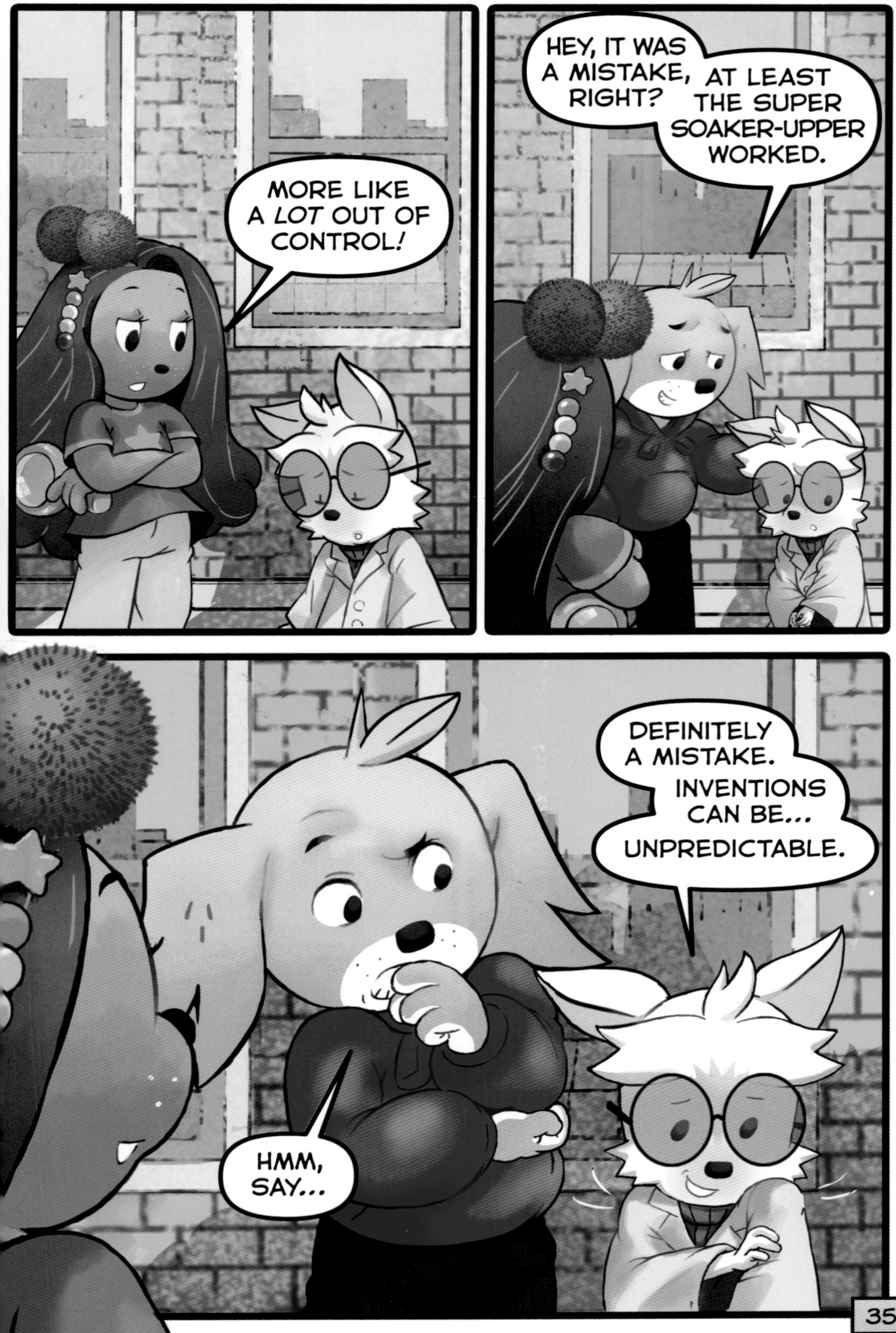
MORE LIKE A *LOT* OUT OF CONTROL!
HEY, IT WAS A MISTAKE, RIGHT?
AT LEAST THE SUPER SOAKER-UPPER WORKED.
DEFINITELY A MISTAKE.
INVENTIONS CAN BE...
UNPREDICTABLE.
HMM, SAY...

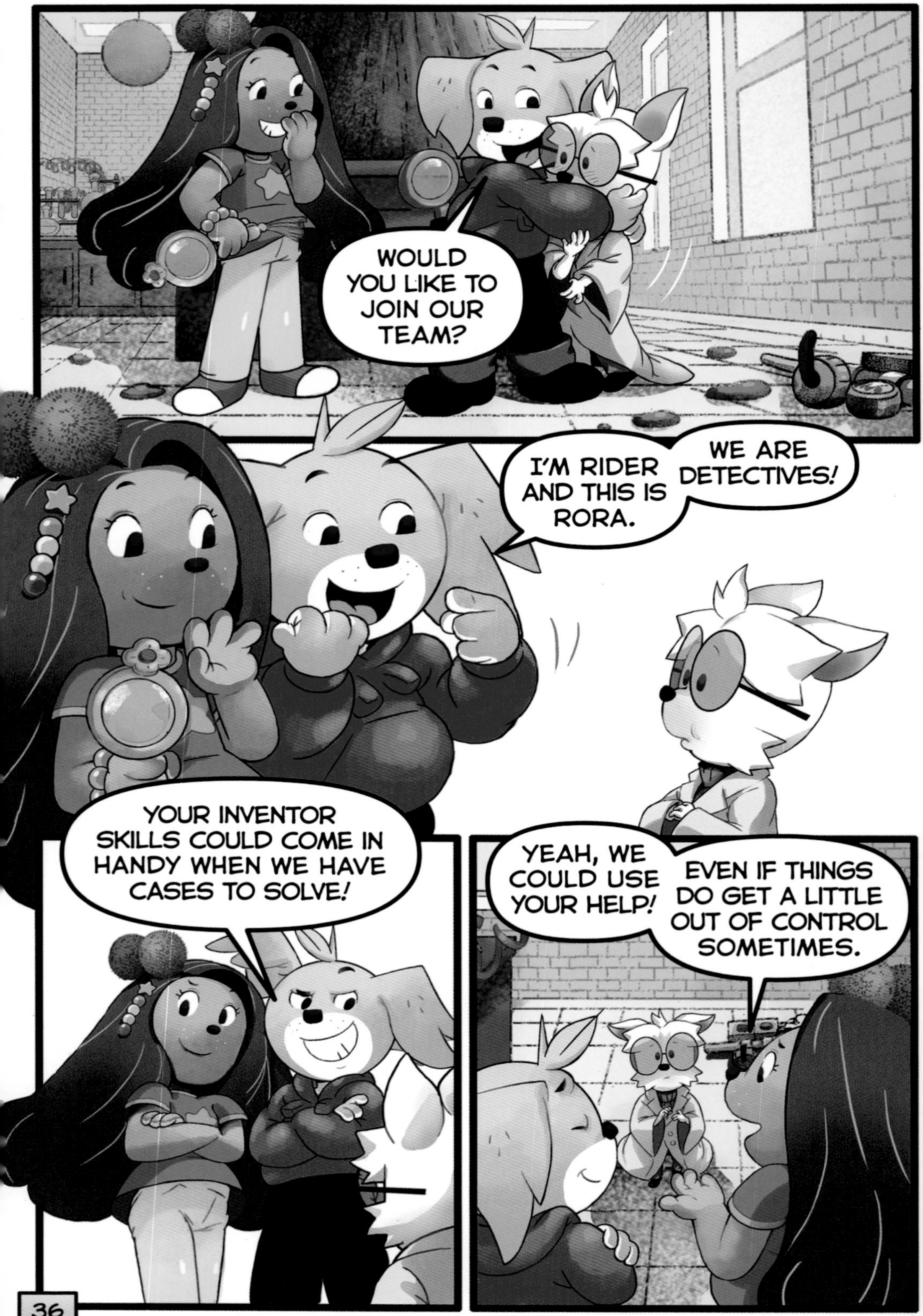
WOULD YOU LIKE TO JOIN OUR TEAM?
I'M RIDER AND THIS IS RORA.
WE ARE DETECTIVES!
YOUR INVENTOR SKILLS COULD COME IN HANDY WHEN WE HAVE CASES TO SOLVE!
YEAH, WE COULD USE YOUR HELP!
EVEN IF THINGS DO GET A LITTLE OUT OF CONTROL SOMETIMES.

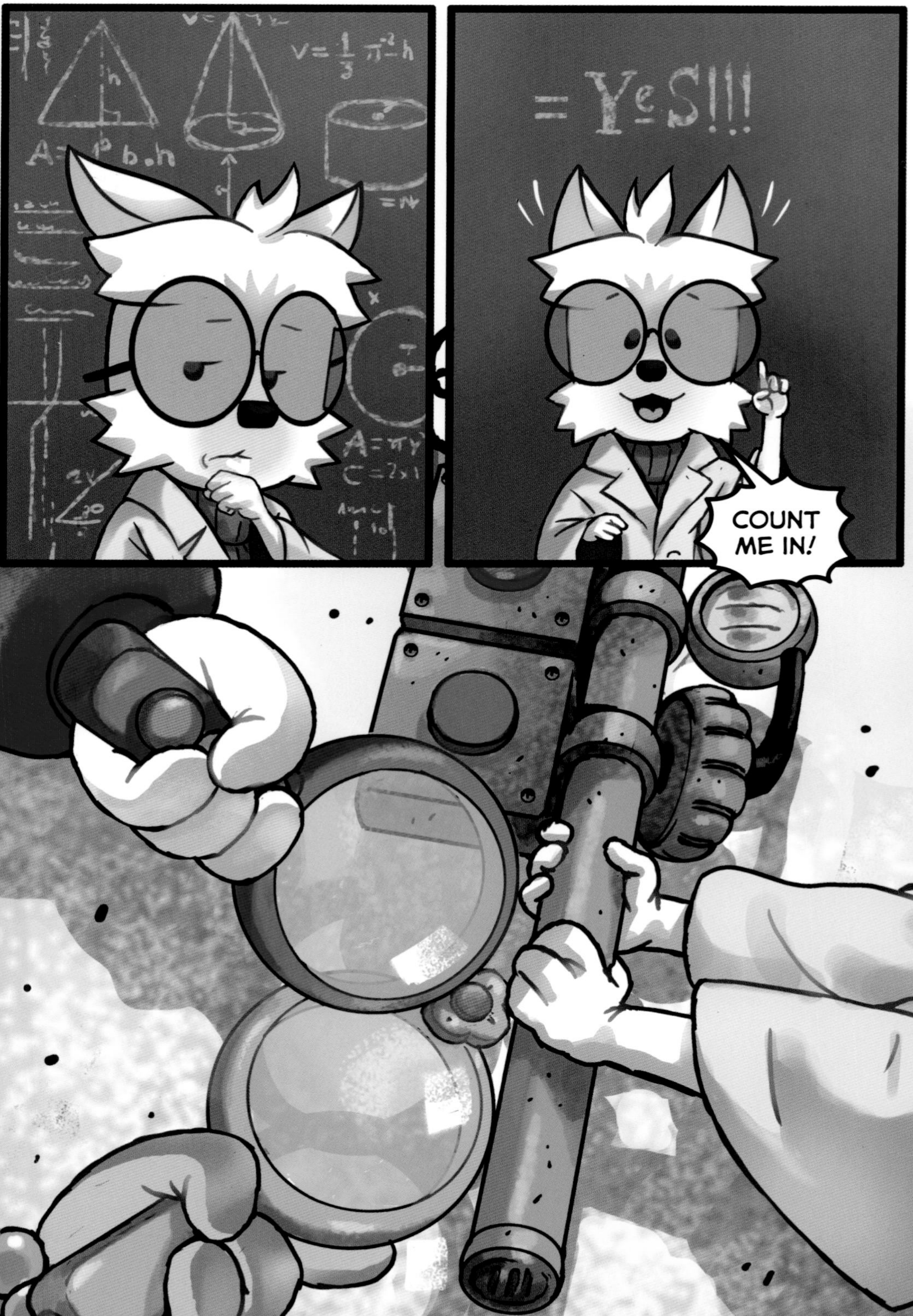
= YeS!!!
COUNT ME IN!

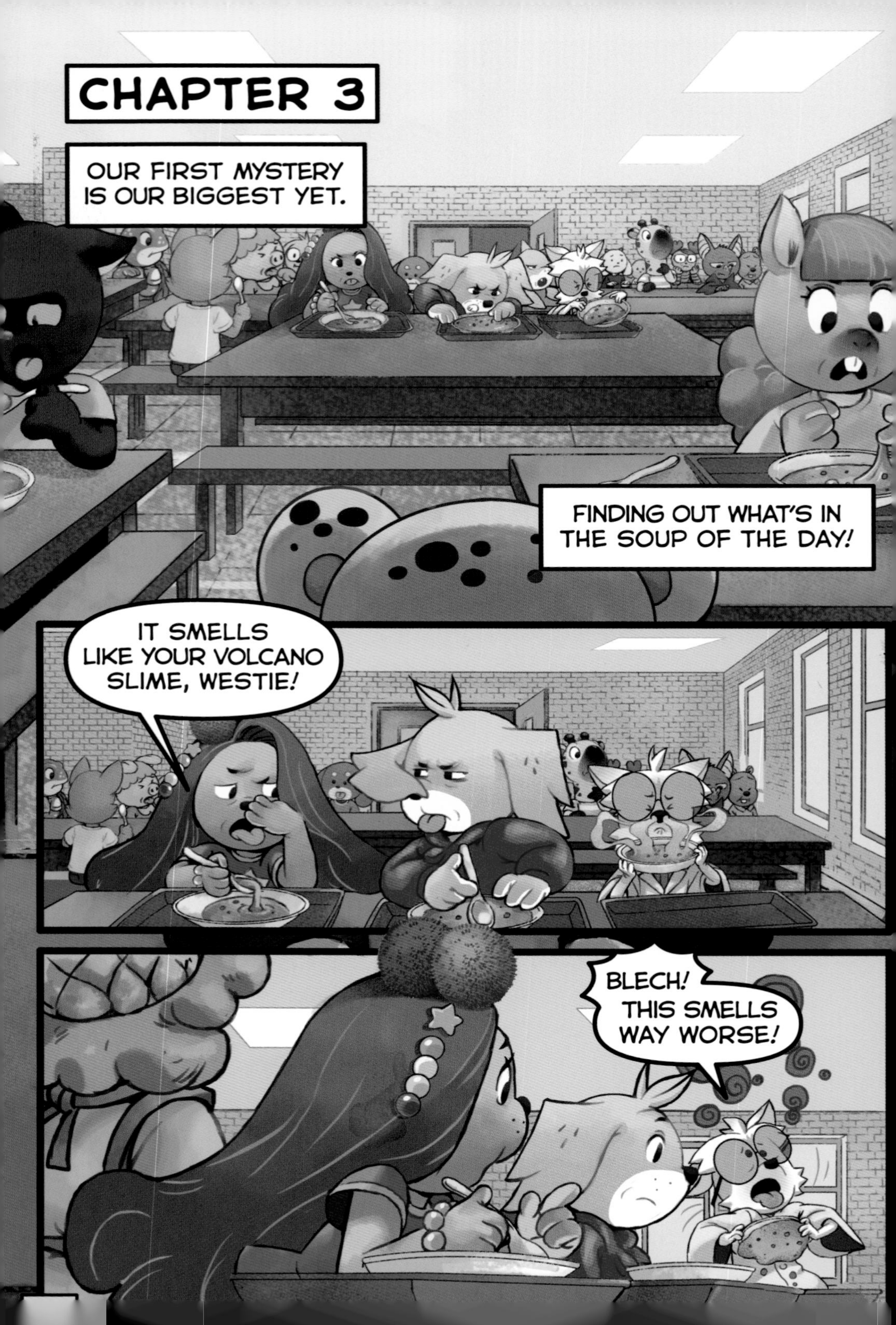
CHAPTER 3
OUR FIRST MYSTERY IS OUR BIGGEST YET.
FINDING OUT WHAT'S IN THE SOUP OF THE DAY!
IT SMELLS LIKE YOUR VOLCANO SLIME, WESTIE!
BLECH! THIS SMELLS WAY WORSE!

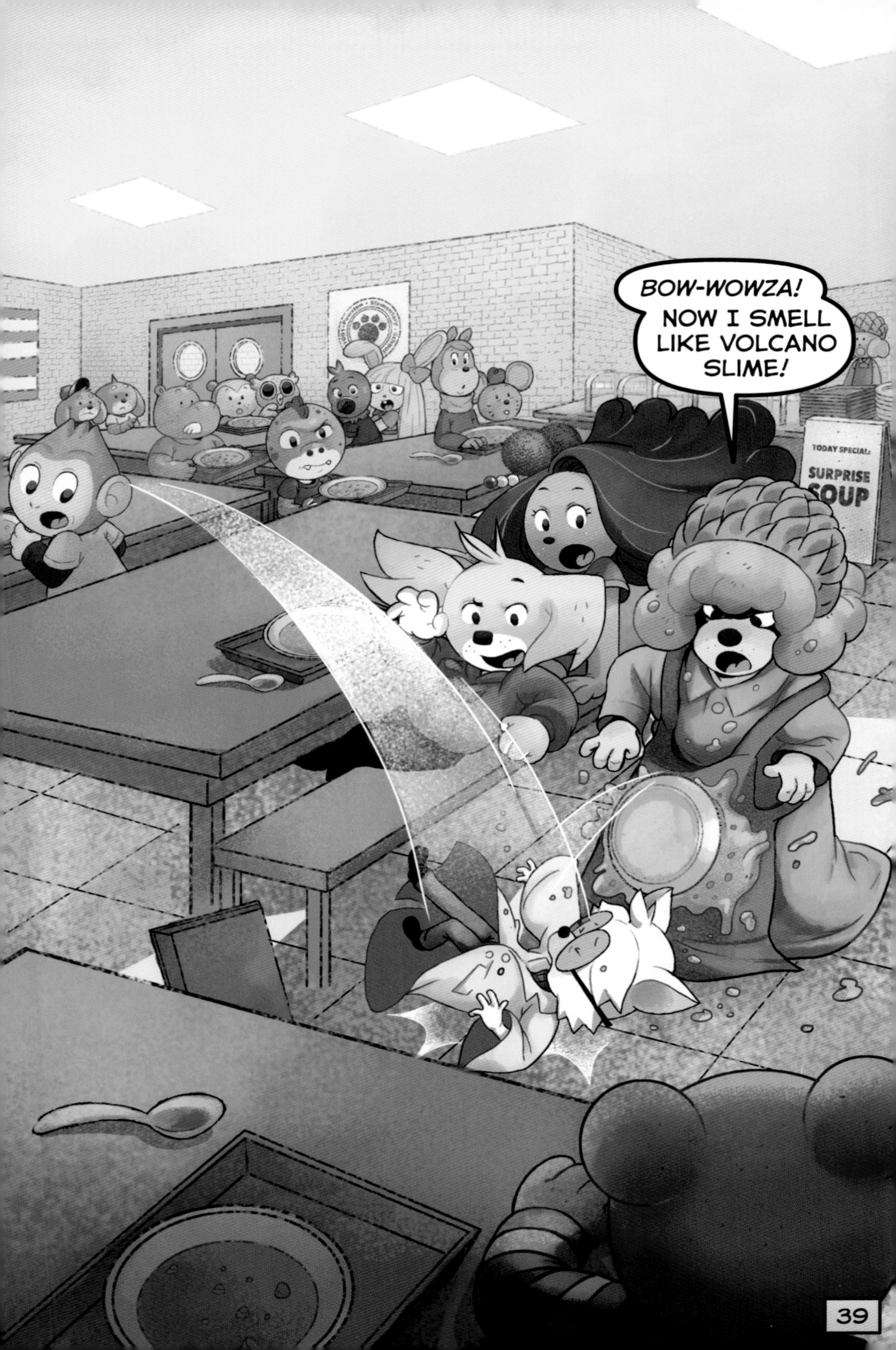
BOW-WOWZA! NOW I SMELL LIKE VOLCANO SLIME!
TODAY SPECIAL: SURPRISE SOUP

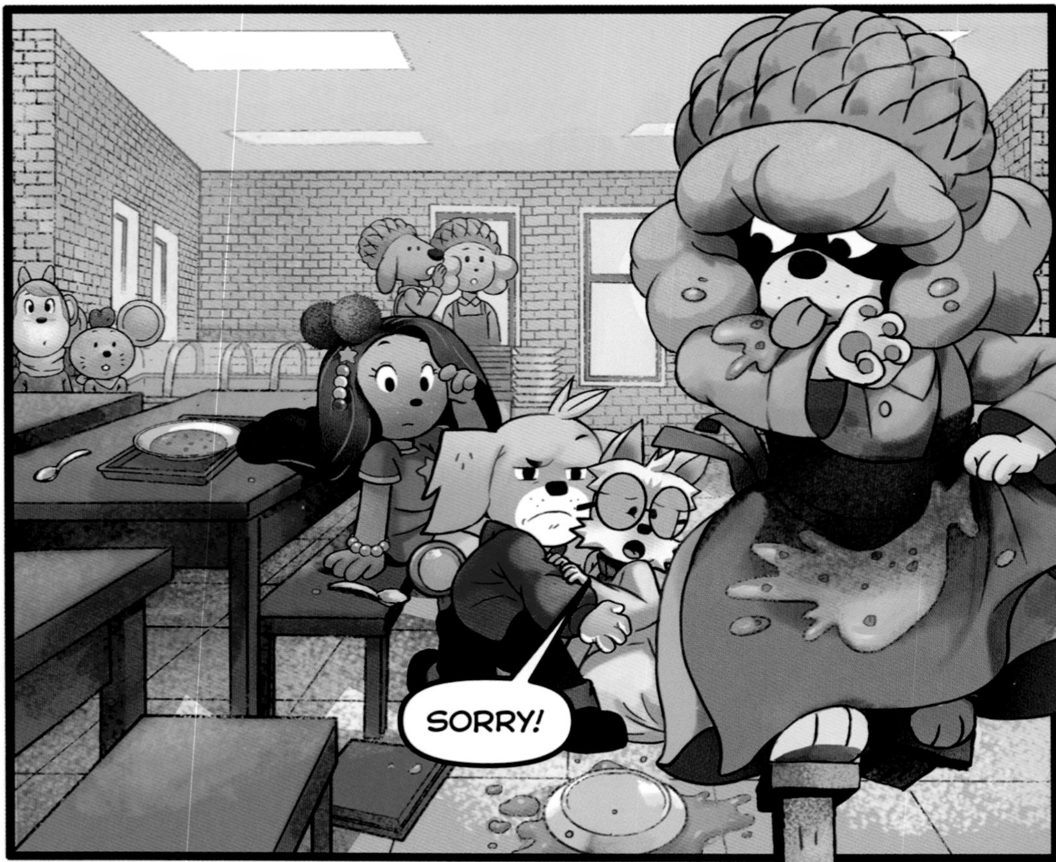
SORRY!

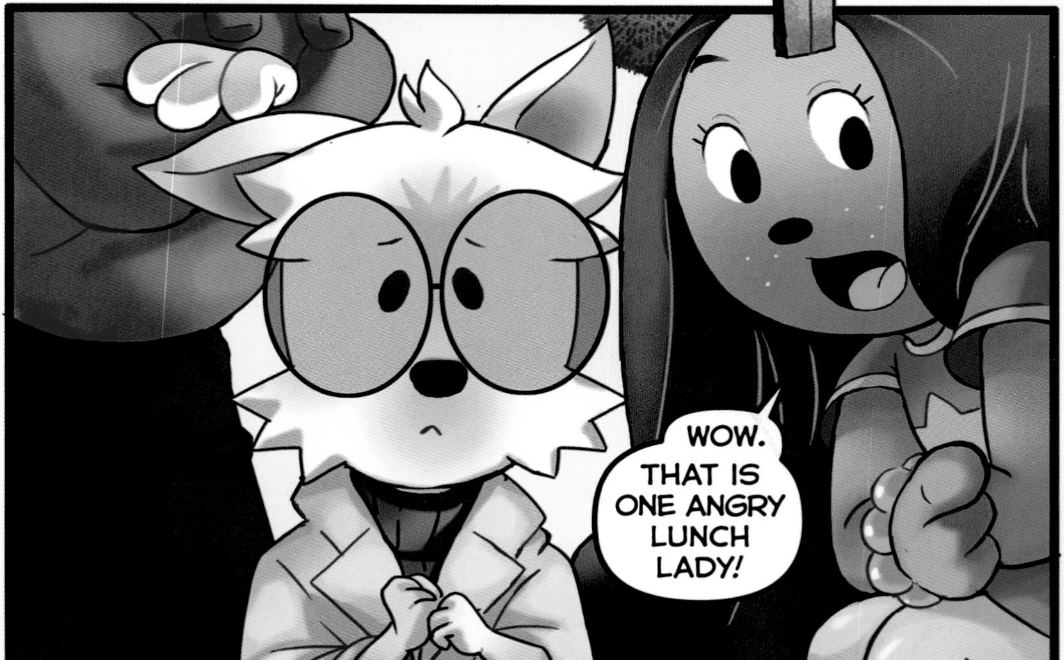
WOW. THAT IS ONE ANGRY LUNCH LADY!

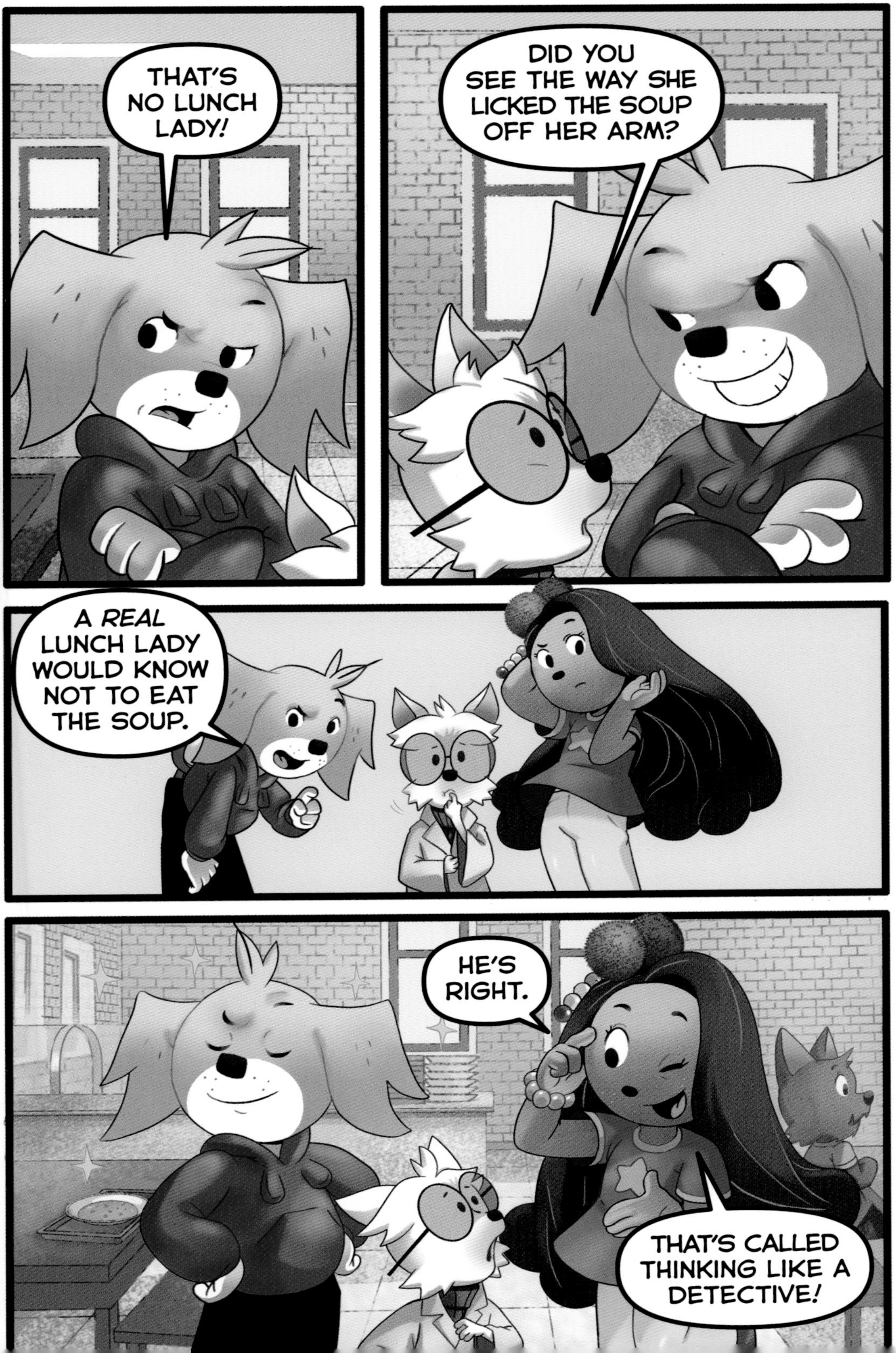
THAT'S NO LUNCH LADY!
DID YOU SEE THE WAY SHE LICKED THE SOUP OFF HER ARM?
A *REAL* LUNCH LADY WOULD KNOW NOT TO EAT THE SOUP.
HE'S RIGHT.
THAT'S CALLED THINKING LIKE A DETECTIVE!

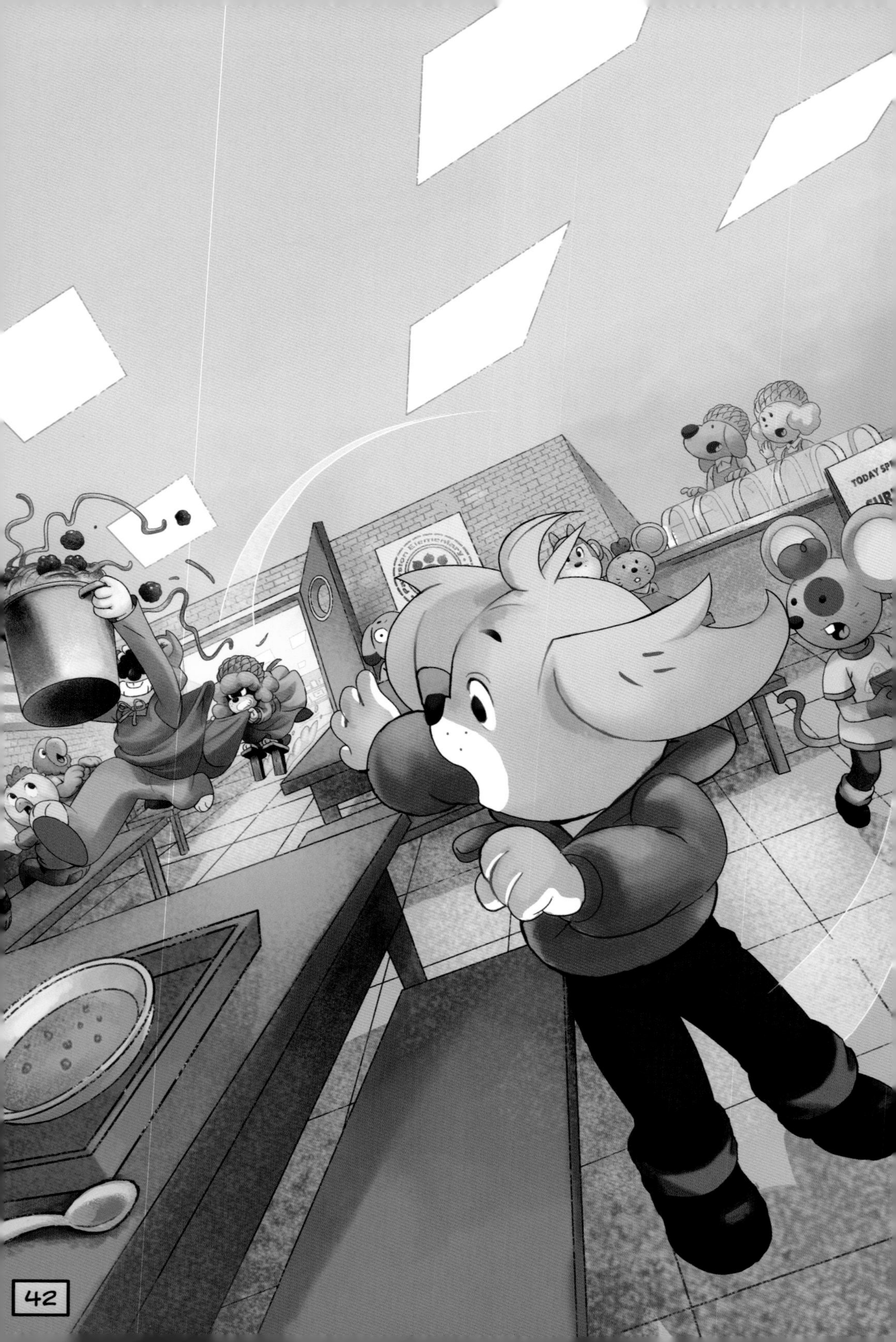

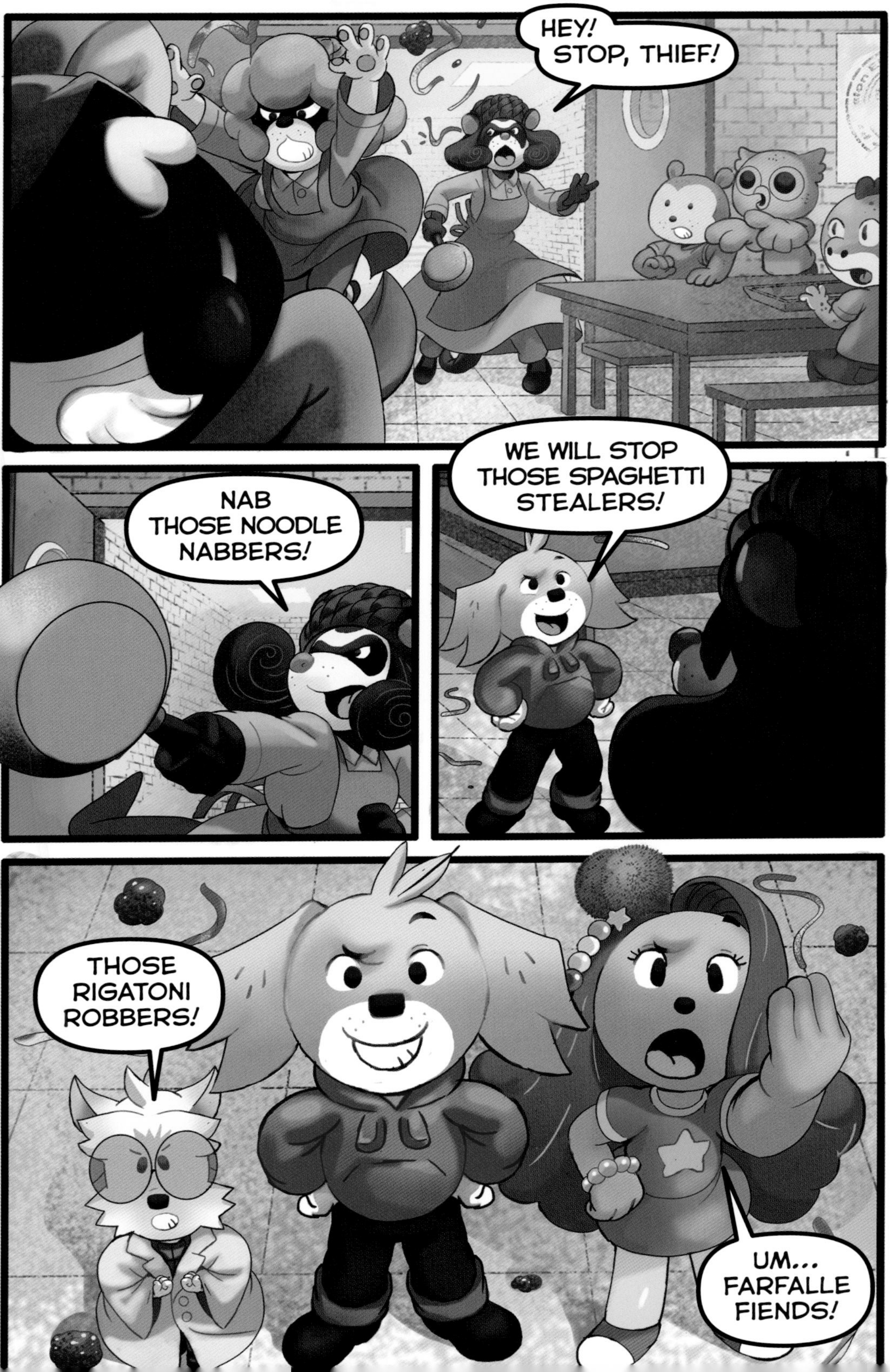
HEY! STOP, THIEF!
NAB THOSE NOODLE NABBERS!
WE WILL STOP THOSE SPAGHETTI STEALERS!
THOSE RIGATONI ROBBERS!
UM... FARFALLE FIENDS!

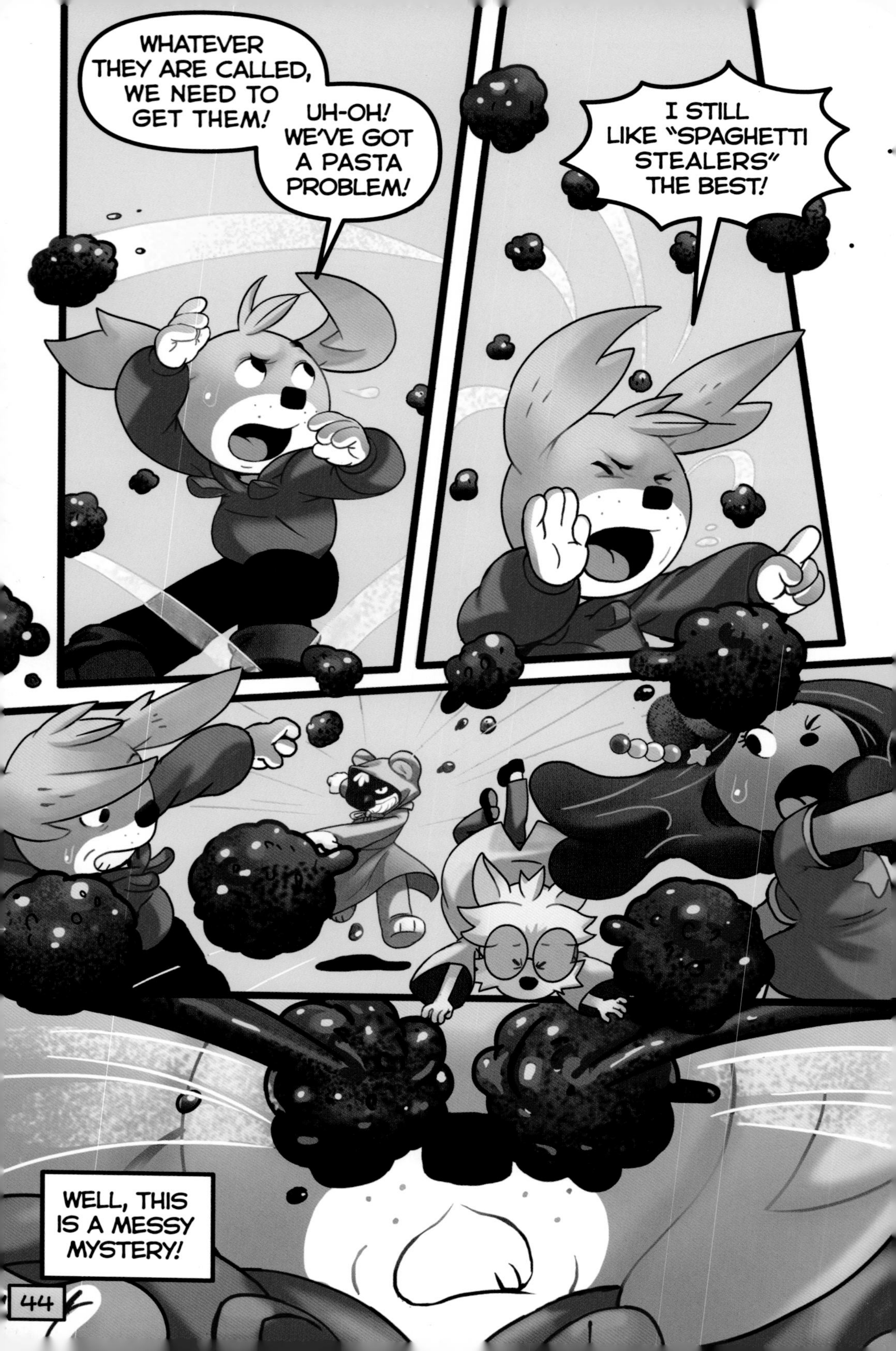
WHATEVER THEY ARE CALLED, WE NEED TO GET THEM!
UH-OH! WE'VE GOT A PASTA PROBLEM!
I STILL LIKE "SPAGHETTI STEALERS" THE BEST!
WELL, THIS IS A MESSY MYSTERY!

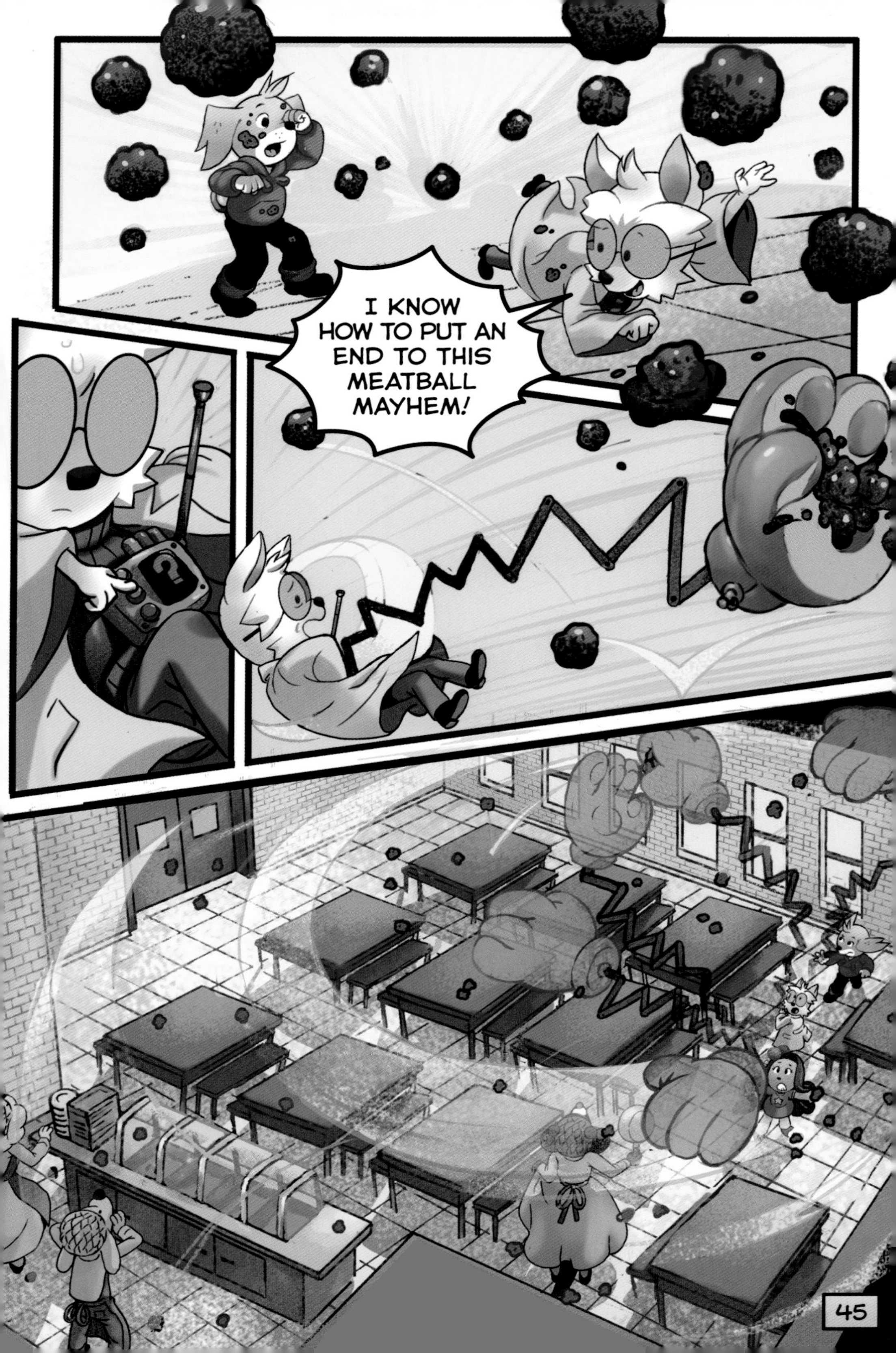
I KNOW HOW TO PUT AN END TO THIS MEATBALL MAYHEM!

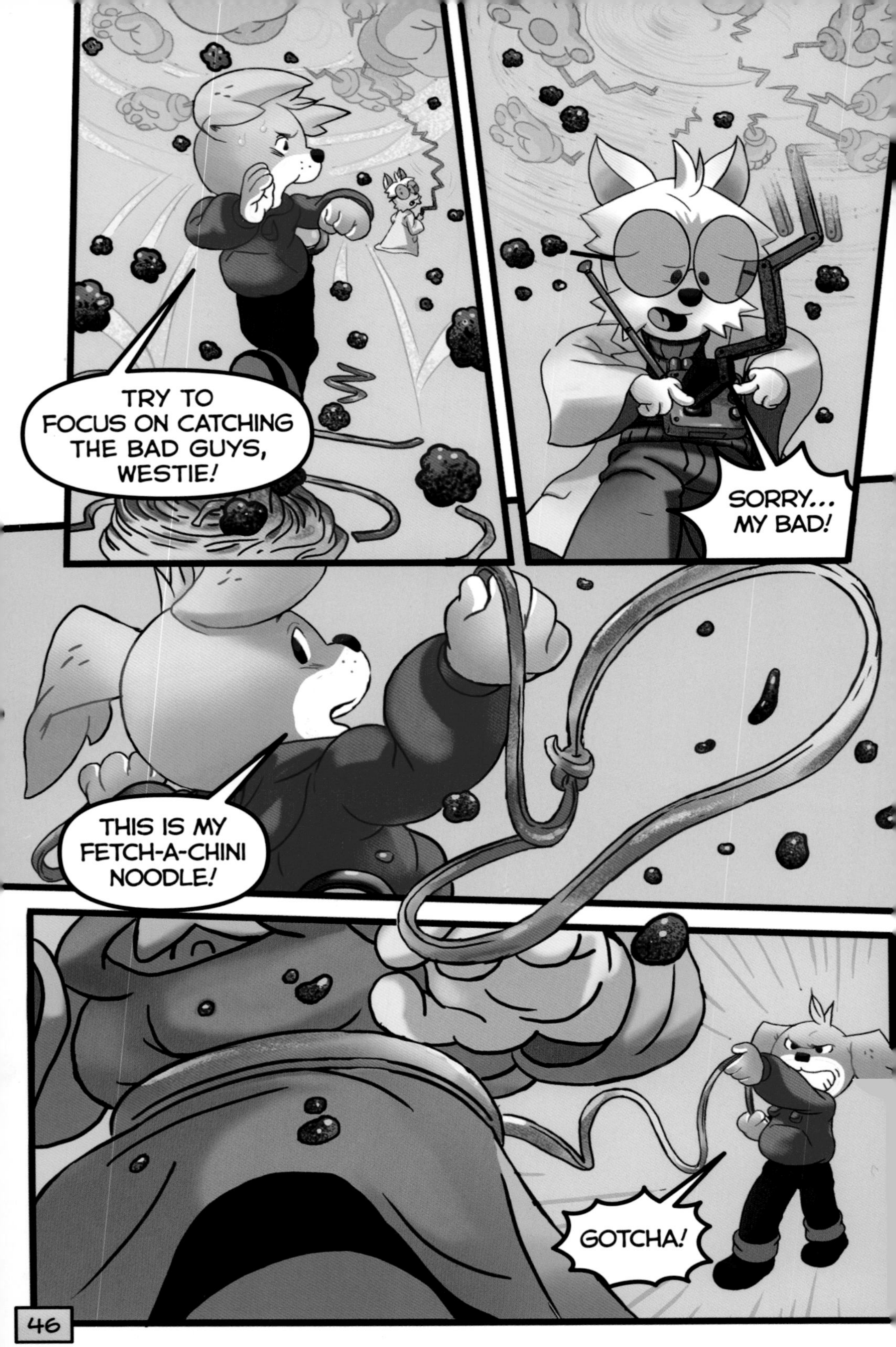
TRY TO FOCUS ON CATCHING THE BAD GUYS, WESTIE!
SORRY... MY BAD!
THIS IS MY FETCH-A-CHINI NOODLE!
GOTCHA!

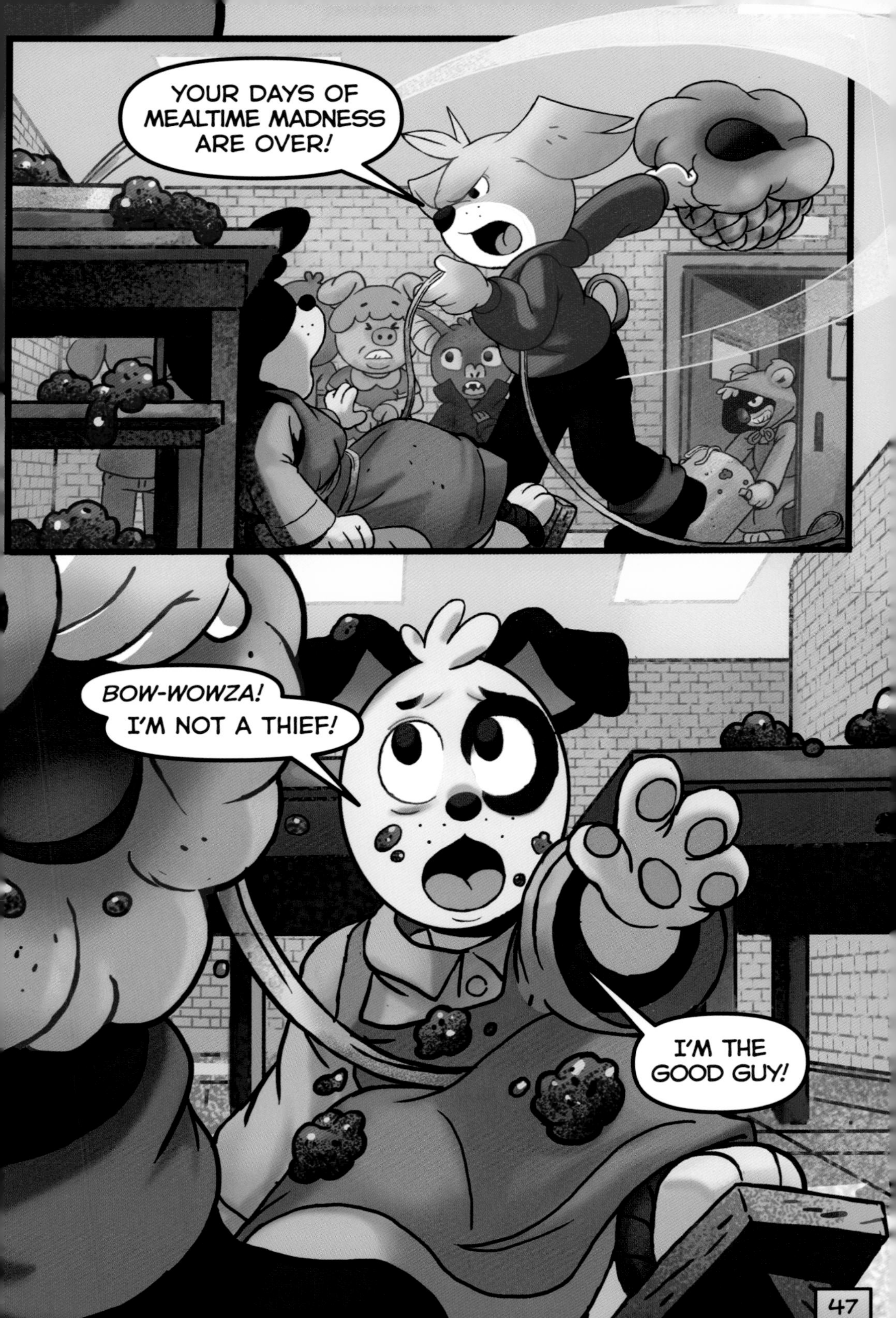
YOUR DAYS OF MEALTIME MADNESS ARE OVER!
BOW-WOWZA! I'M NOT A THIEF!
I'M THE GOOD GUY!

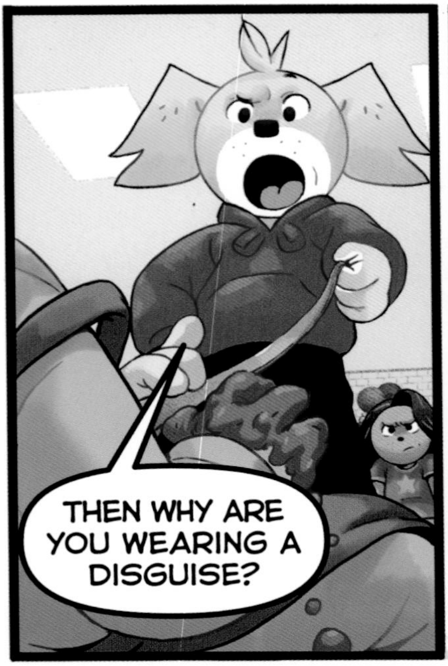
THEN WHY ARE YOU WEARING A DISGUISE?

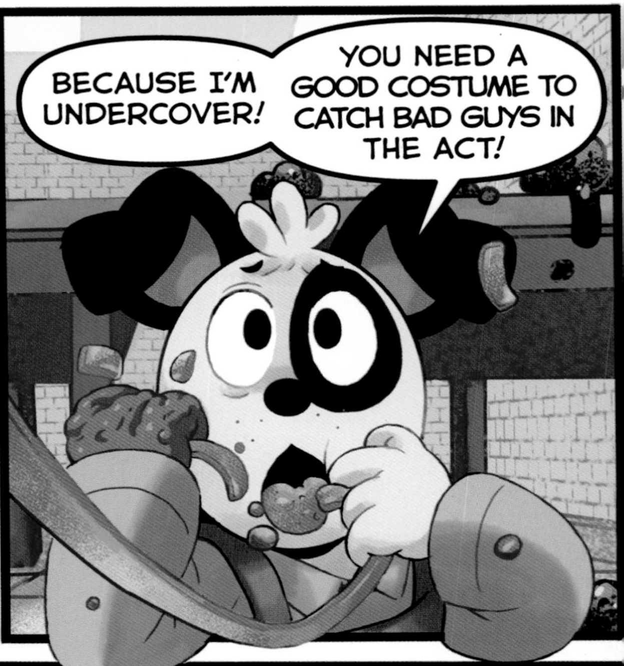
BECAUSE I'M UNDERCOVER!
YOU NEED A GOOD COSTUME TO CATCH BAD GUYS IN THE ACT!

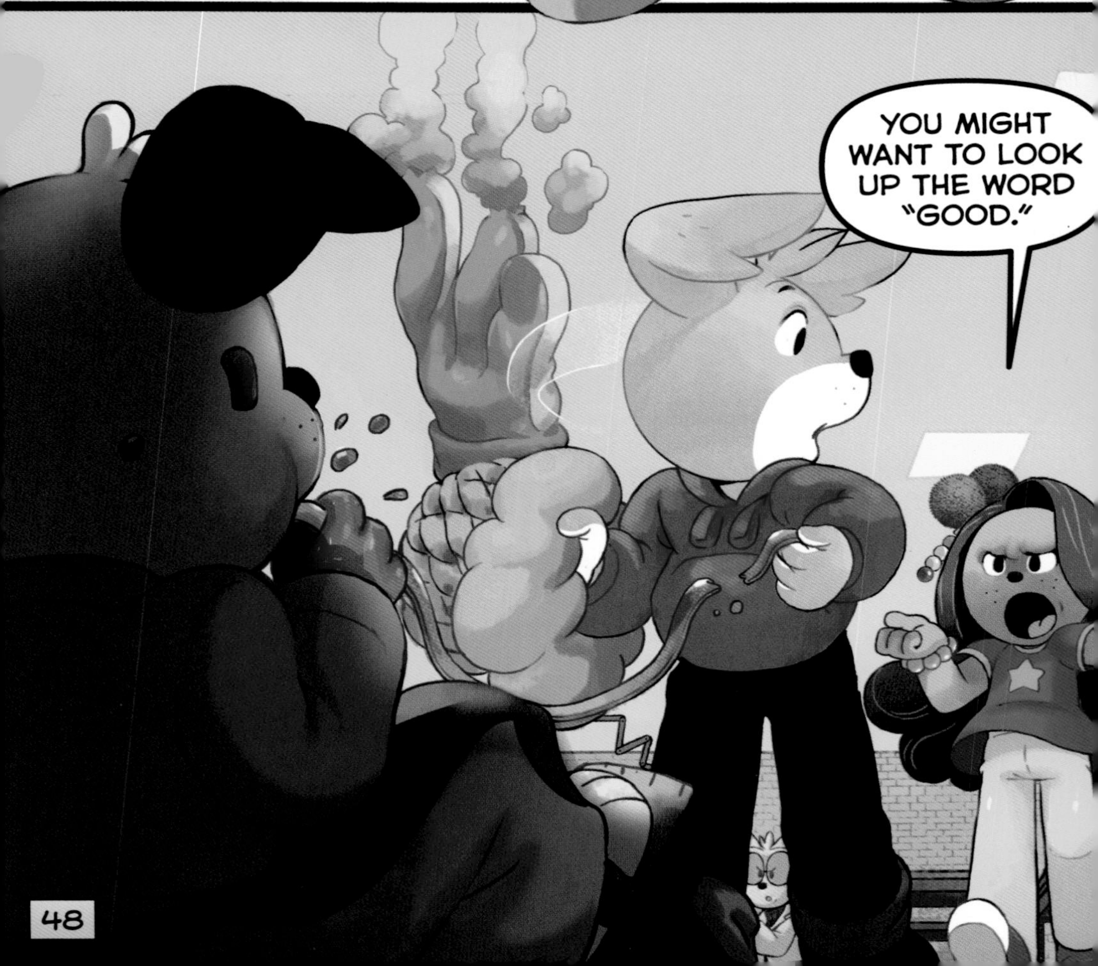
YOU MIGHT WANT TO LOOK UP THE WORD "GOOD."

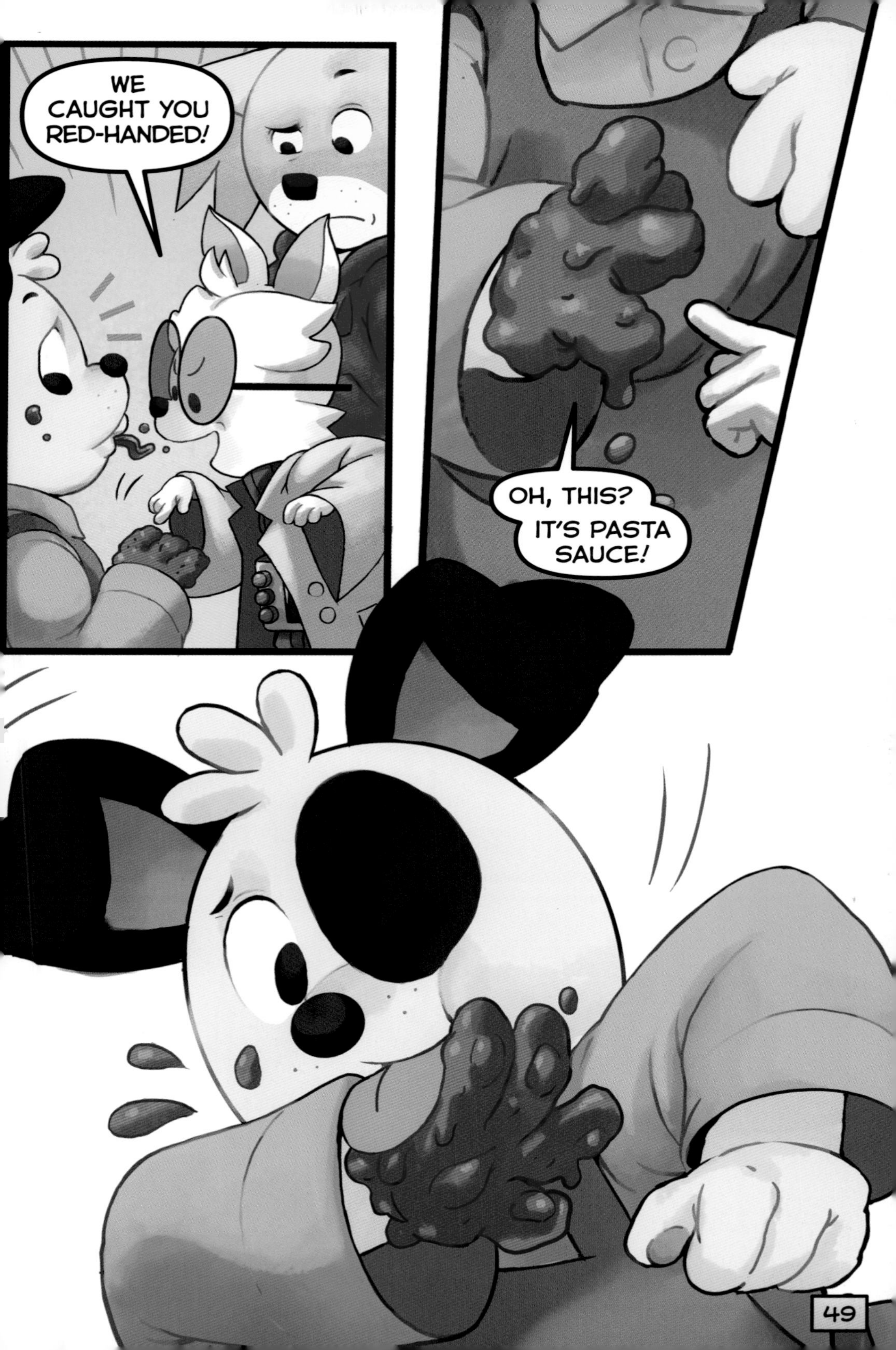
WE CAUGHT YOU RED-HANDED!
OH, THIS? IT'S PASTA SAUCE!

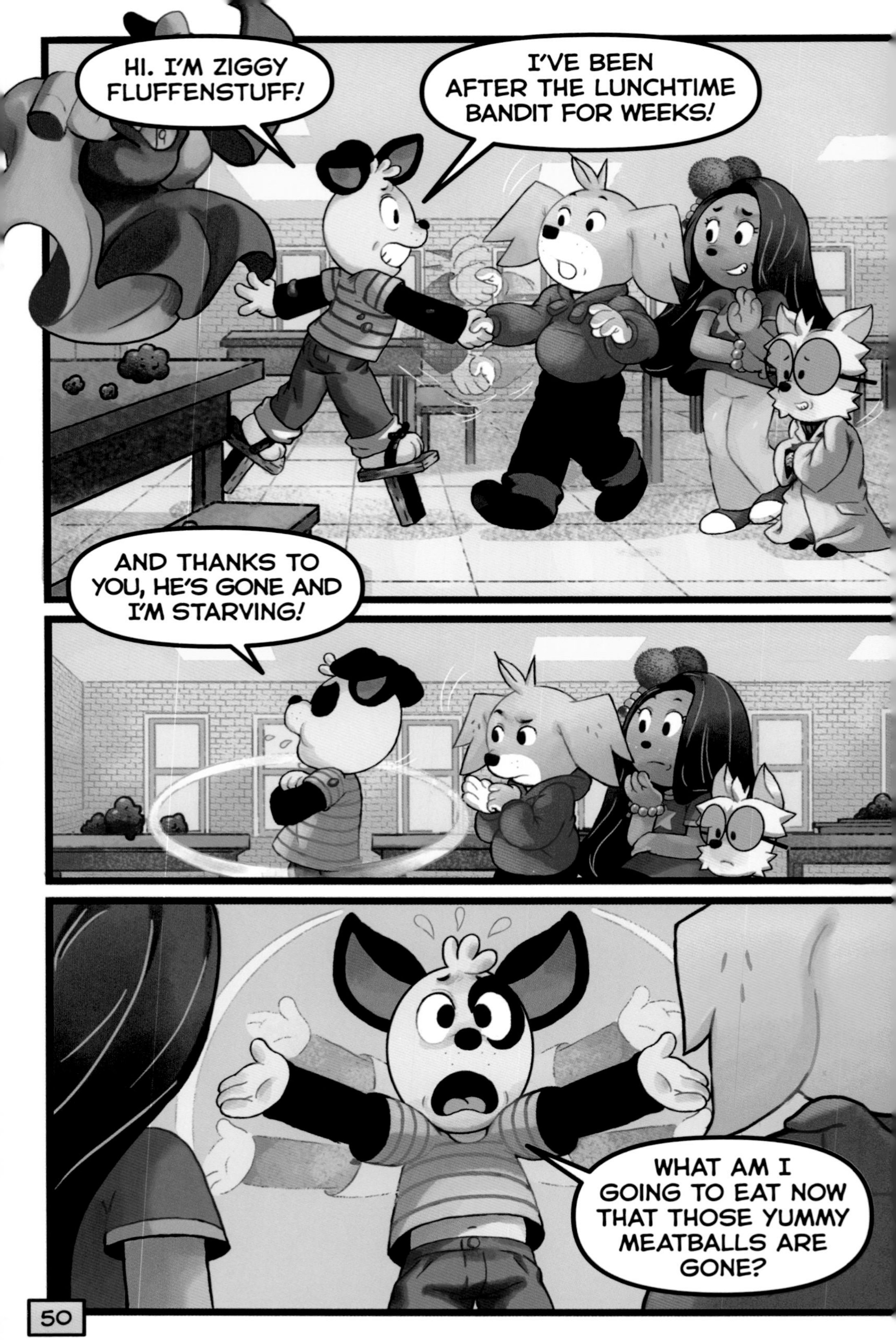
HI. I'M ZIGGY FLUFFENSTUFF!
I'VE BEEN AFTER THE LUNCHTIME BANDIT FOR WEEKS!
AND THANKS TO YOU, HE'S GONE AND I'M STARVING!
WHAT AM I GOING TO EAT NOW THAT THOSE YUMMY MEATBALLS ARE GONE?

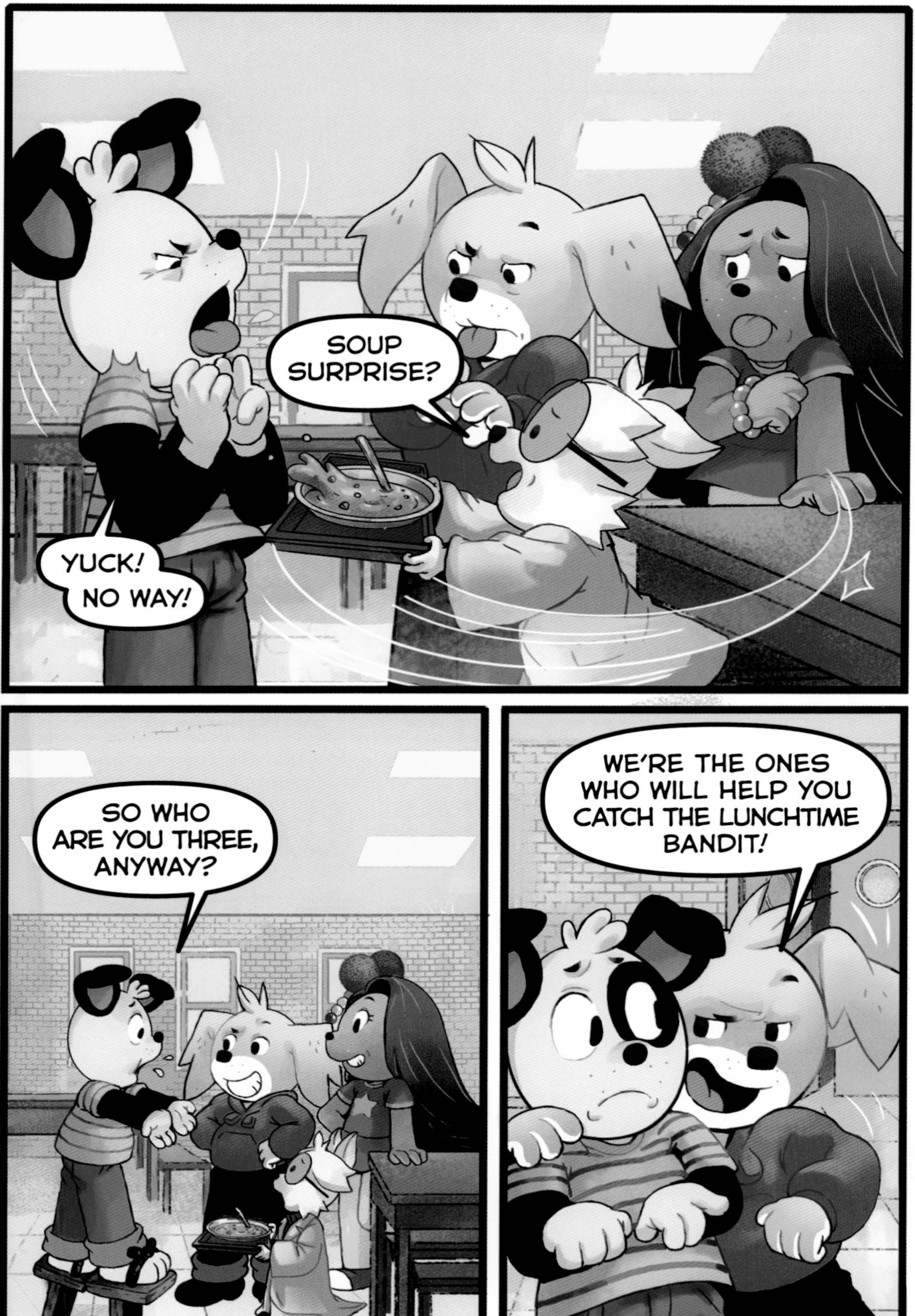
SOUP SURPRISE?
YUCK! NO WAY!
SO WHO ARE YOU THREE, ANYWAY?
WE'RE THE ONES WHO WILL HELP YOU CATCH THE LUNCHTIME BANDIT!

CHAPTER 4

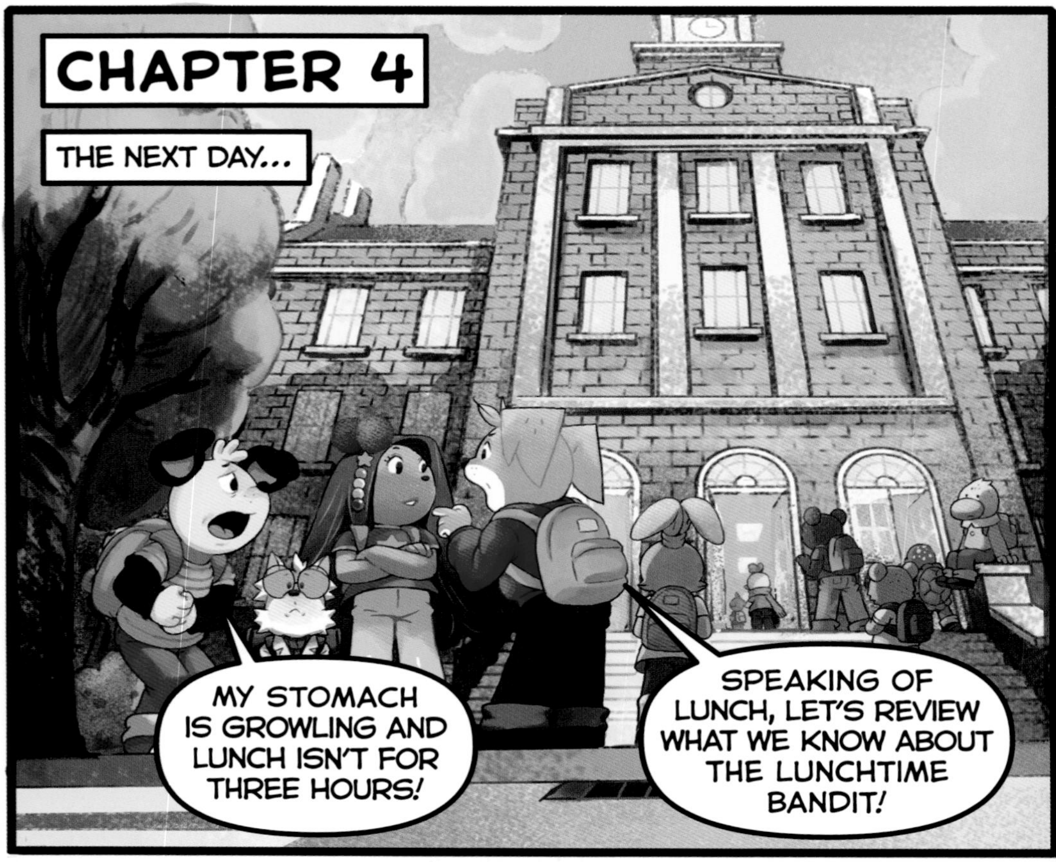
THE NEXT DAY...
MY STOMACH IS GROWLING AND LUNCH ISN'T FOR THREE HOURS!
SPEAKING OF LUNCH, LET'S REVIEW WHAT WE KNOW ABOUT THE LUNCHTIME BANDIT!

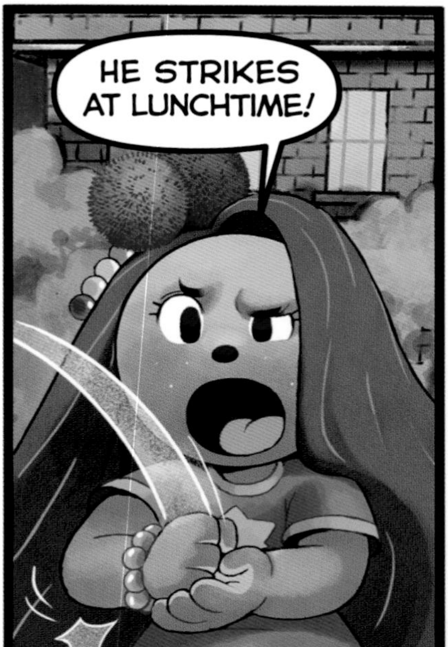
HE STRIKES AT LUNCHTIME!

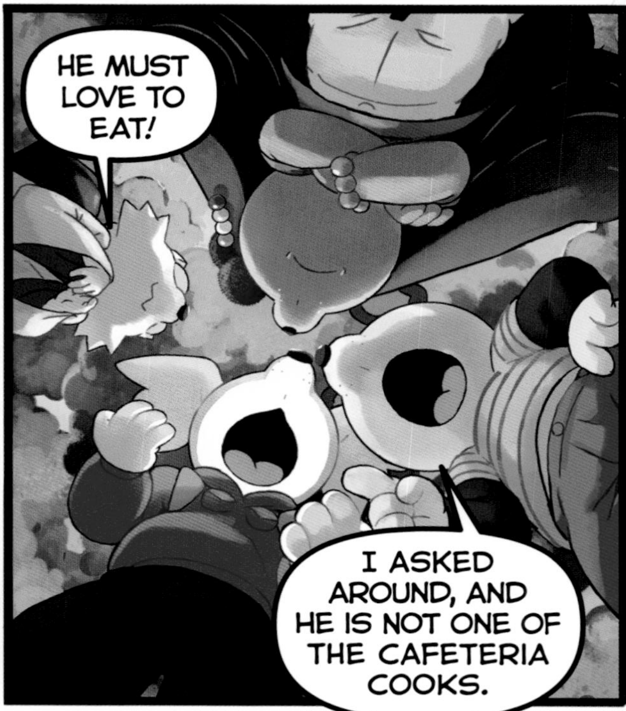
HE MUST LOVE TO EAT!
I ASKED AROUND, AND HE IS NOT ONE OF THE CAFETERIA COOKS.

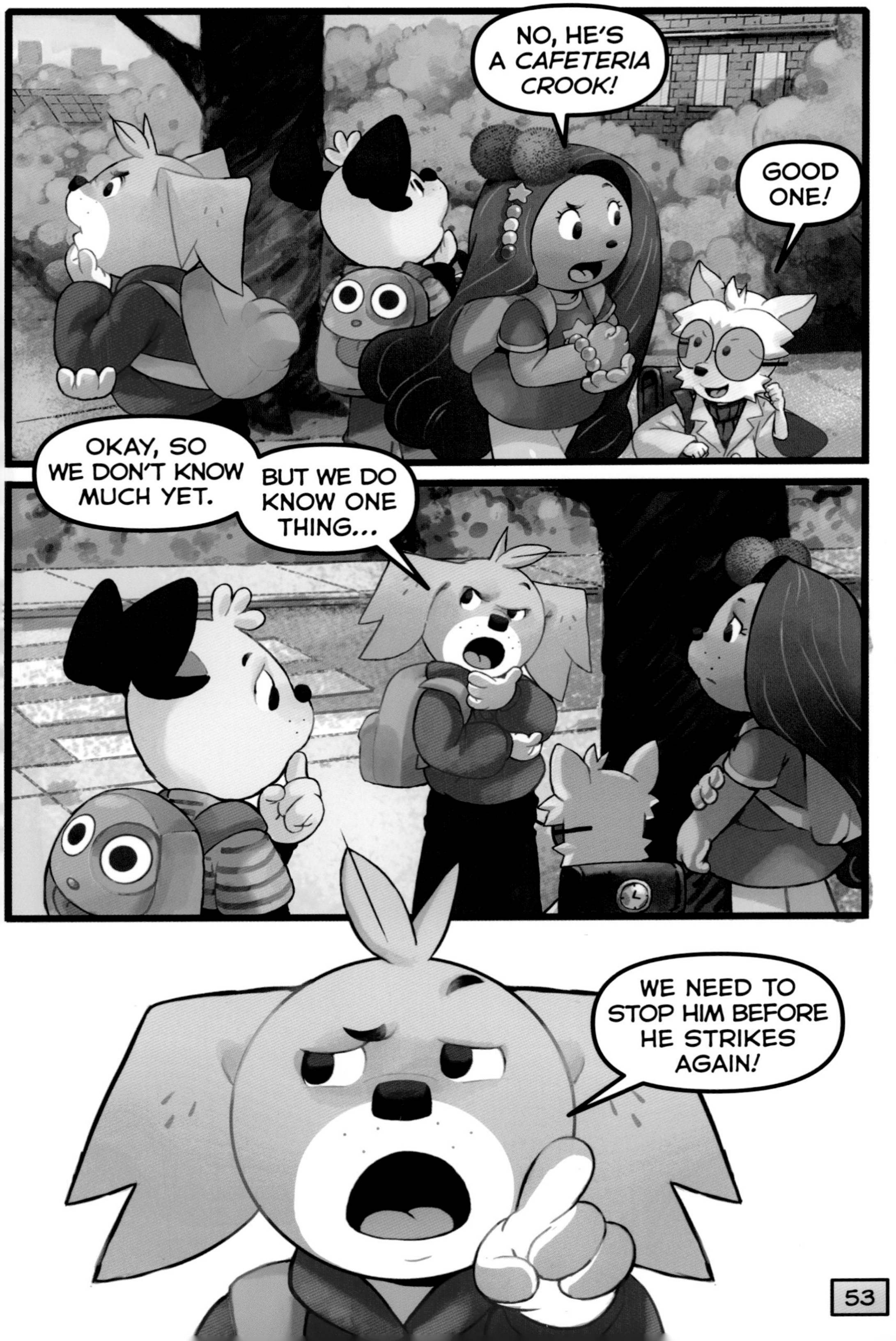
NO, HE'S A CAFETERIA CROOK!
GOOD ONE!
OKAY, SO WE DON'T KNOW MUCH YET.
BUT WE DO KNOW ONE THING...
WE NEED TO STOP HIM BEFORE HE STRIKES AGAIN!

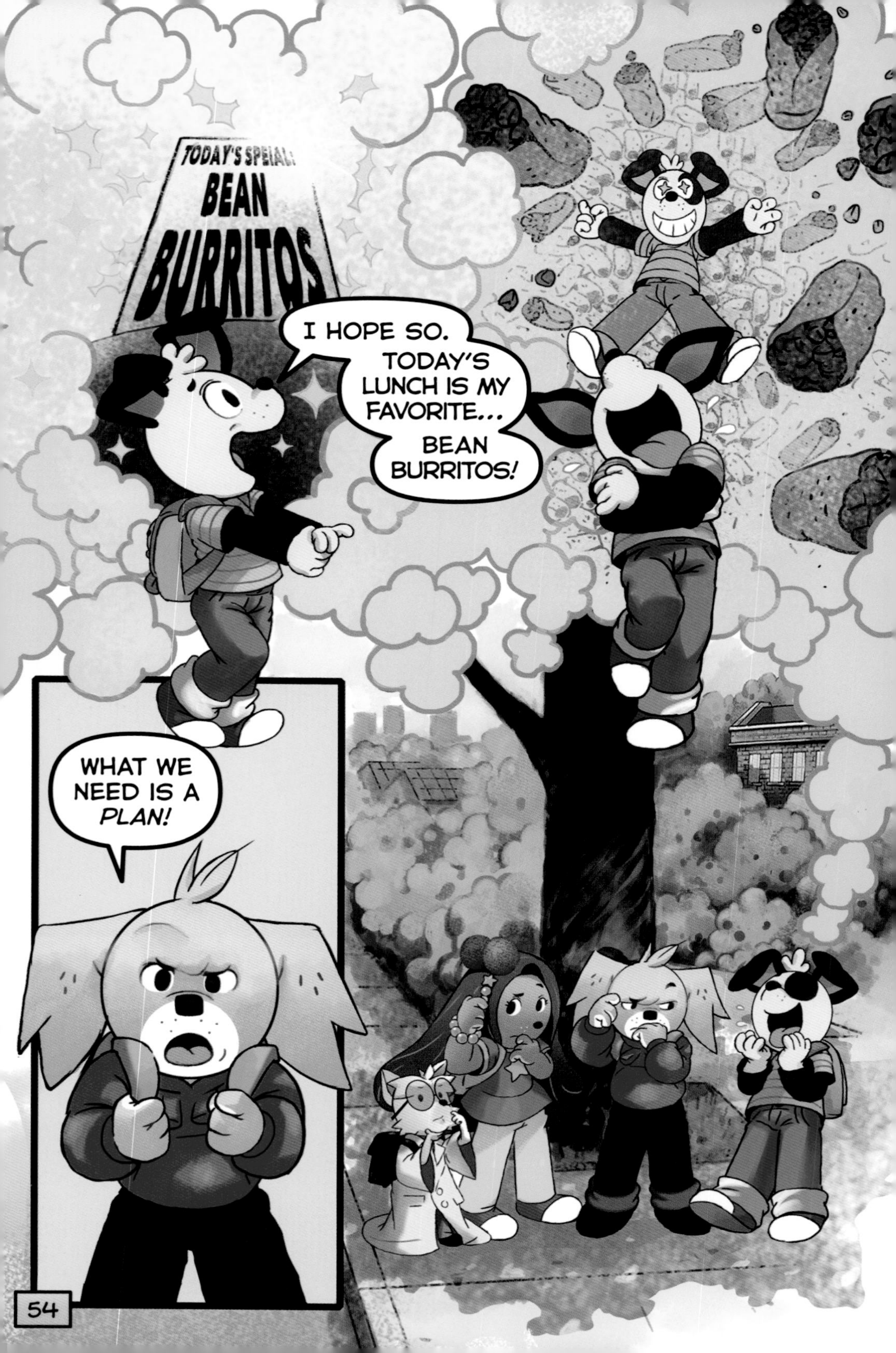
TODAY'S SPEIAL:
BEAN
BURRITOS
I HOPE SO.
TODAY'S LUNCH IS MY FAVORITE...
BEAN BURRITOS!
WHAT WE NEED IS A *PLAN!*

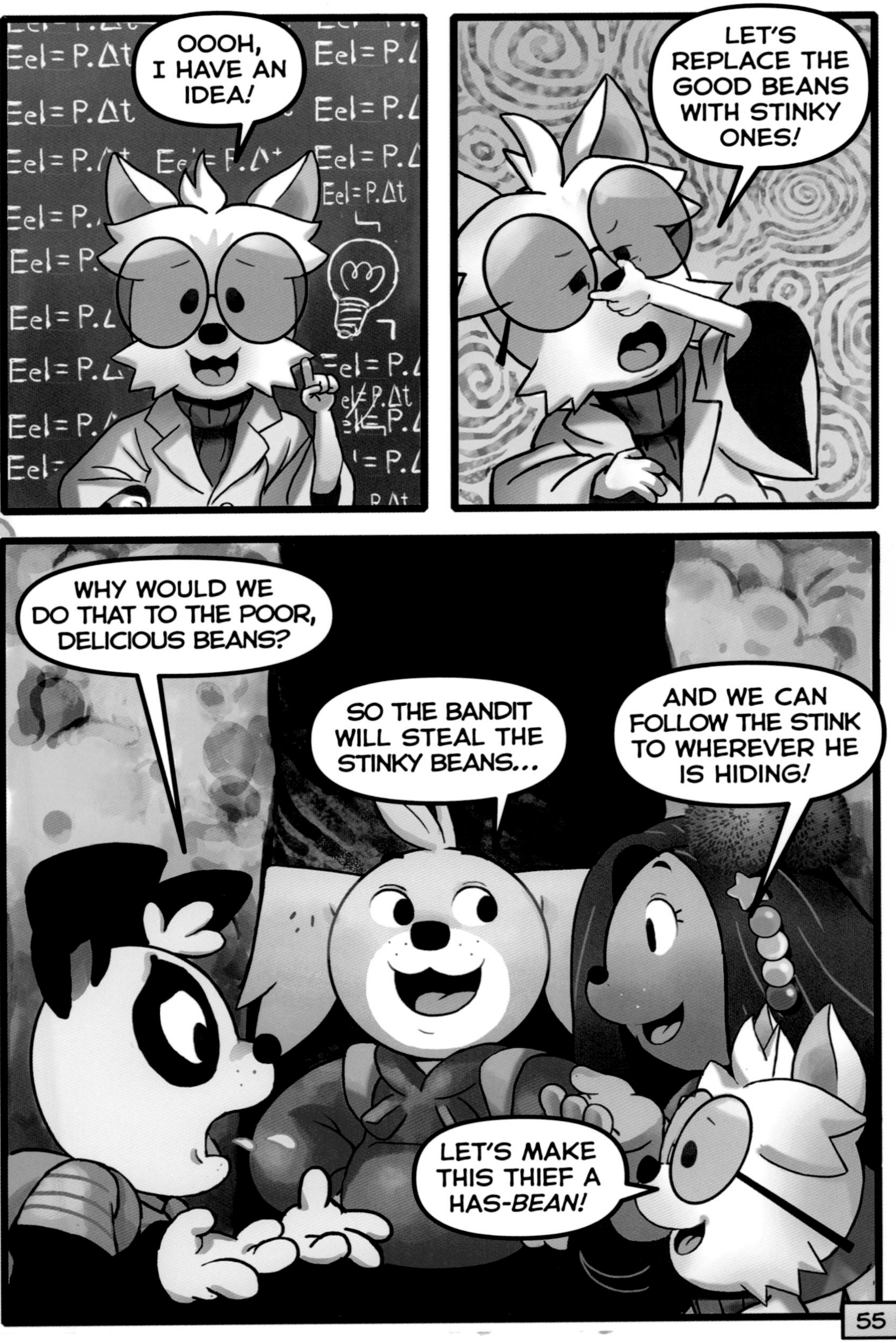
OOOH, I HAVE AN IDEA!
LET'S REPLACE THE GOOD BEANS WITH STINKY ONES!
WHY WOULD WE DO THAT TO THE POOR, DELICIOUS BEANS?
SO THE BANDIT WILL STEAL THE STINKY BEANS...
AND WE CAN FOLLOW THE STINK TO WHEREVER HE IS HIDING!
LET'S MAKE THIS THIEF A HAS-*BEAN*!

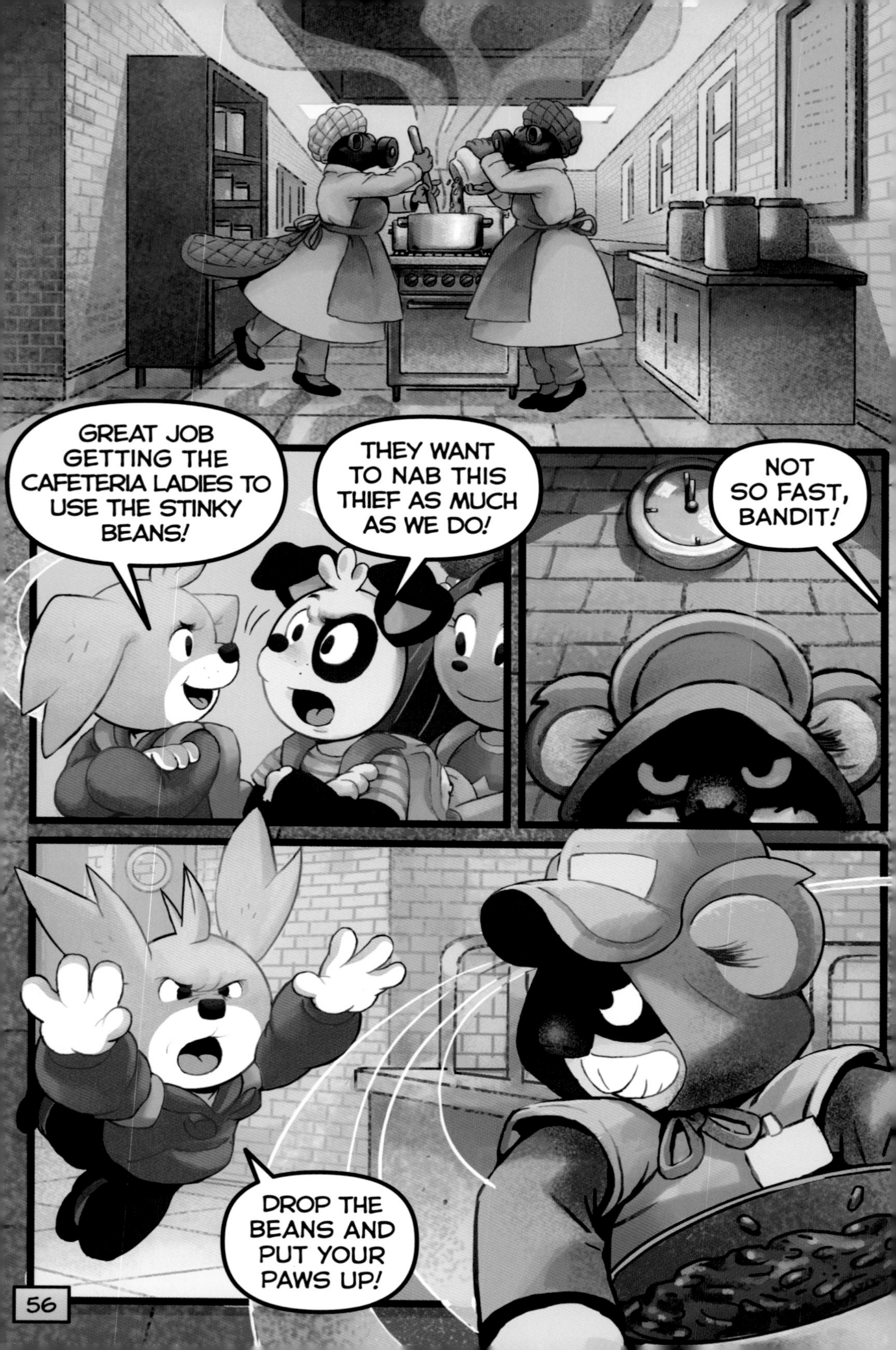
GREAT JOB GETTING THE CAFETERIA LADIES TO USE THE STINKY BEANS!
THEY WANT TO NAB THIS THIEF AS MUCH AS WE DO!
NOT SO FAST, BANDIT!
DROP THE BEANS AND PUT YOUR PAWS UP!

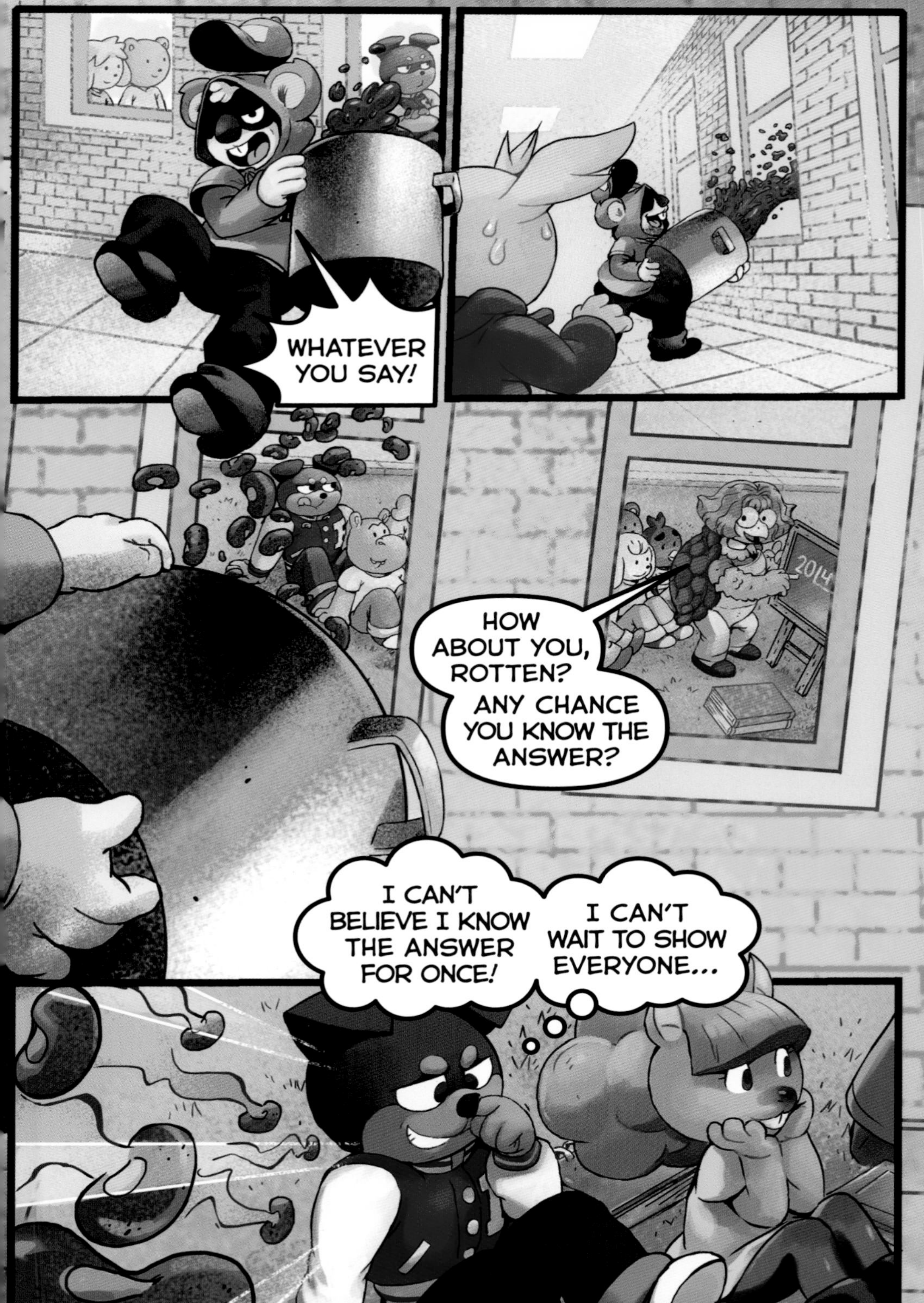
WHATEVER YOU SAY!
2014
HOW ABOUT YOU, ROTTEN?
ANY CHANCE YOU KNOW THE ANSWER?
I CAN'T BELIEVE I KNOW THE ANSWER FOR ONCE!
I CAN'T WAIT TO SHOW EVERYONE...

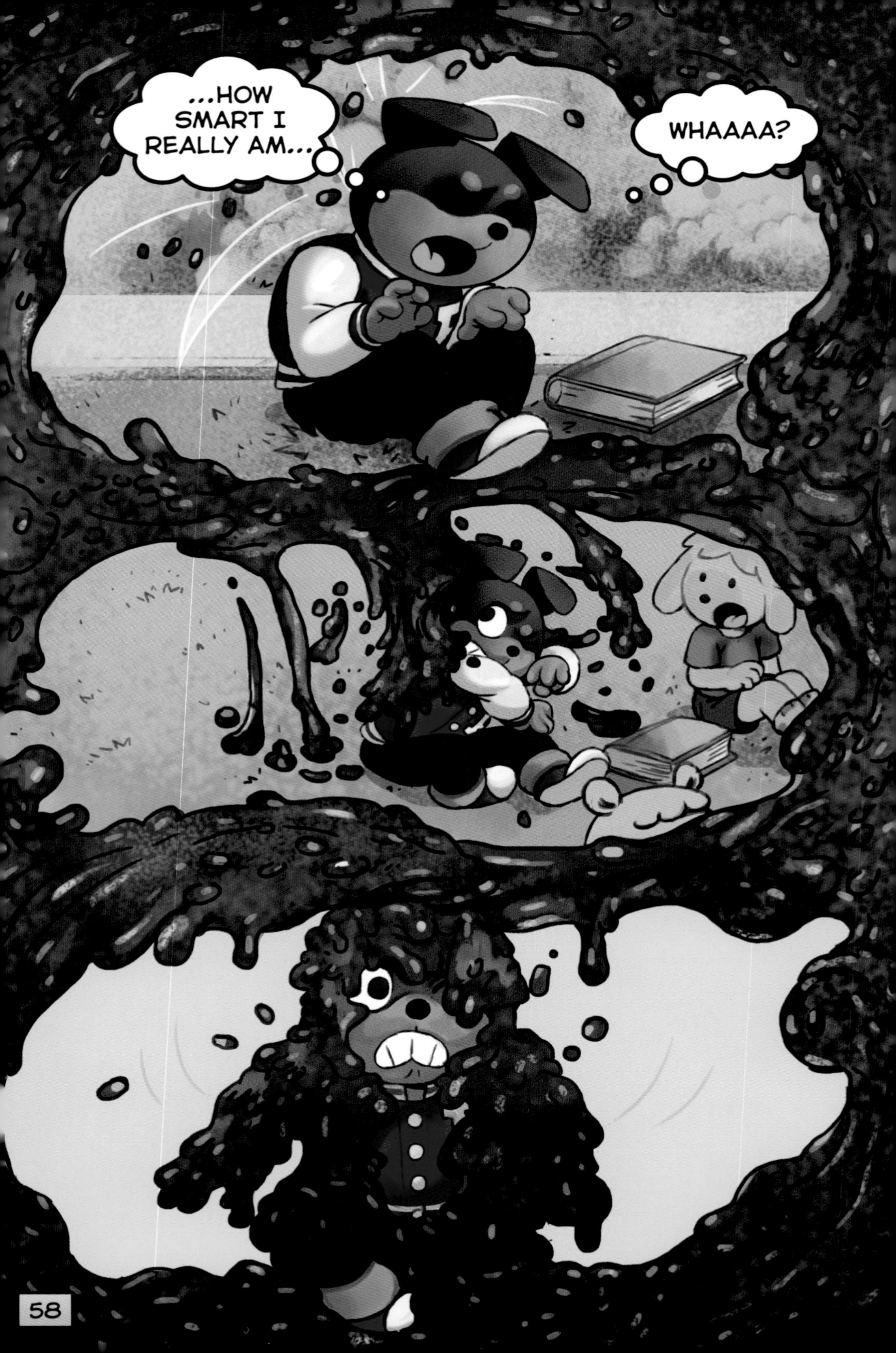
...HOW SMART I REALLY AM...
WHAAAA?

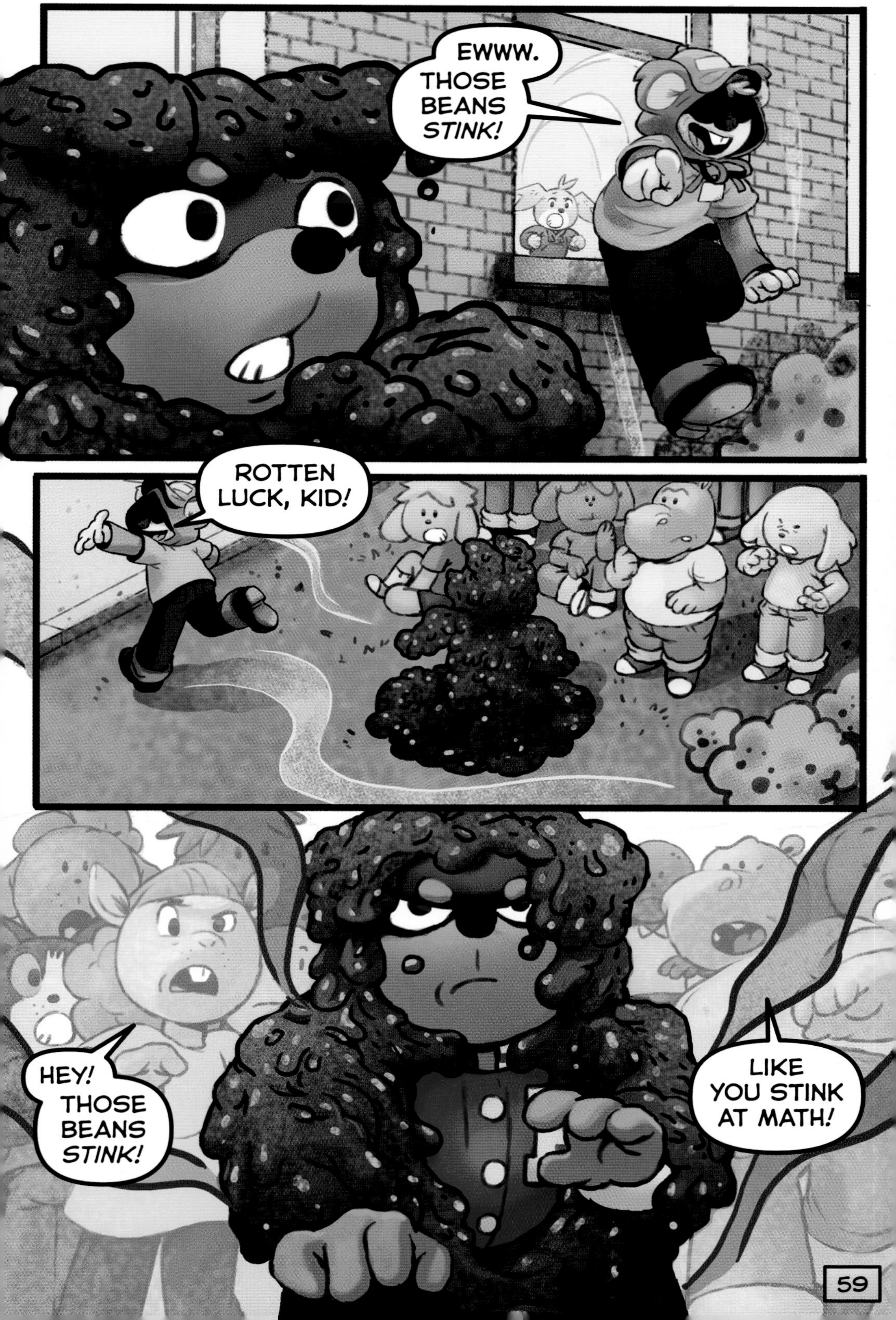
EWWW. THOSE BEANS STINK!
ROTTEN LUCK, KID!
HEY! THOSE BEANS STINK!
LIKE YOU STINK AT MATH!

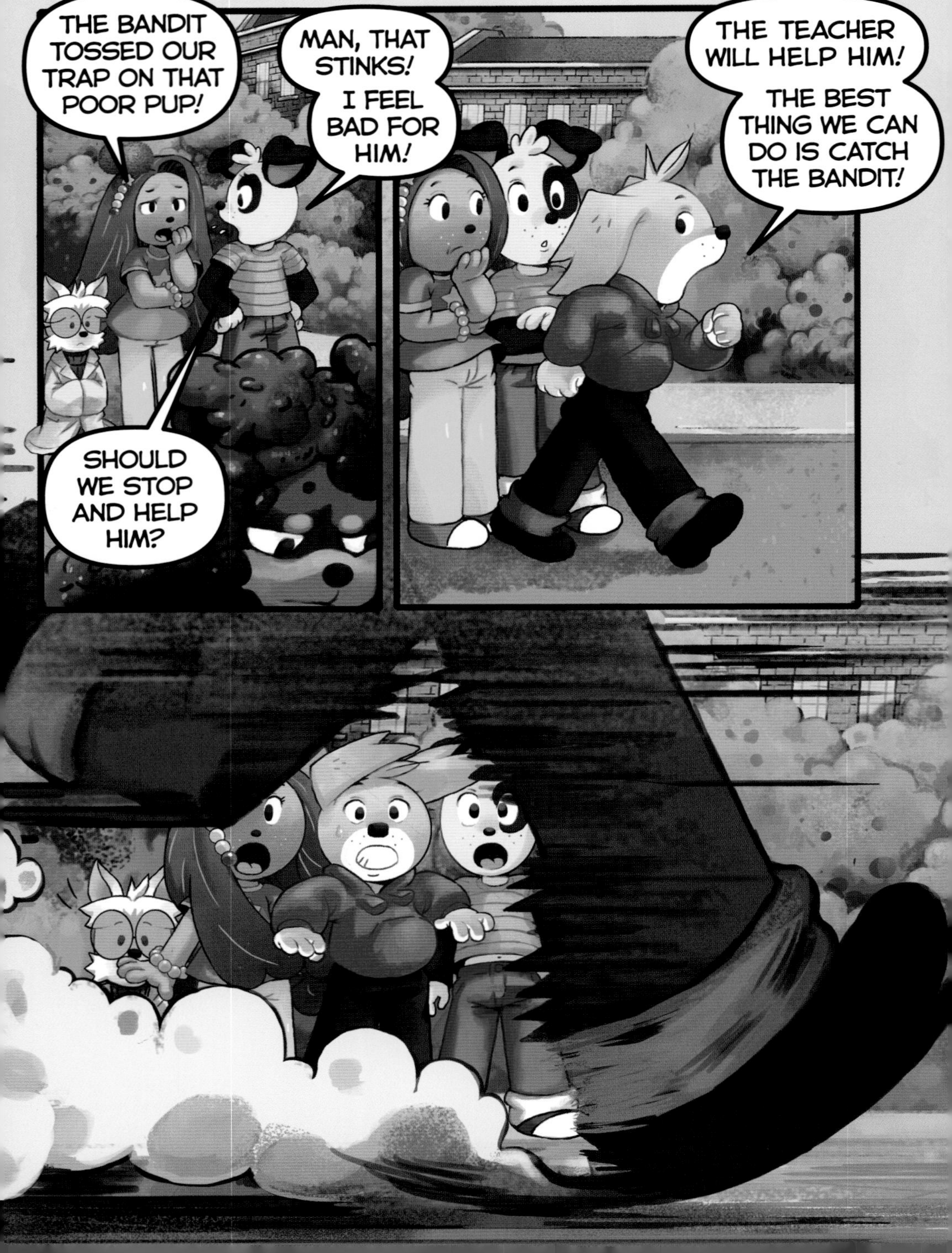
THE BANDIT TOSSED OUR TRAP ON THAT POOR PUP!
MAN, THAT STINKS!
I FEEL BAD FOR HIM!
SHOULD WE STOP AND HELP HIM?
THE TEACHER WILL HELP HIM!
THE BEST THING WE CAN DO IS CATCH THE BANDIT!

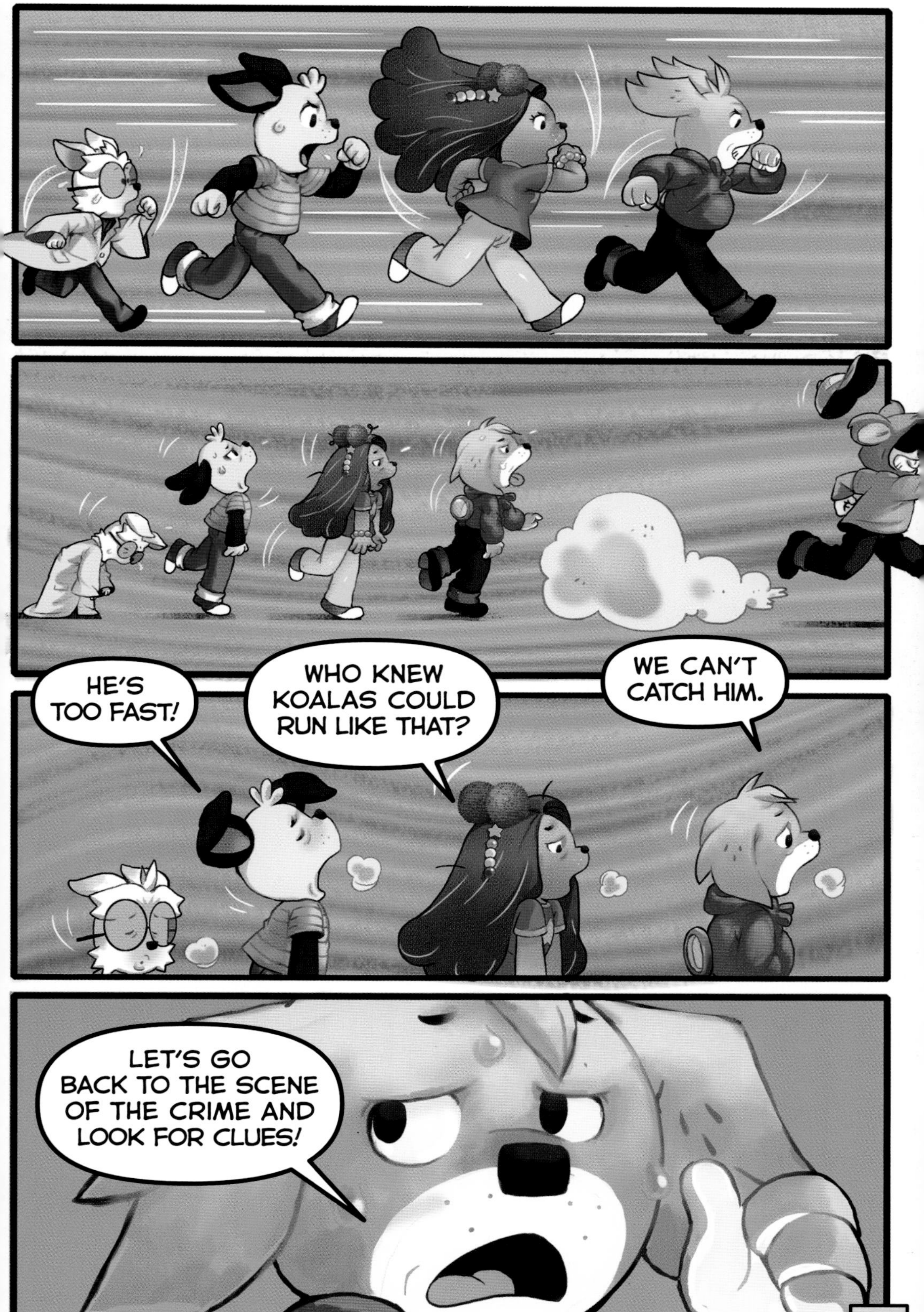

HE'S TOO FAST!
WHO KNEW KOALAS COULD RUN LIKE THAT?
WE CAN'T CATCH HIM.
LET'S GO BACK TO THE SCENE OF THE CRIME AND LOOK FOR CLUES!

CHAPTER 5

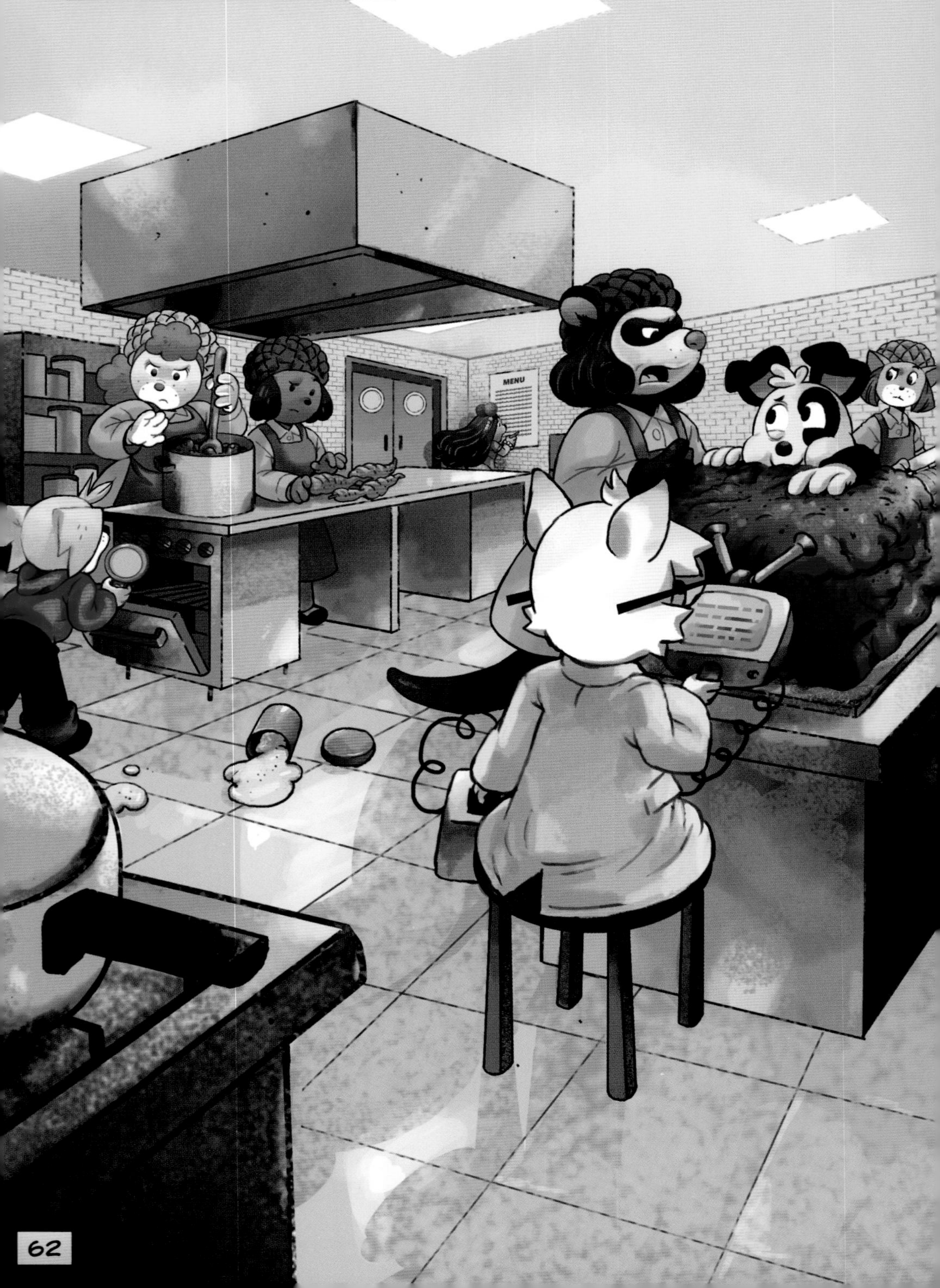
MENU

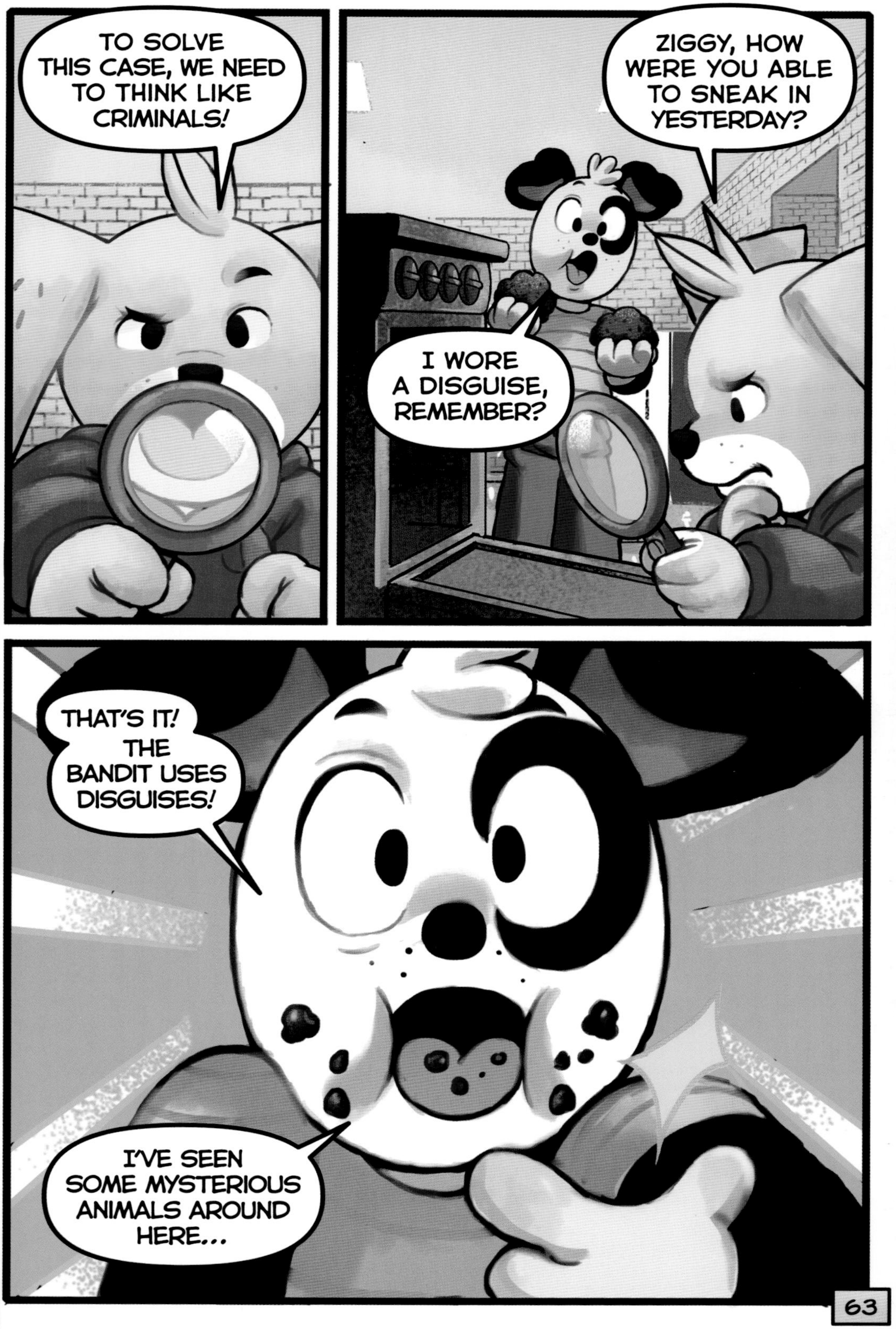
TO SOLVE THIS CASE, WE NEED TO THINK LIKE CRIMINALS!
ZIGGY, HOW WERE YOU ABLE TO SNEAK IN YESTERDAY?
I WORE A DISGUISE, REMEMBER?
THAT'S IT! THE BANDIT USES DISGUISES!
I'VE SEEN SOME MYSTERIOUS ANIMALS AROUND HERE...

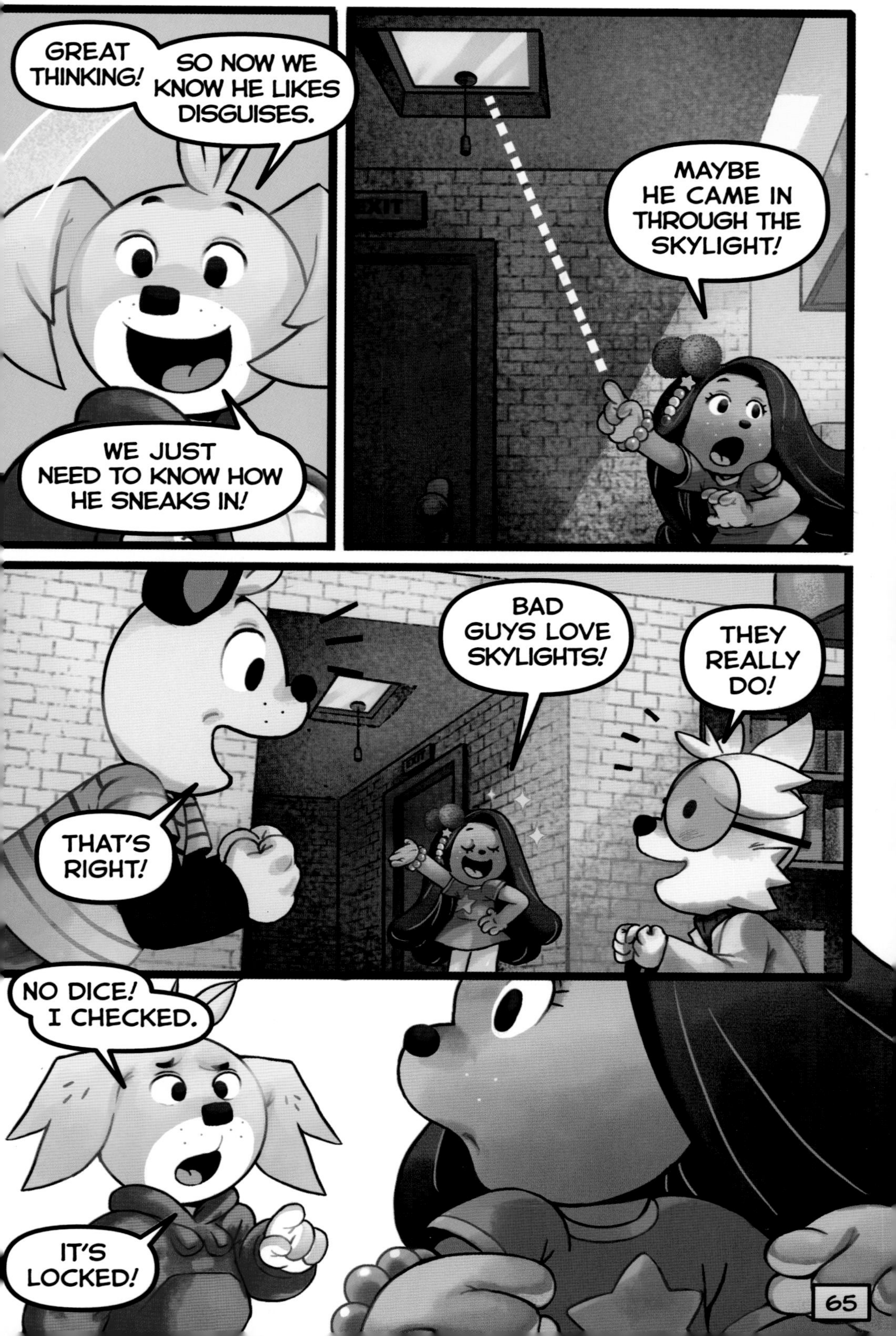
GREAT THINKING!
SO NOW WE KNOW HE LIKES DISGUISES.
WE JUST NEED TO KNOW HOW HE SNEAKS IN!
MAYBE HE CAME IN THROUGH THE SKYLIGHT!
EXIT
BAD GUYS LOVE SKYLIGHTS!
THEY REALLY DO!
THAT'S RIGHT!
NO DICE! I CHECKED.
IT'S LOCKED!

68

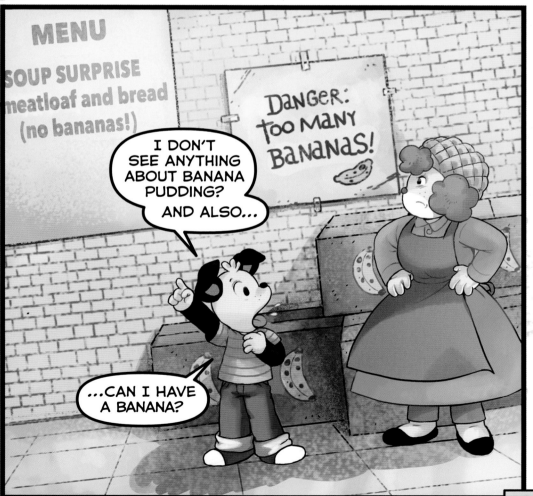

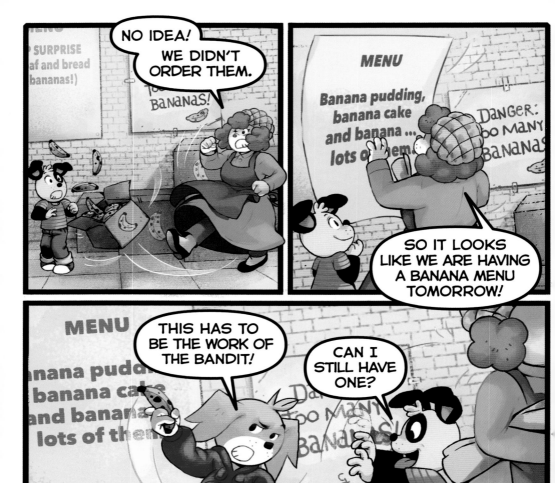

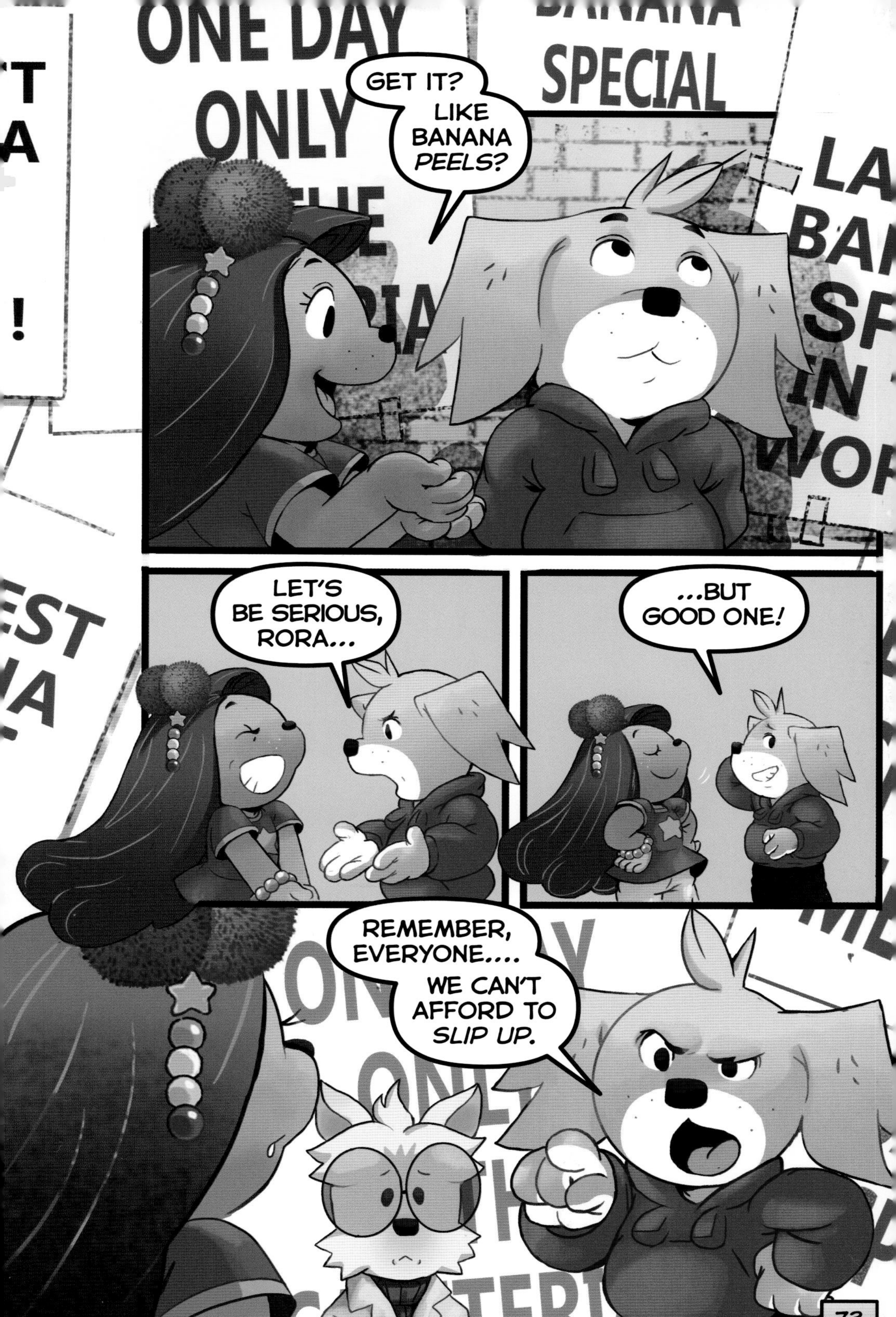

ONE DAY ONLY
SPECIAL
GET IT? LIKE BANANA *PEELS?*
LET'S BE SERIOUS, RORA...
...BUT GOOD ONE!
REMEMBER, EVERYONE.... WE CAN'T AFFORD TO *SLIP UP.*

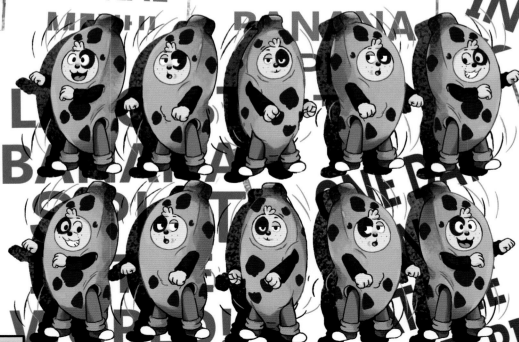

CHAPTER 6

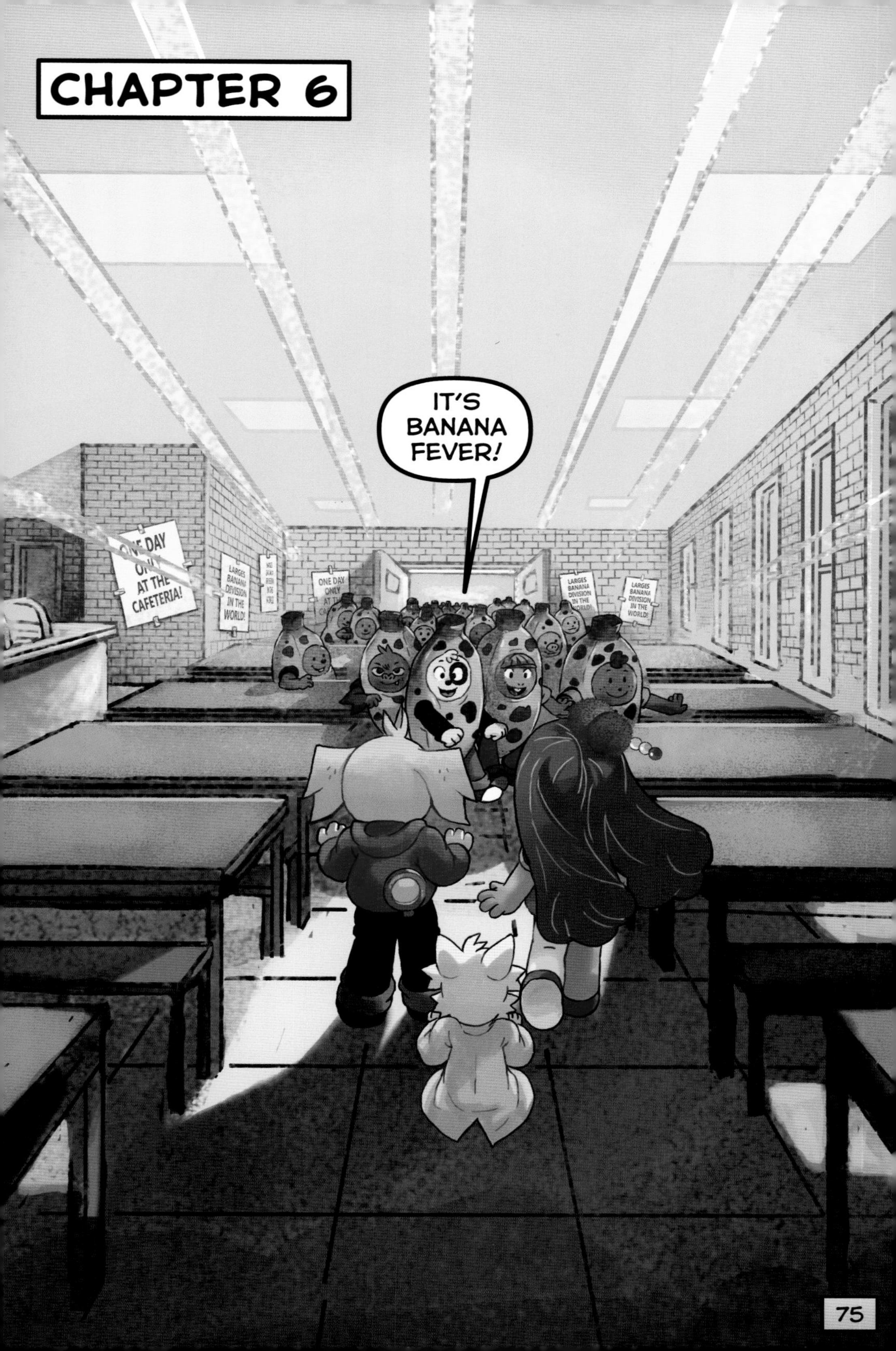
IT'S BANANA FEVER!
LARGES BANANA DIVISION IN THE WORLD!

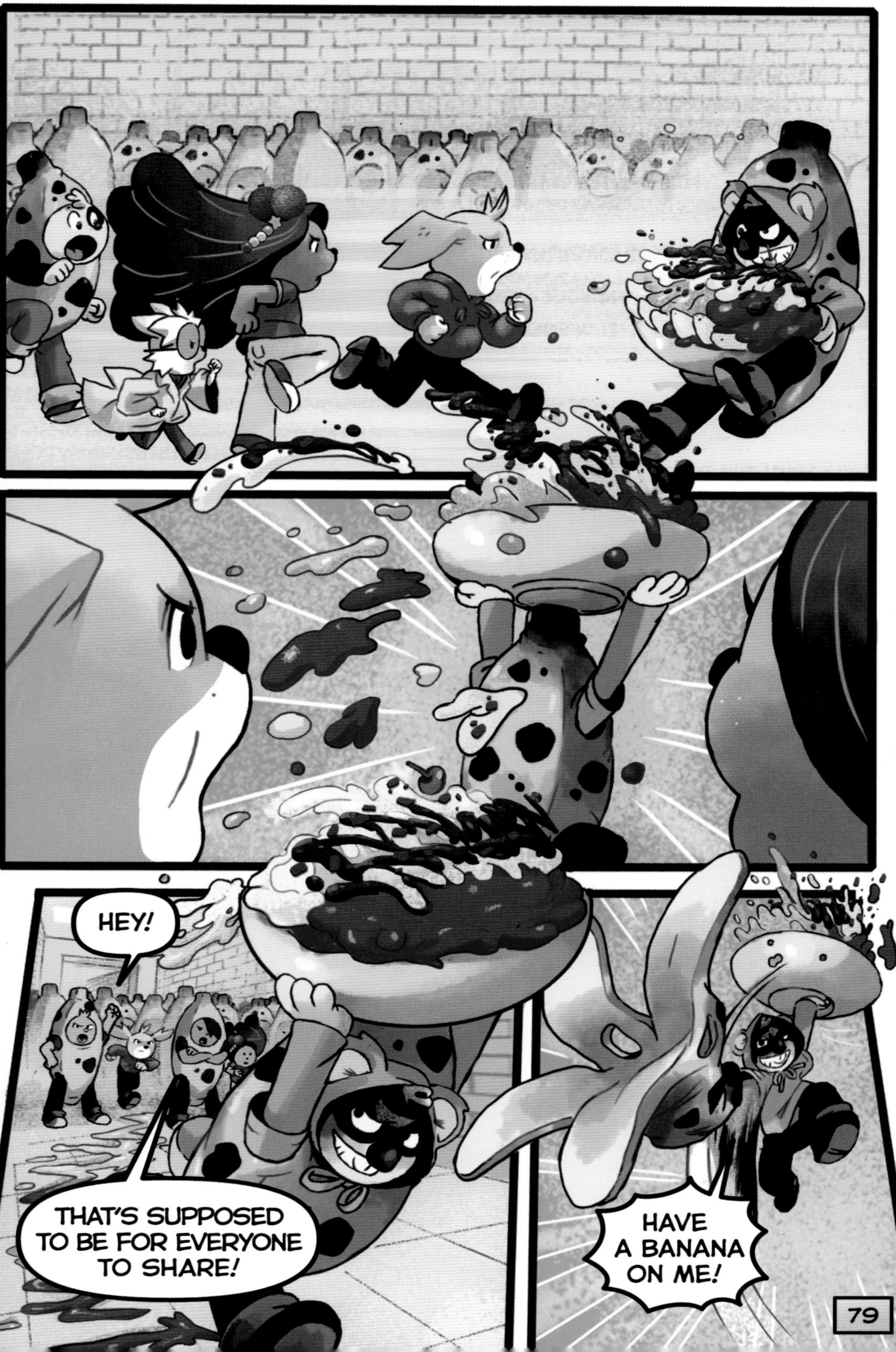
HEY!
THAT'S SUPPOSED TO BE FOR EVERYONE TO SHARE!
HAVE A BANANA ON ME!

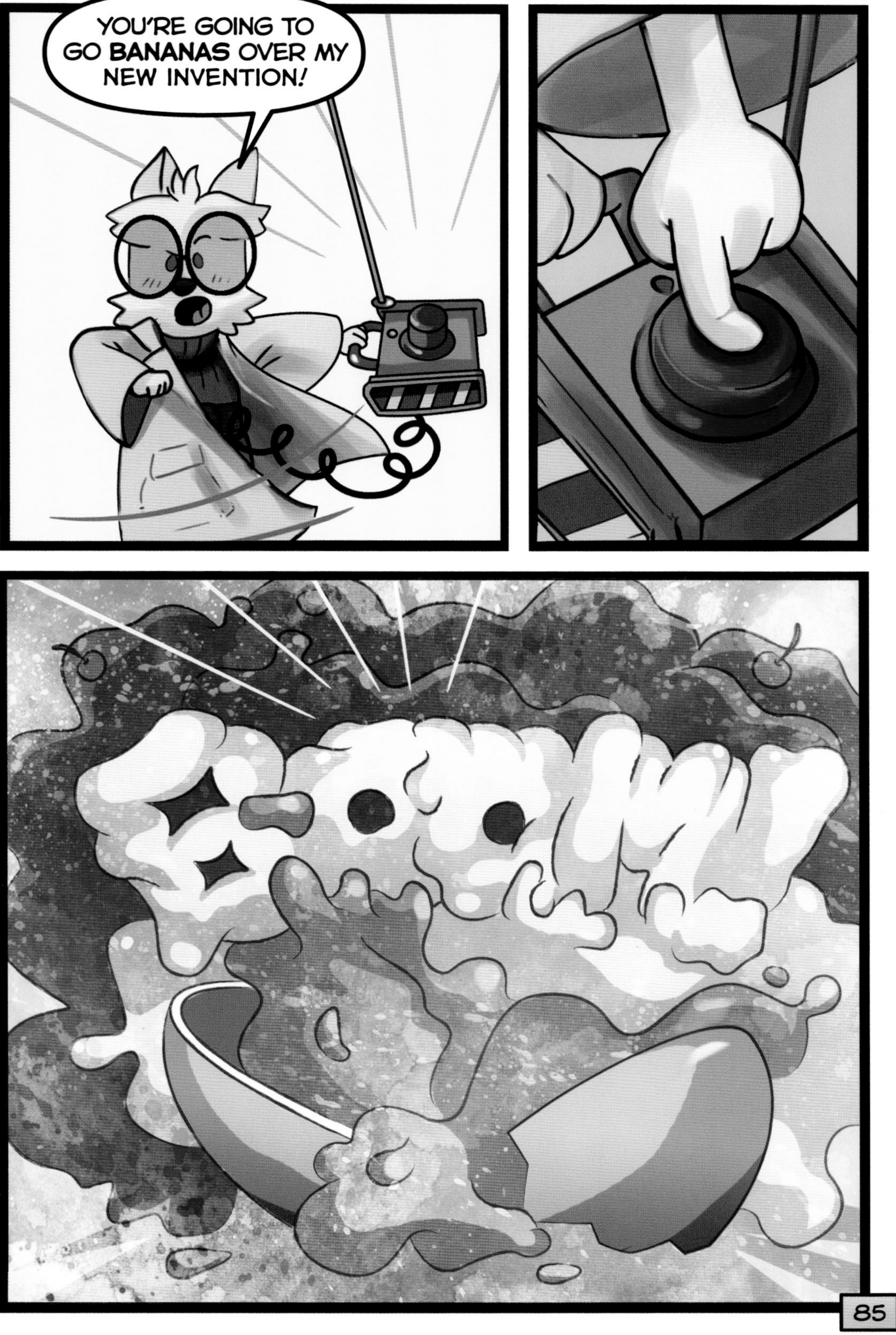
YOU'RE GOING TO GO **BANANAS** OVER MY NEW INVENTION!

CHAPTER 7

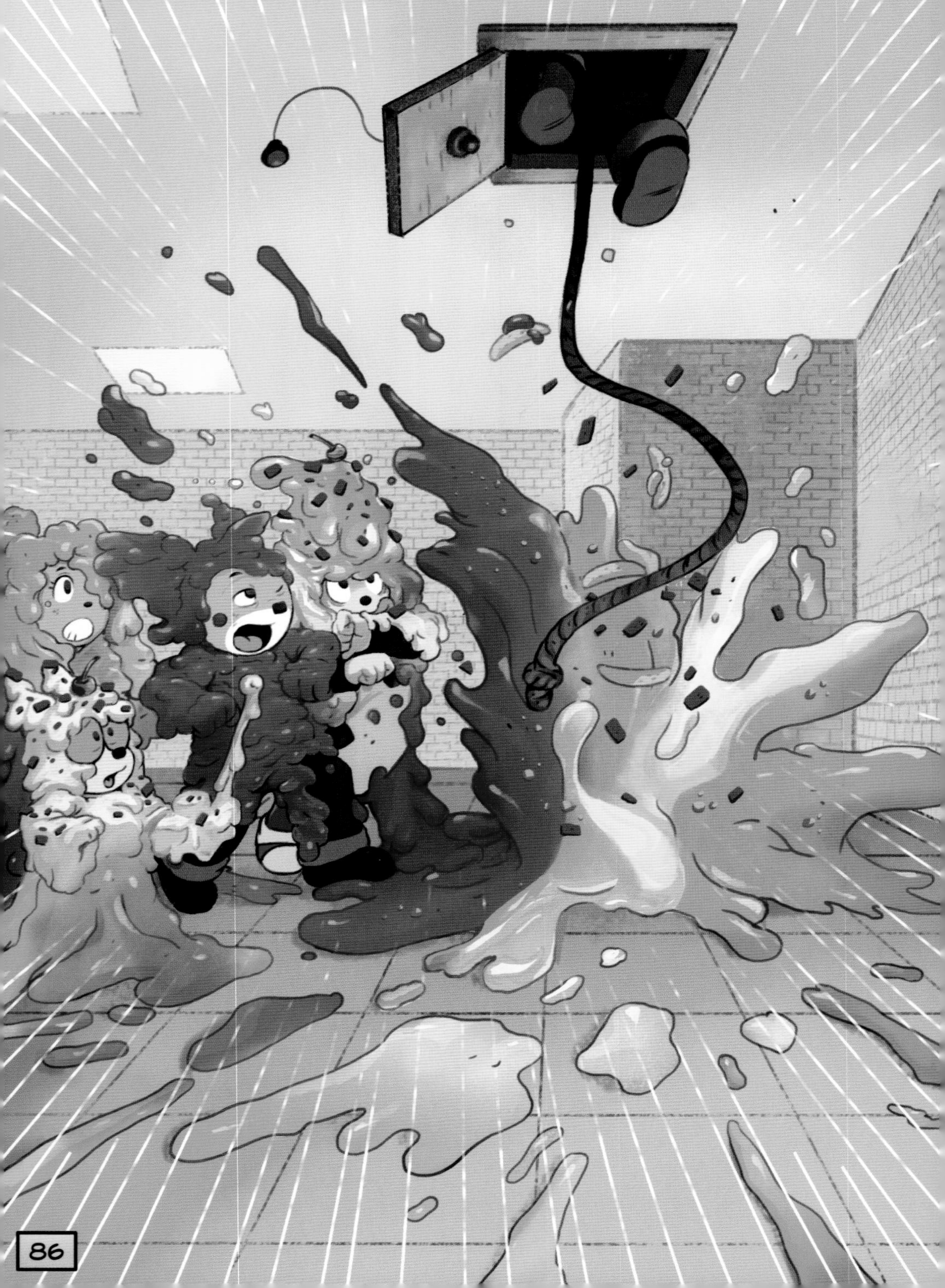

HE ESCAPED!

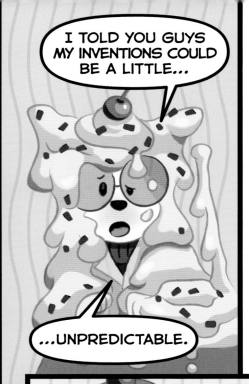

I TOLD YOU GUYS MY INVENTIONS COULD BE A LITTLE...

...UNPREDICTABLE.

AND I TOLD YOU BAD GUYS LOVE SKYLIGHTS!

MMMM... NEEDS MORE FUDGE SAUCE!

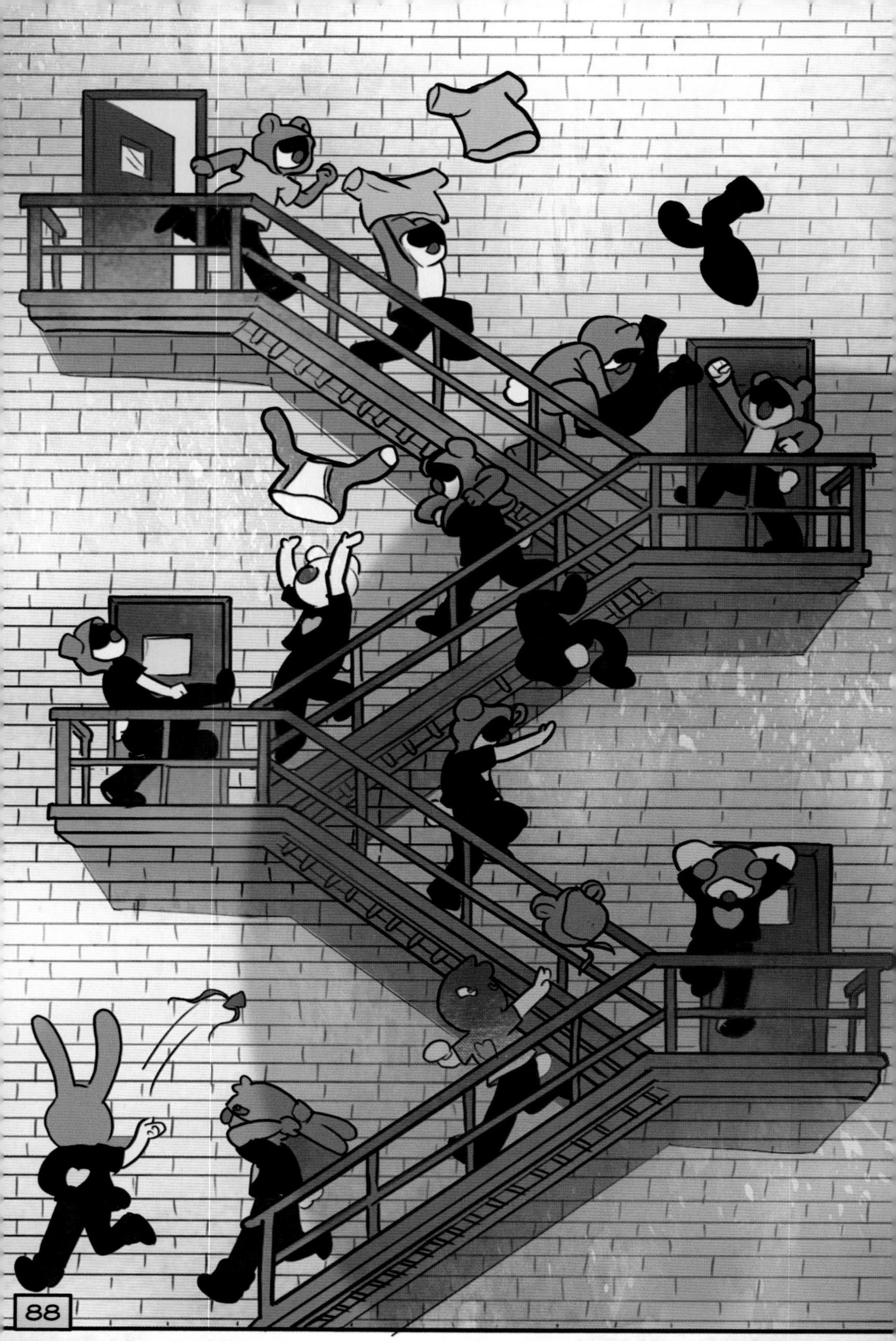

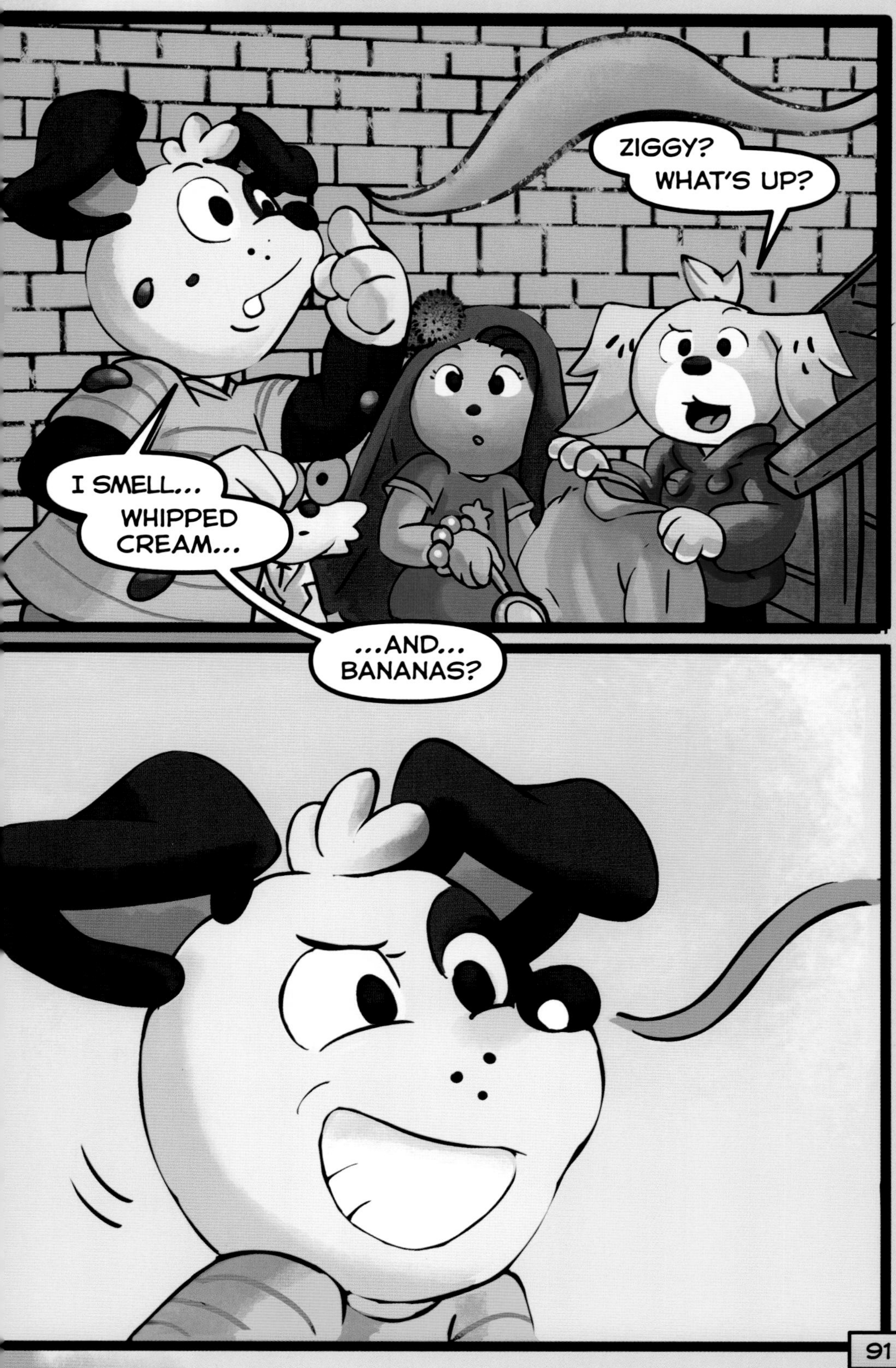
ZIGGY? WHAT'S UP?
I SMELL... WHIPPED CREAM...
...AND... BANANAS?

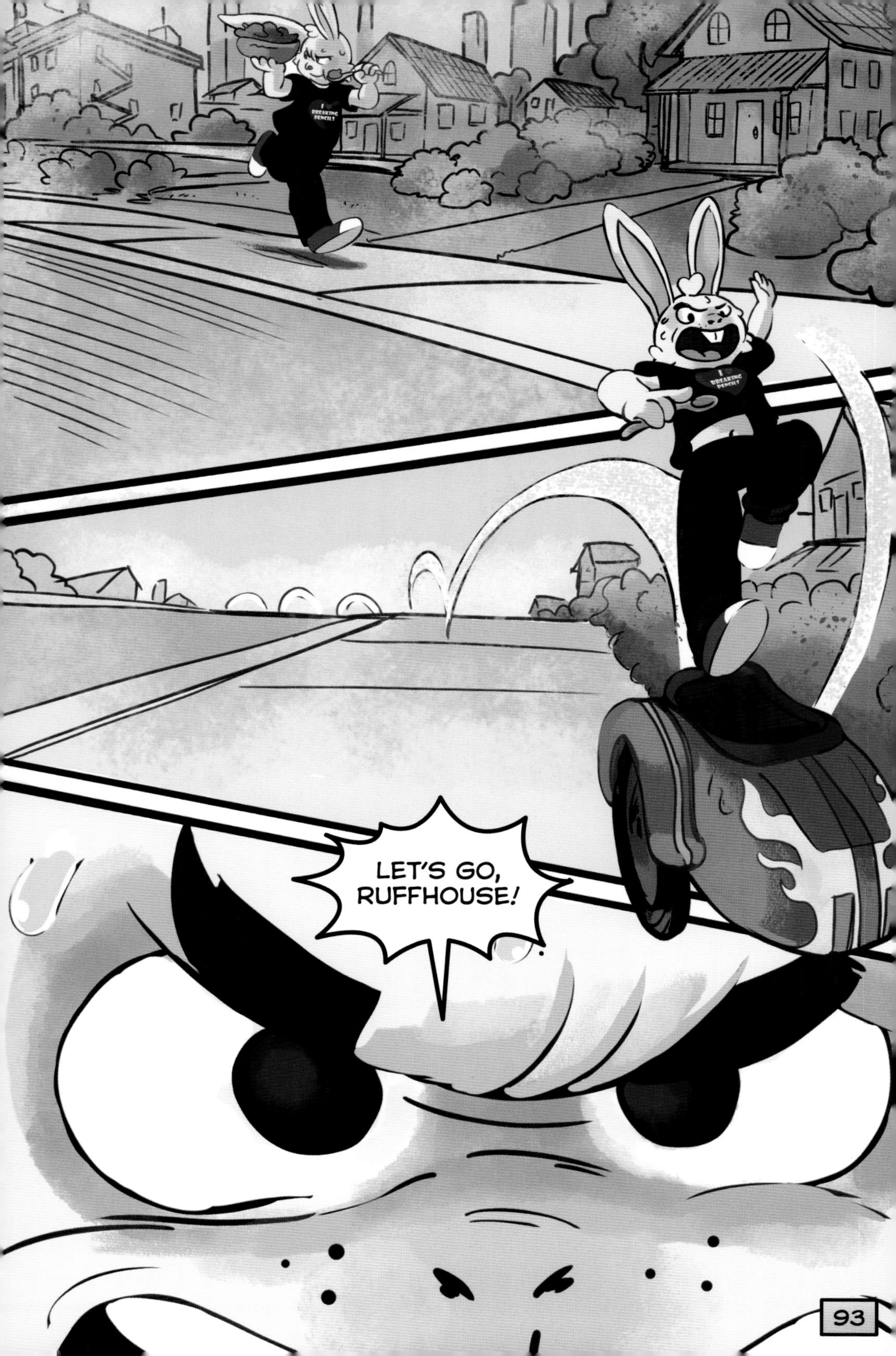
LET'S GO, RUFFHOUSE!

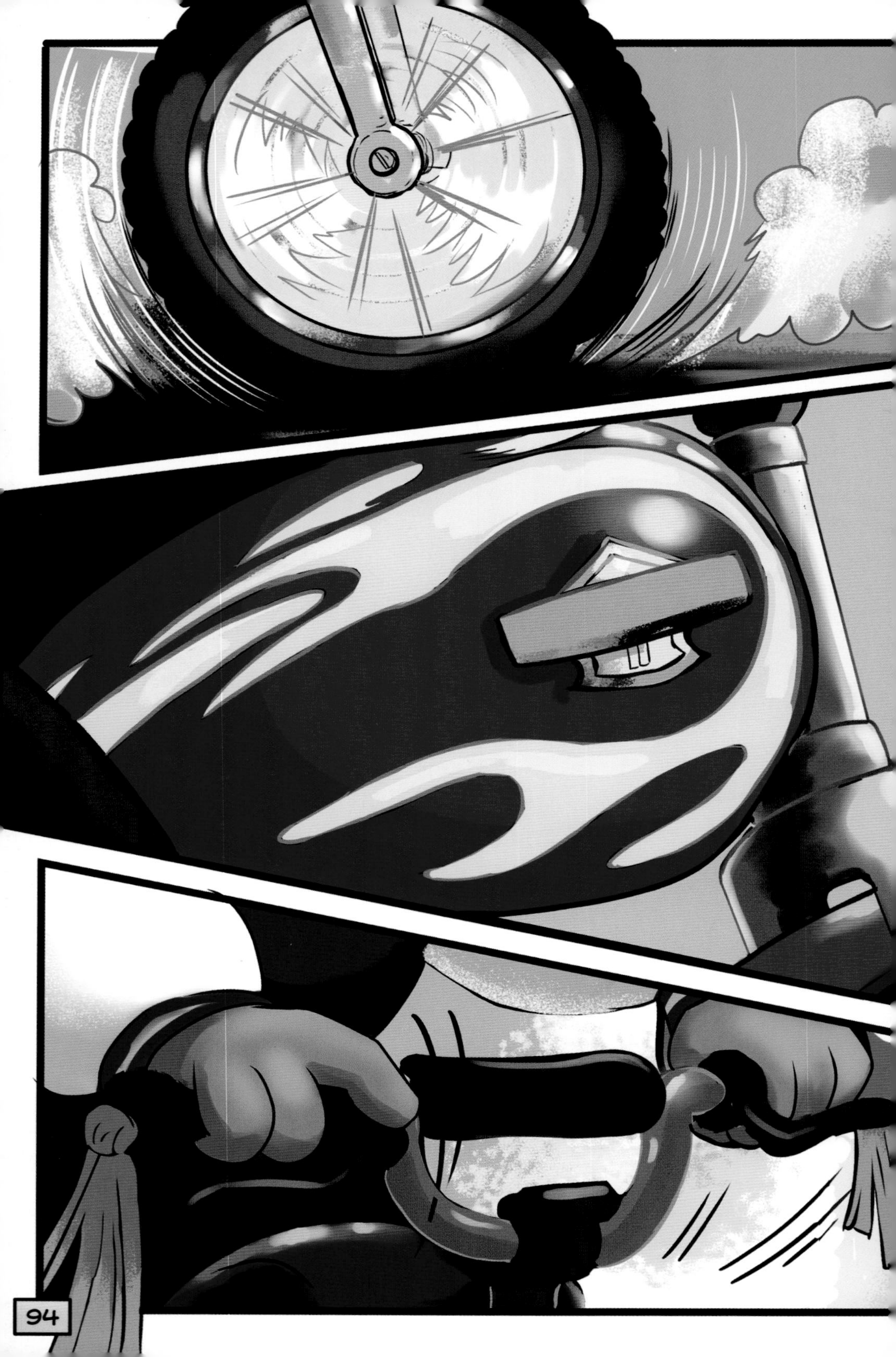

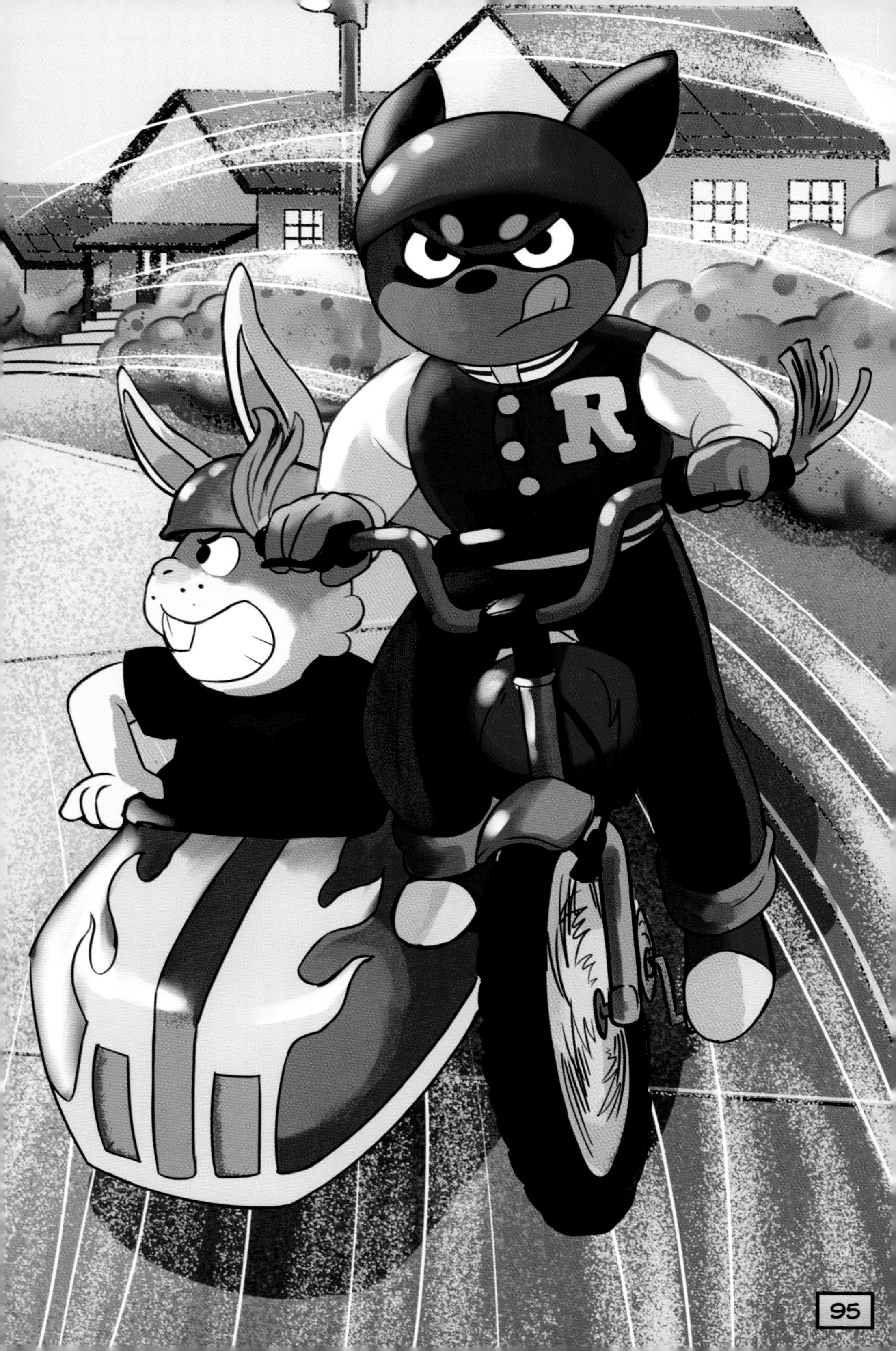

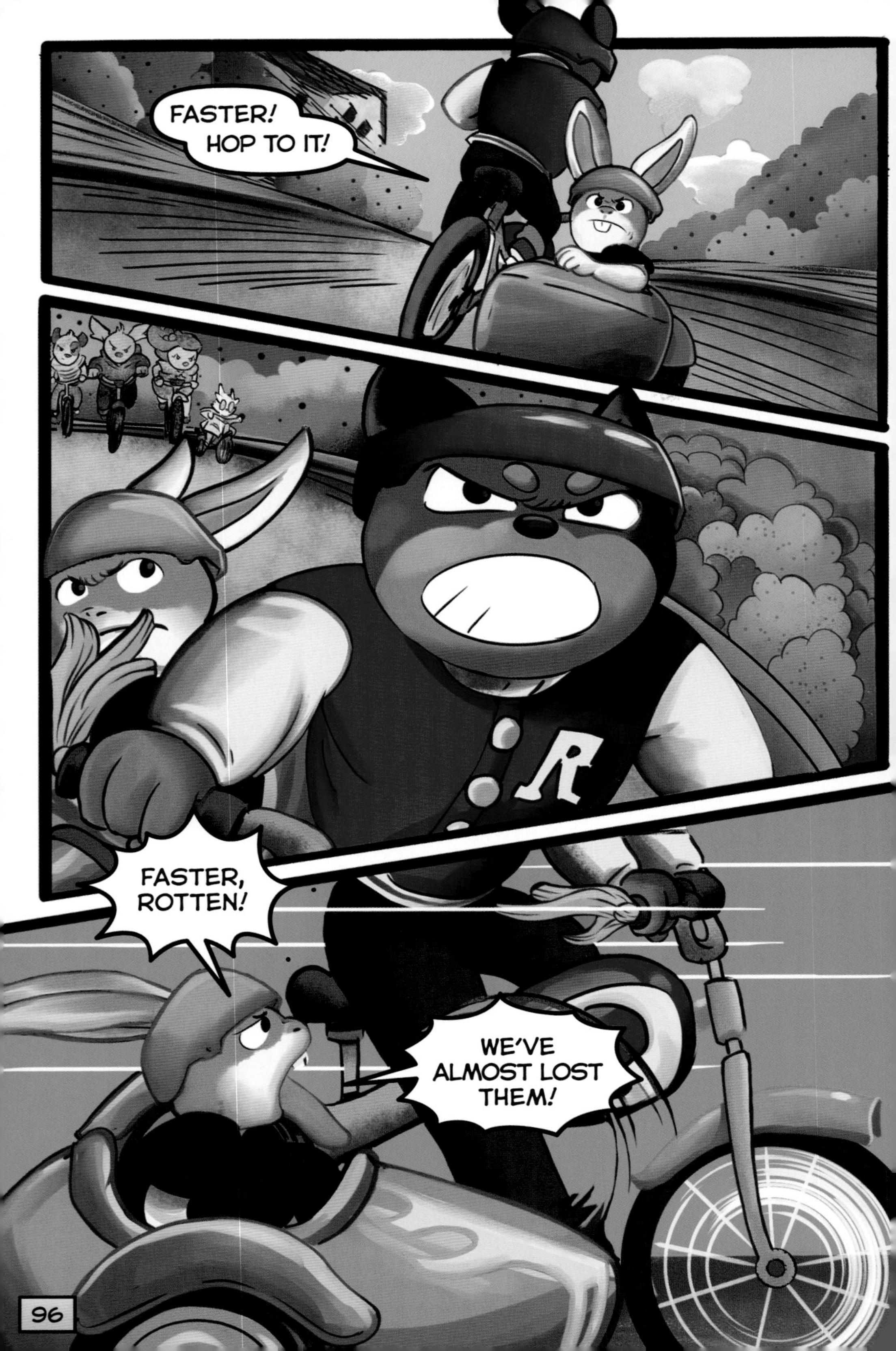
FASTER! HOP TO IT!
FASTER, ROTTEN!
WE'VE ALMOST LOST THEM!

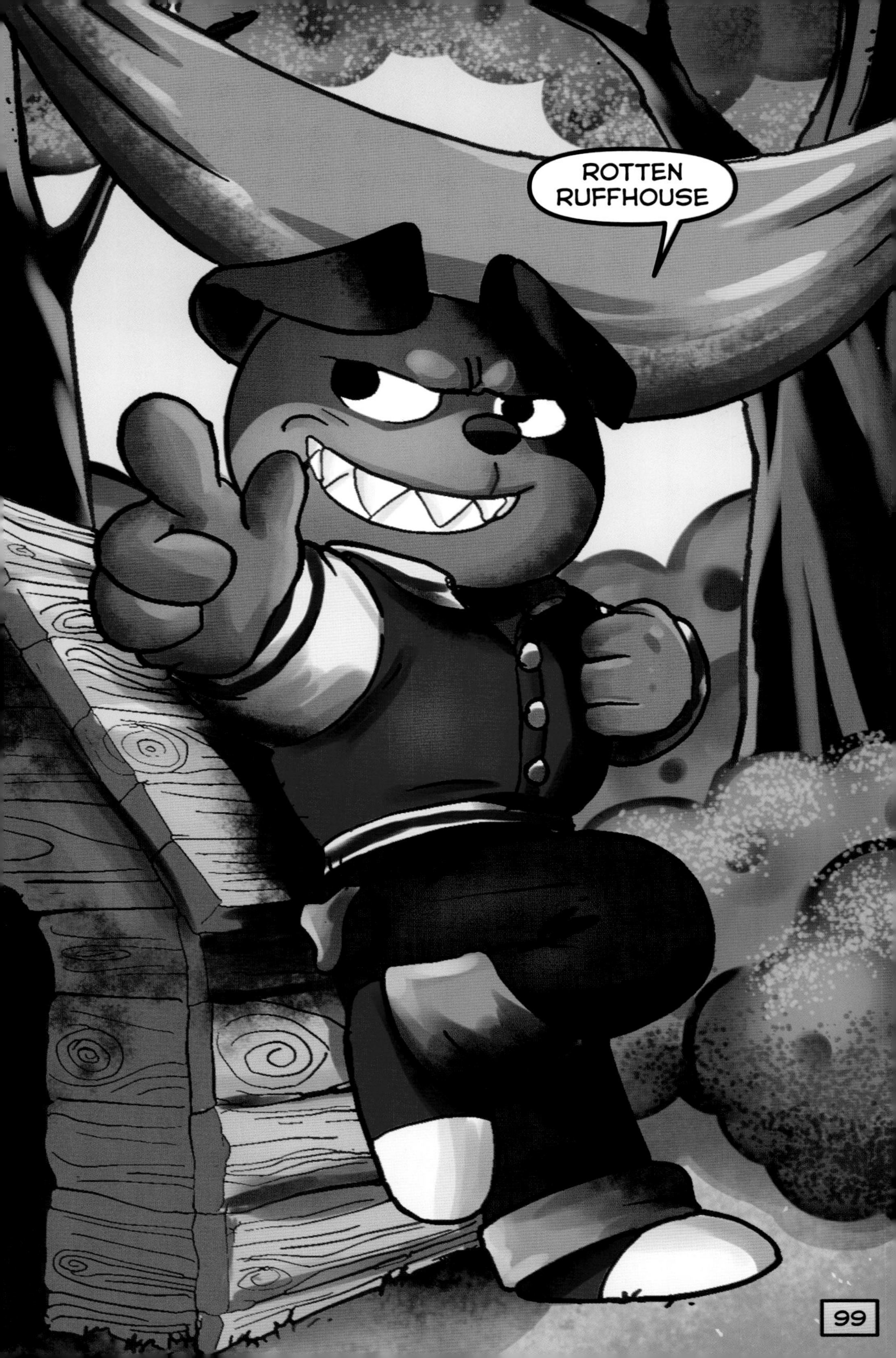
ROTTEN RUFFHOUSE

103

CHAPTER 8

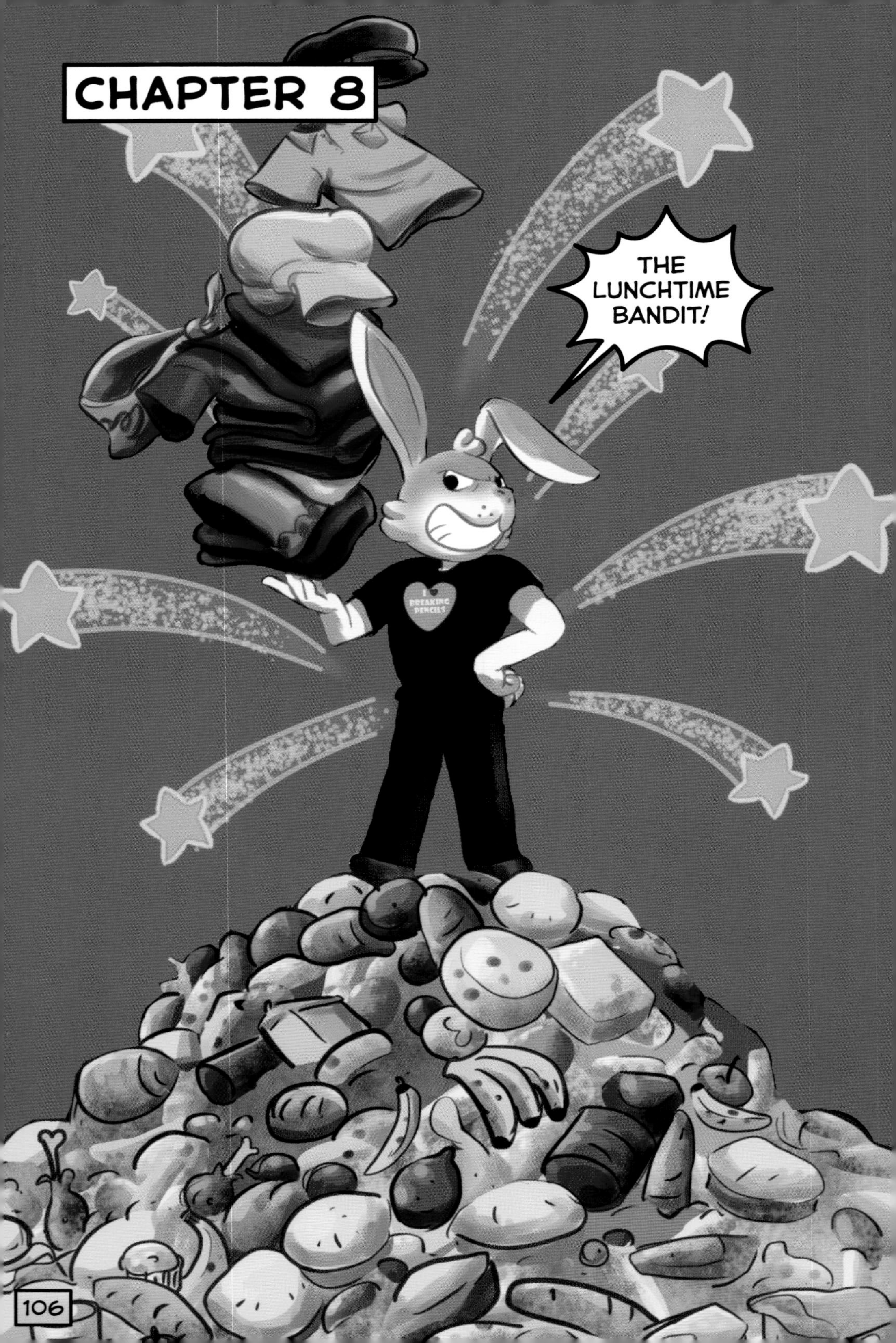
THE LUNCHTIME BANDIT!
I
BREAKING PENCILS

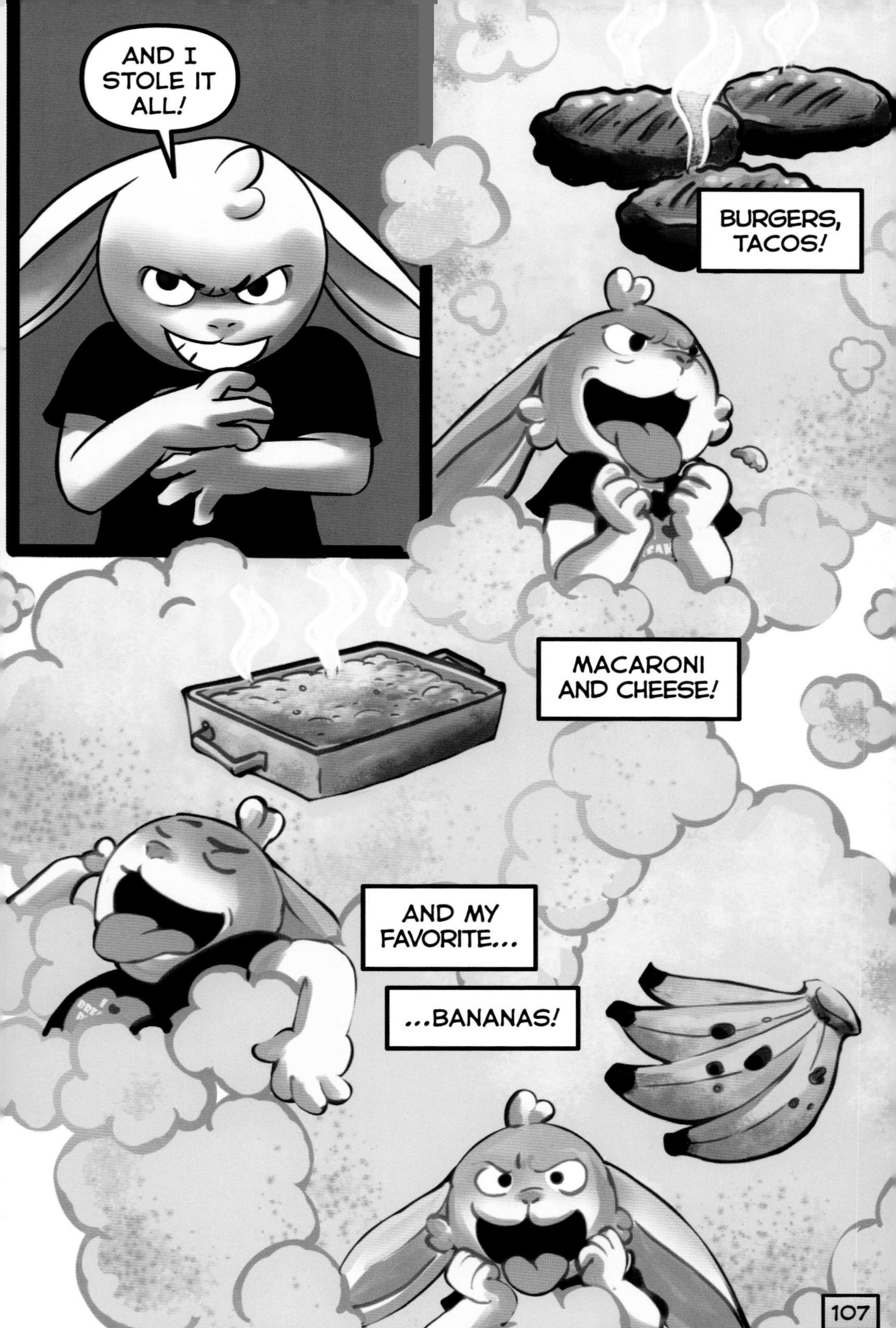
AND I STOLE IT ALL!
BURGERS, TACOS!
MACARONI AND CHEESE!
AND MY FAVORITE...
...BANANAS!

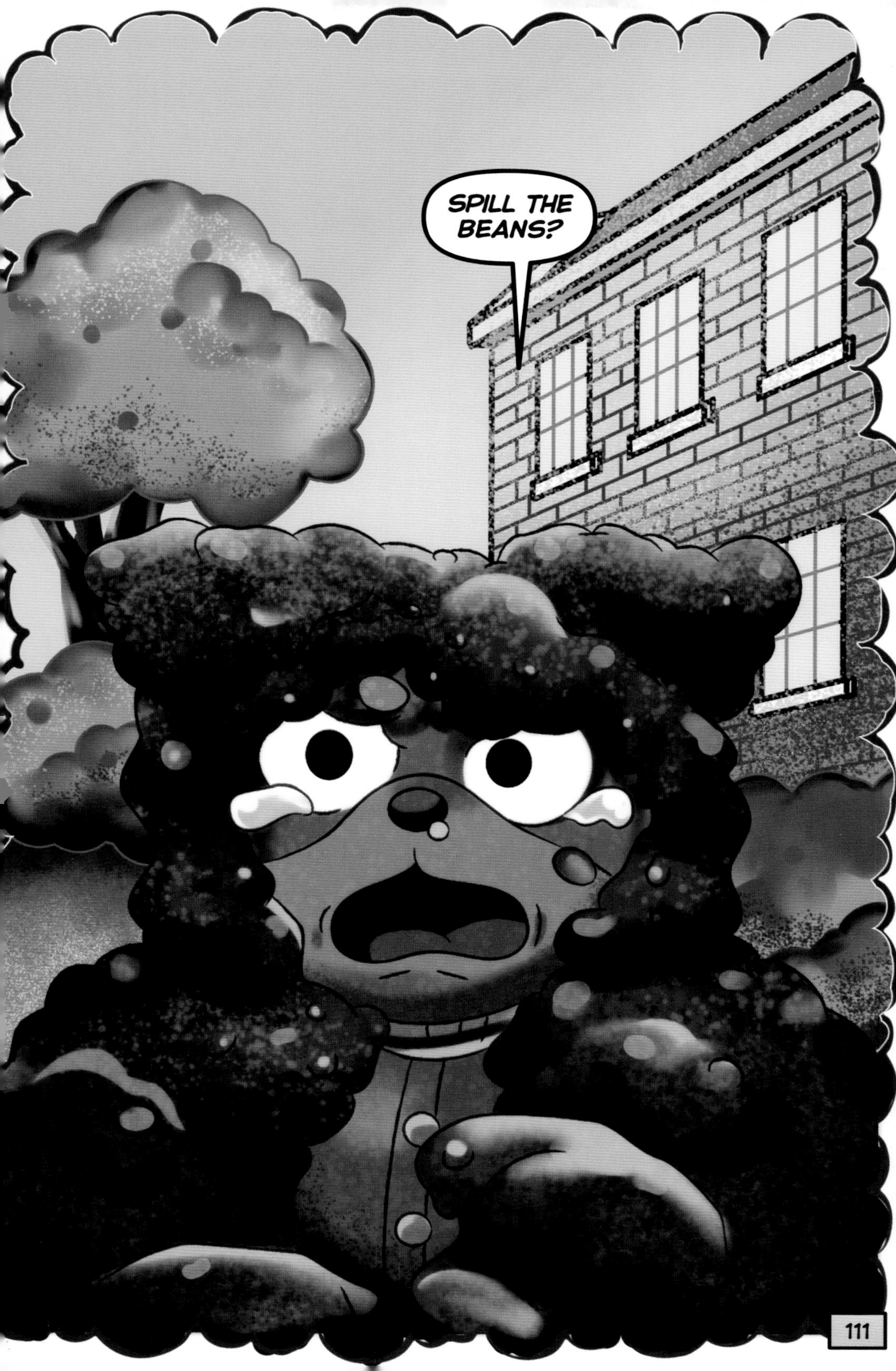
SPILL THE BEANS?

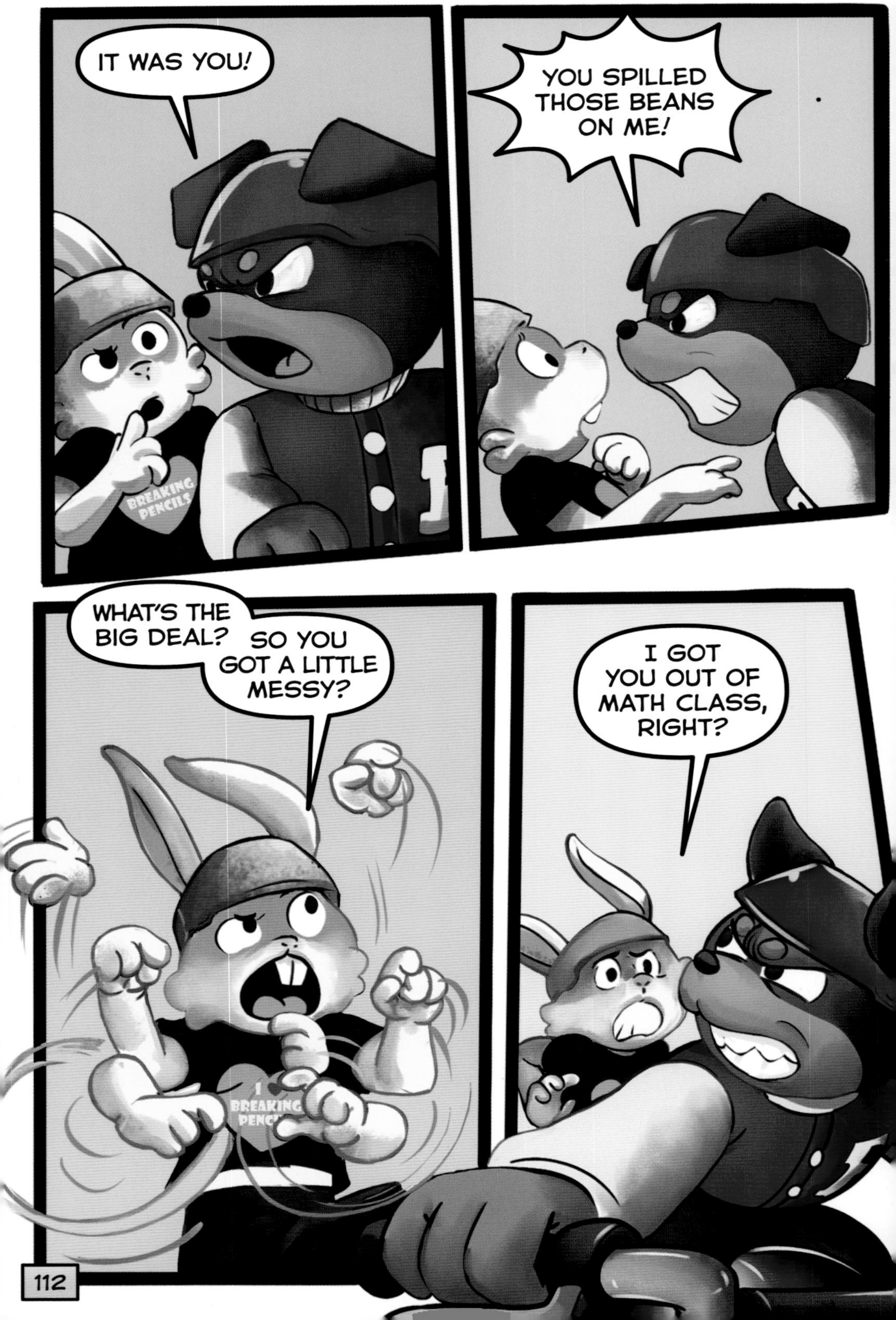
IT WAS YOU!
YOU SPILLED THOSE BEANS ON ME!
BREAKING PENCILS
WHAT'S THE BIG DEAL?
SO YOU GOT A LITTLE MESSY?
I GOT YOU OUT OF MATH CLASS, RIGHT?

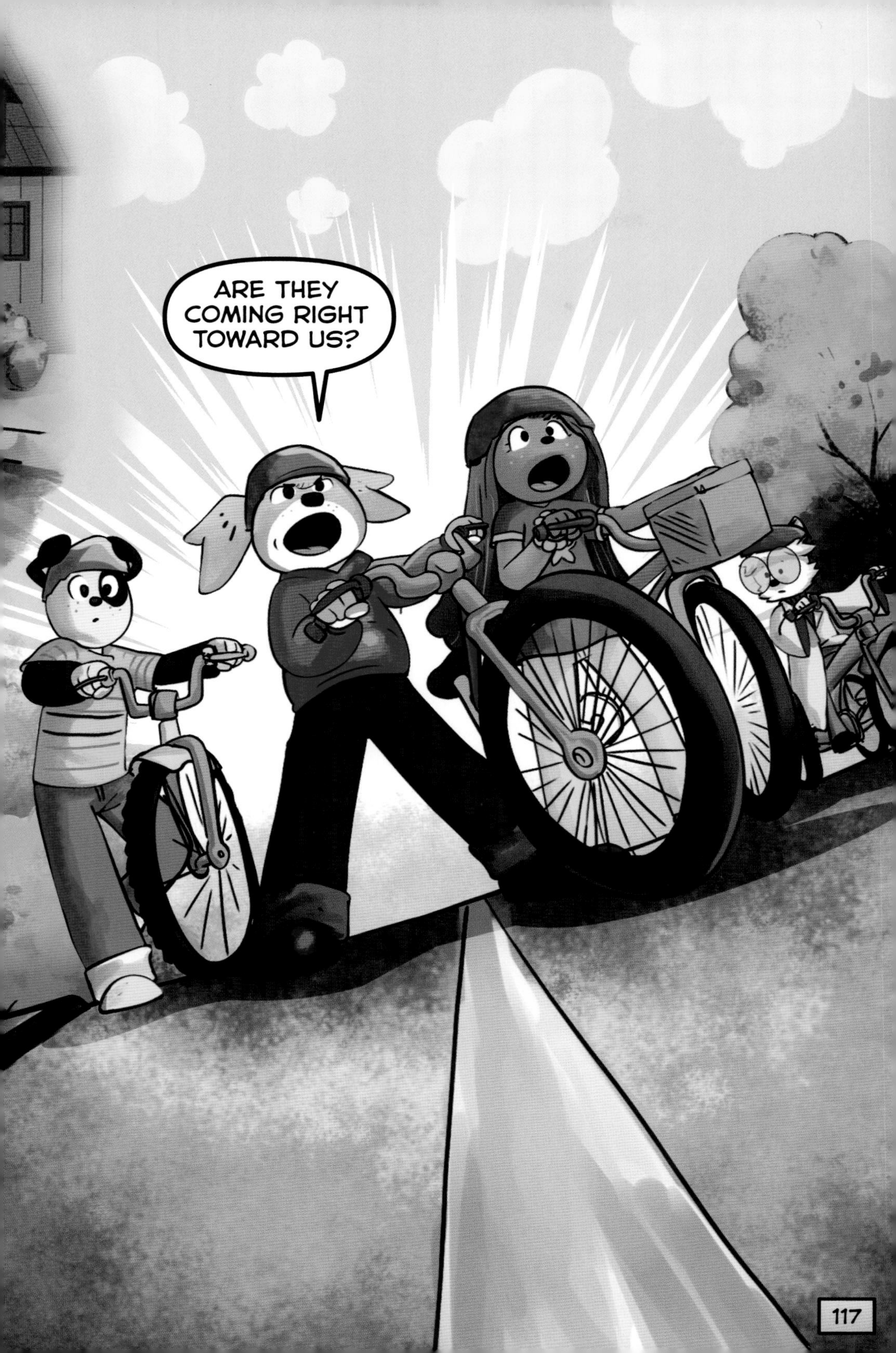
ARE THEY COMING RIGHT TOWARD US?

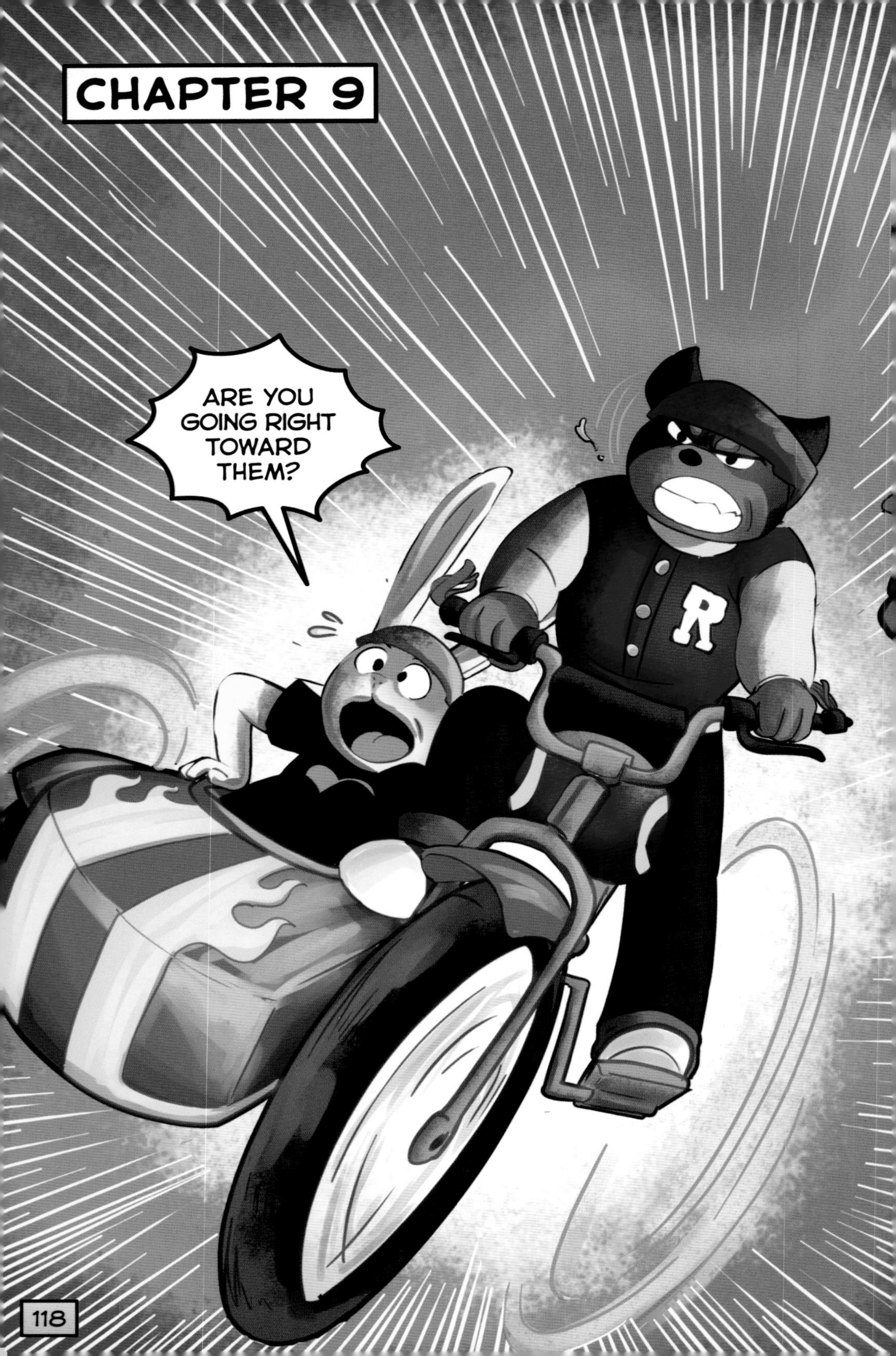
CHAPTER 9
ARE YOU GOING RIGHT TOWARD THEM?

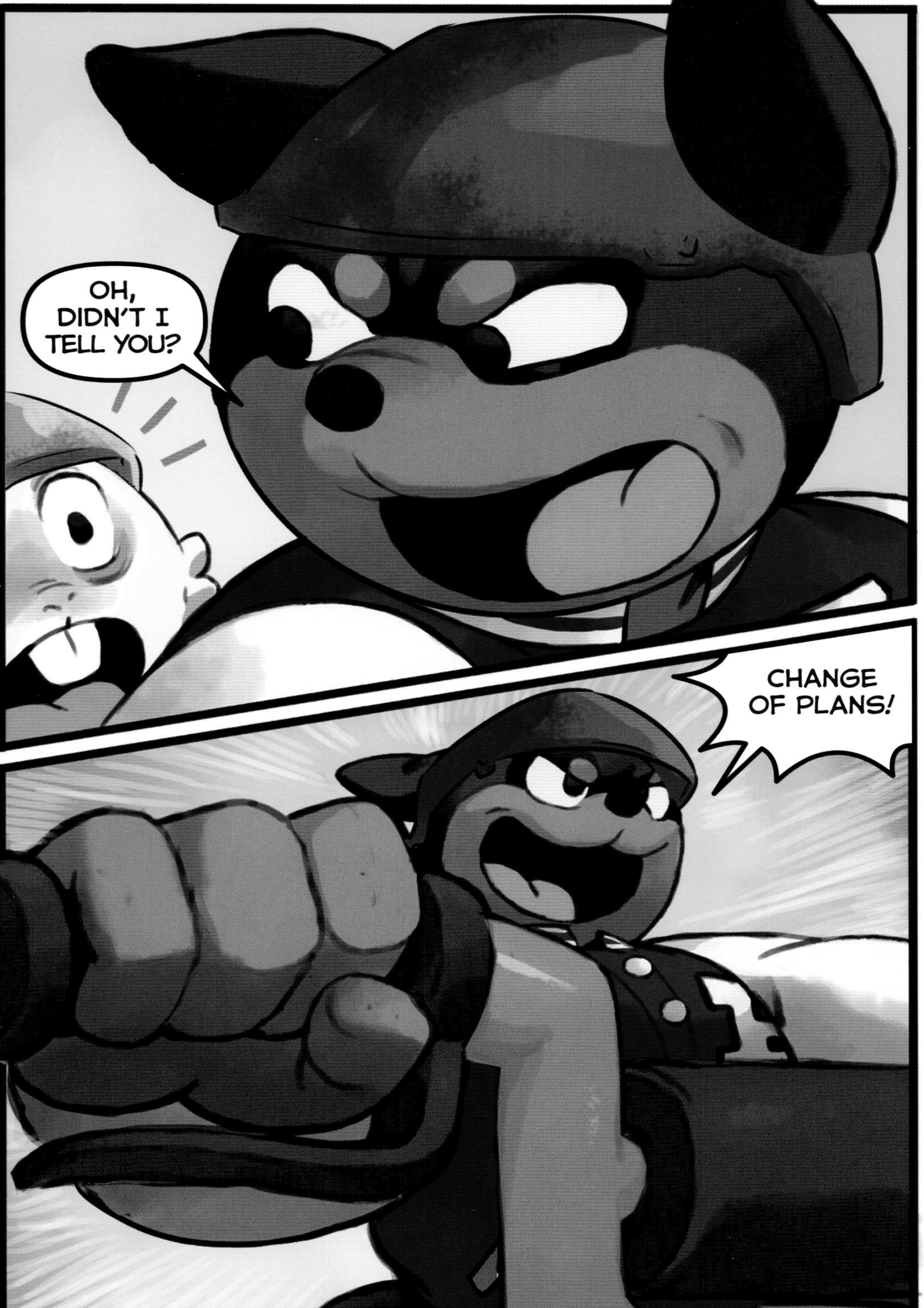
OH, DIDN'T I TELL YOU?
CHANGE OF PLANS!

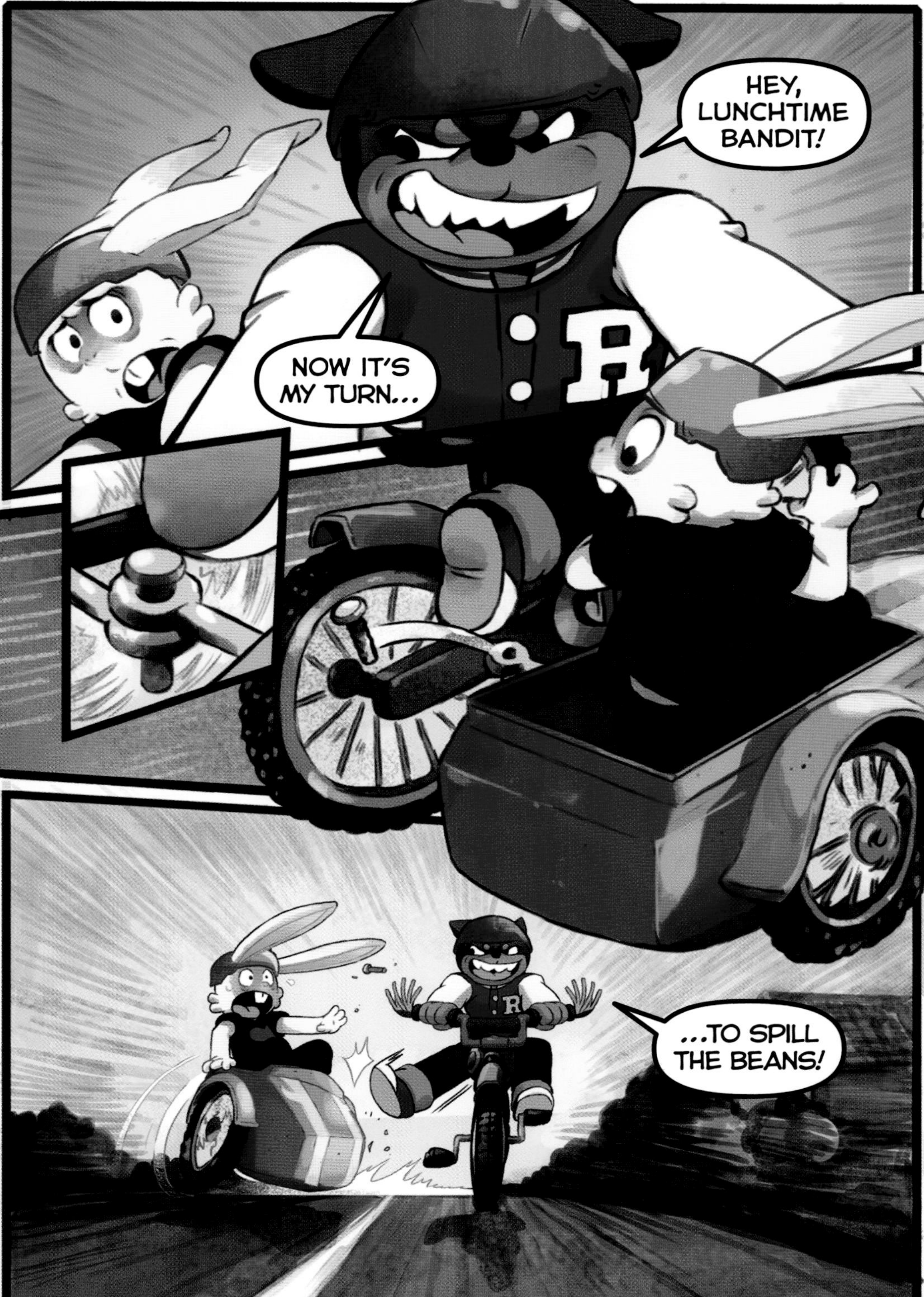
HEY, LUNCHTIME BANDIT!
NOW IT'S MY TURN...
R
R
...TO SPILL THE BEANS!

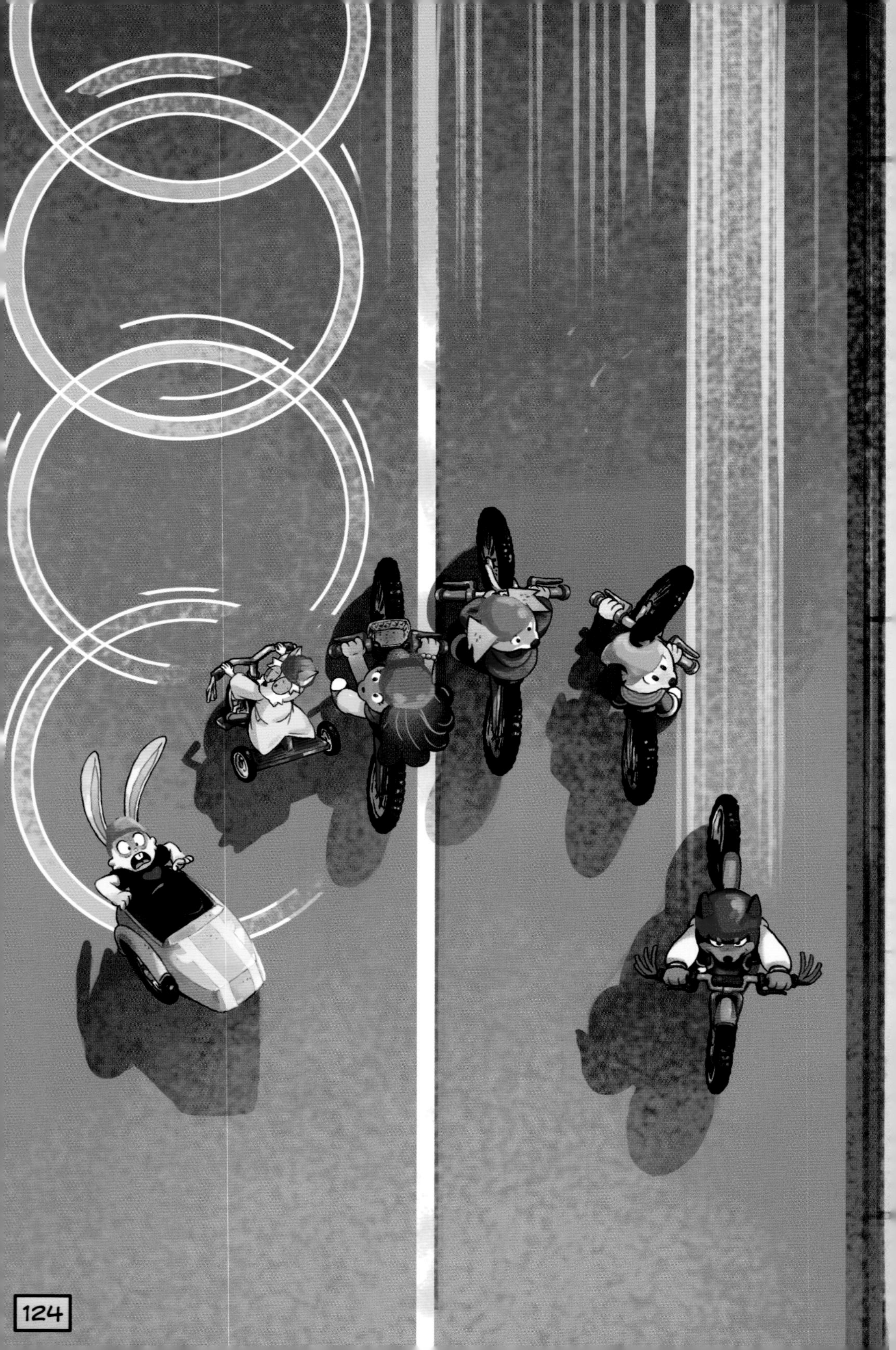

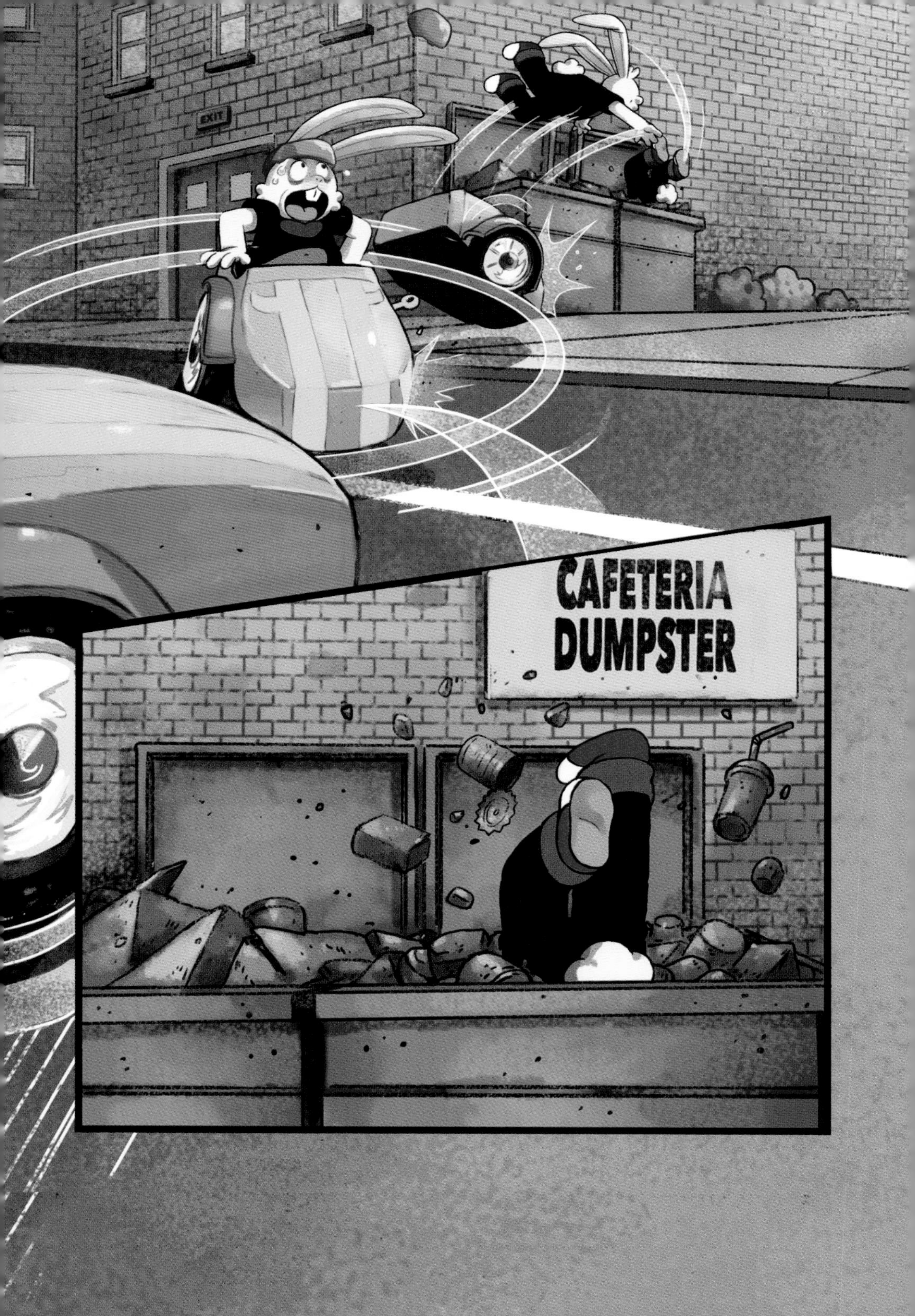
EXIT
CAFETERIA
DUMPSTER

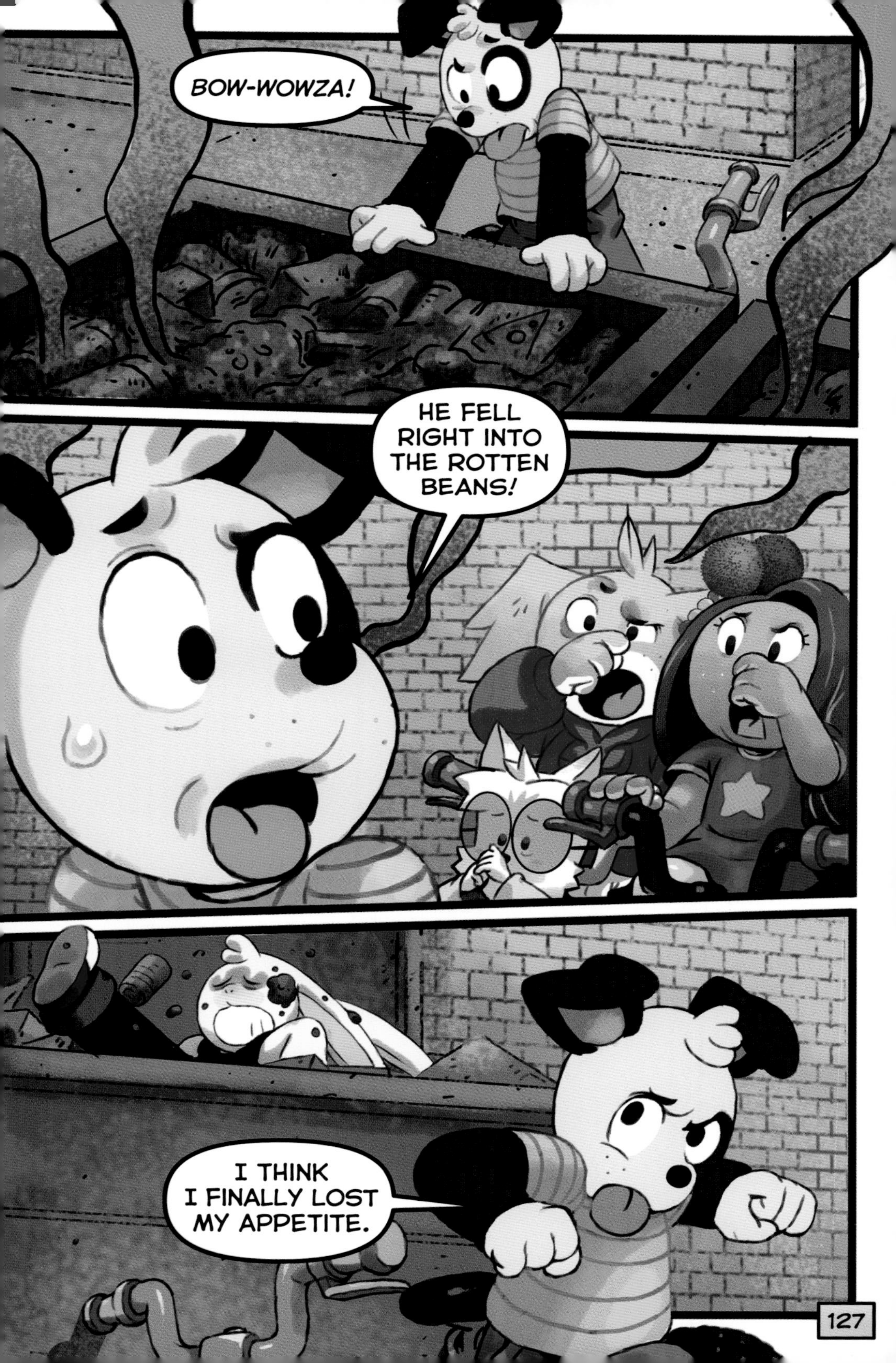
BOW-WOWZA!
HE FELL RIGHT INTO THE ROTTEN BEANS!
I THINK I FINALLY LOST MY APPETITE.

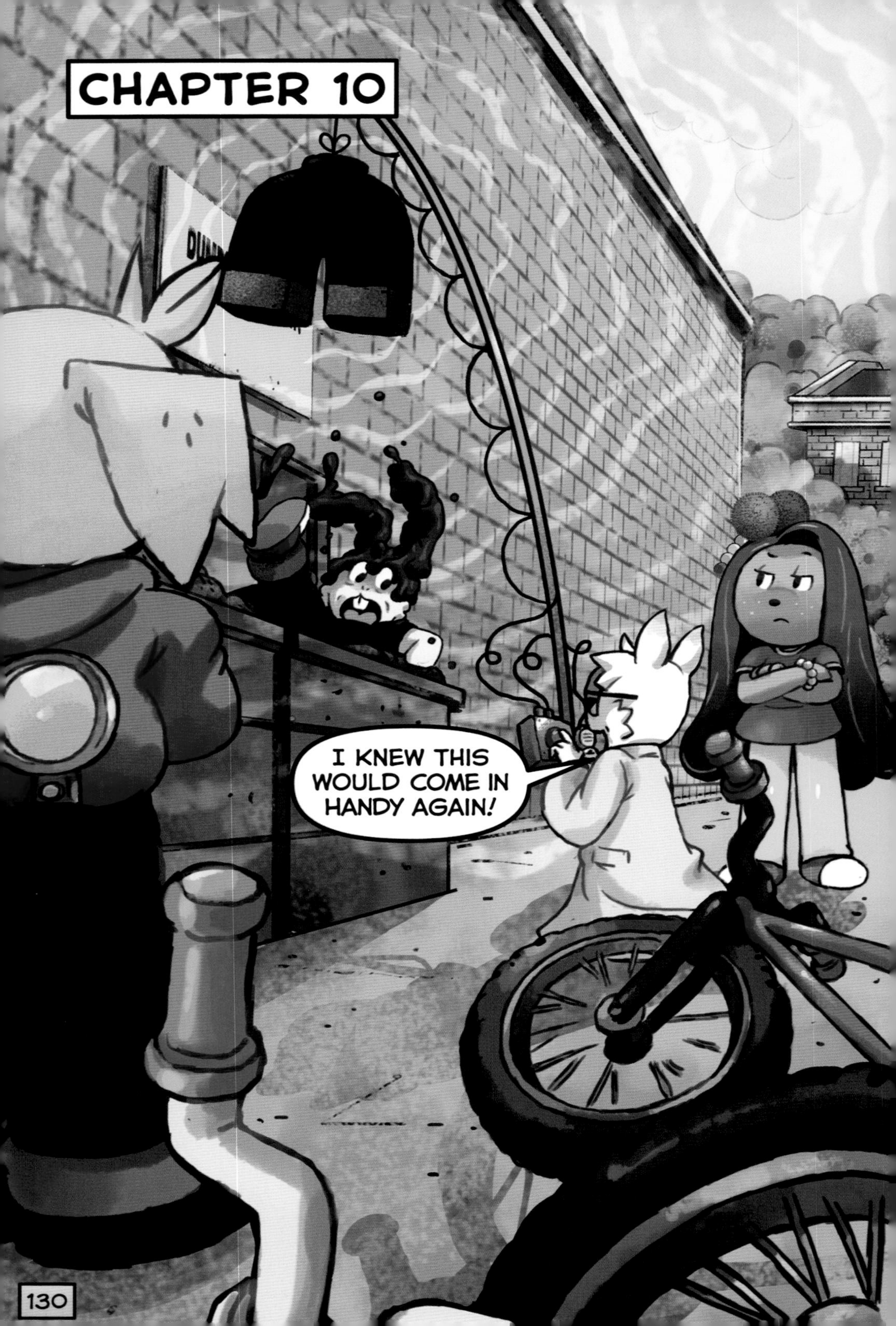
CHAPTER 10
I KNEW THIS WOULD COME IN HANDY AGAIN!

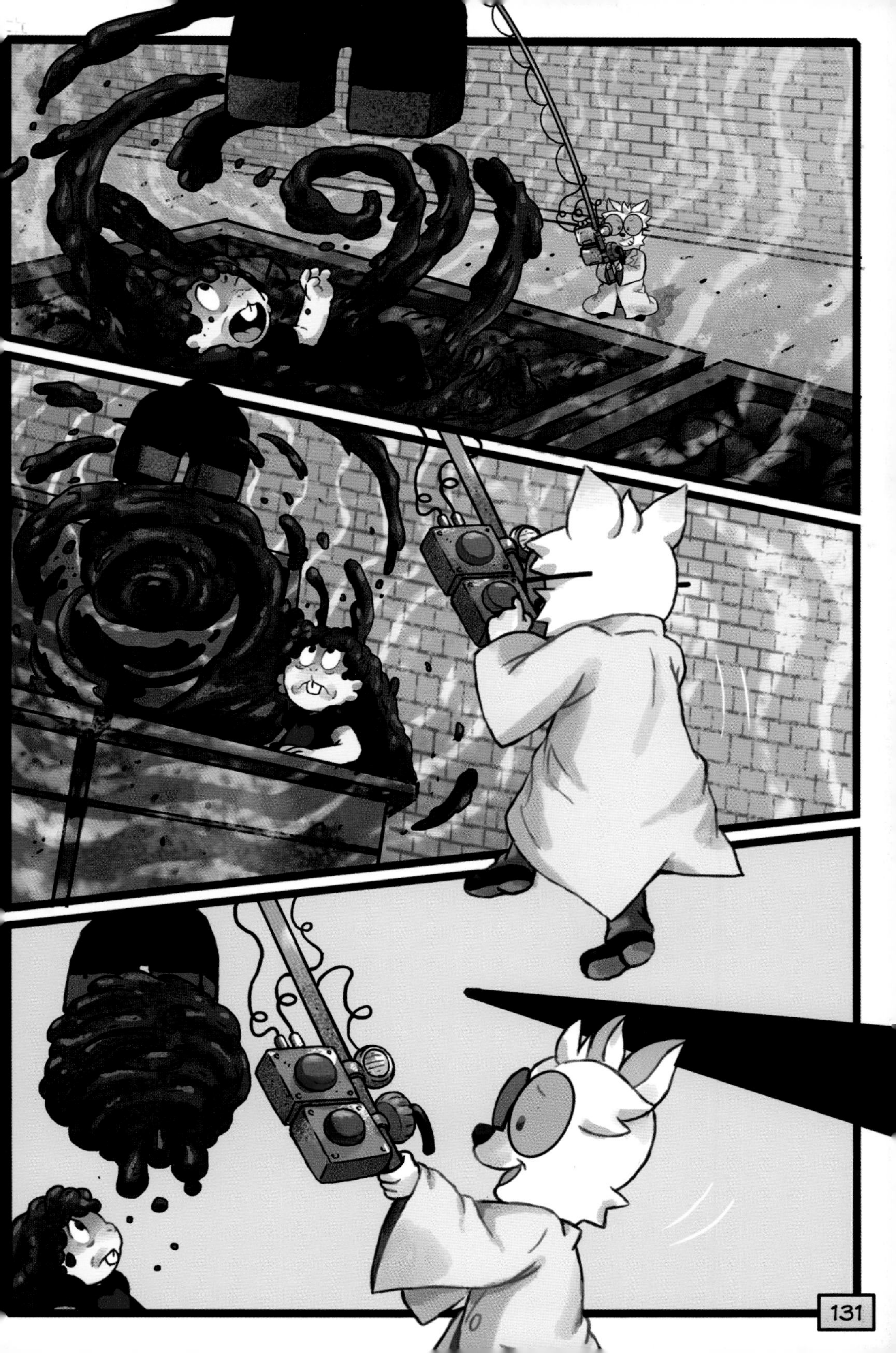

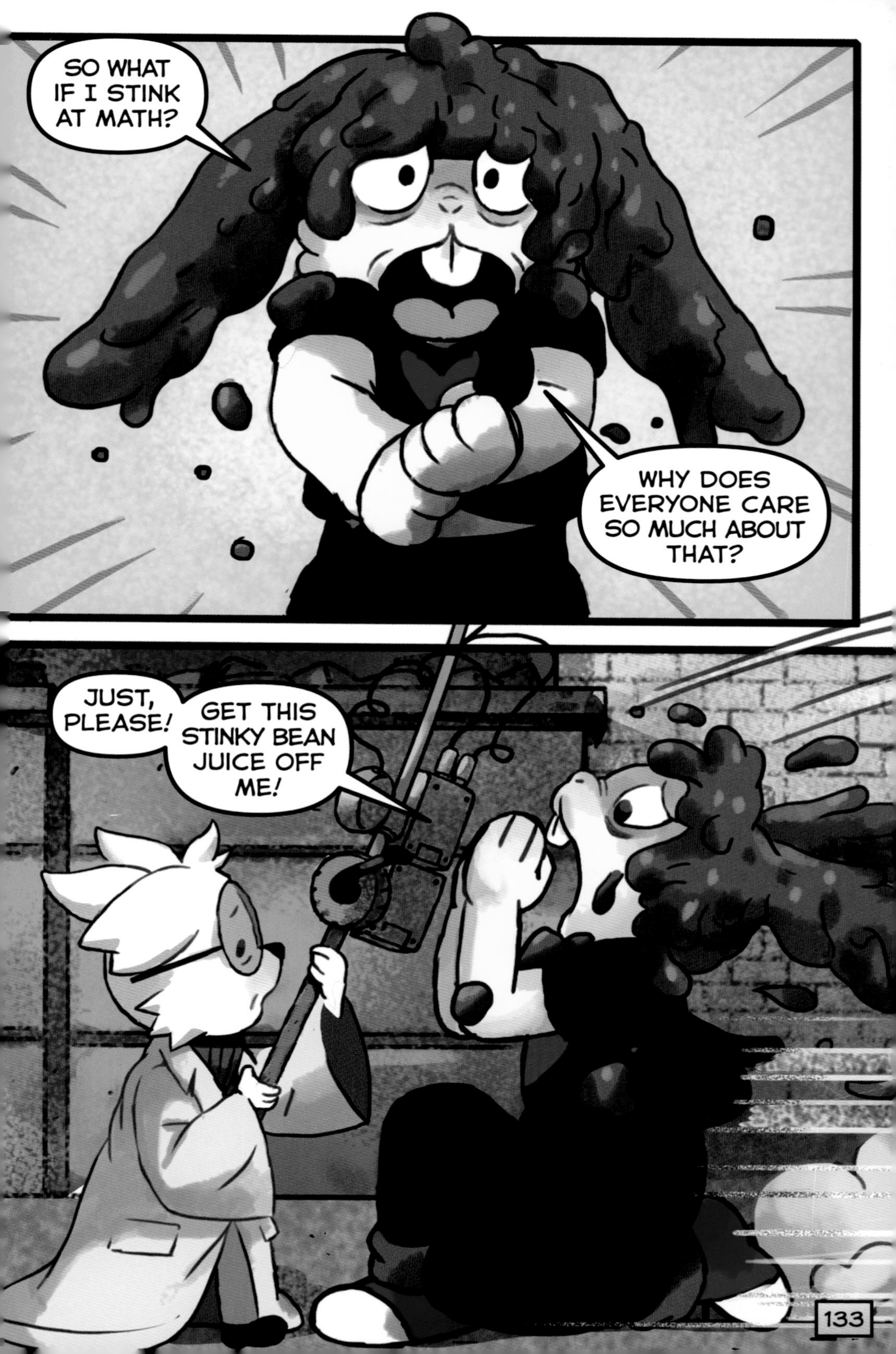

SO WHAT IF I STINK AT MATH?
WHY DOES EVERYONE CARE SO MUCH ABOUT THAT?
JUST, PLEASE!
GET THIS STINKY BEAN JUICE OFF ME!

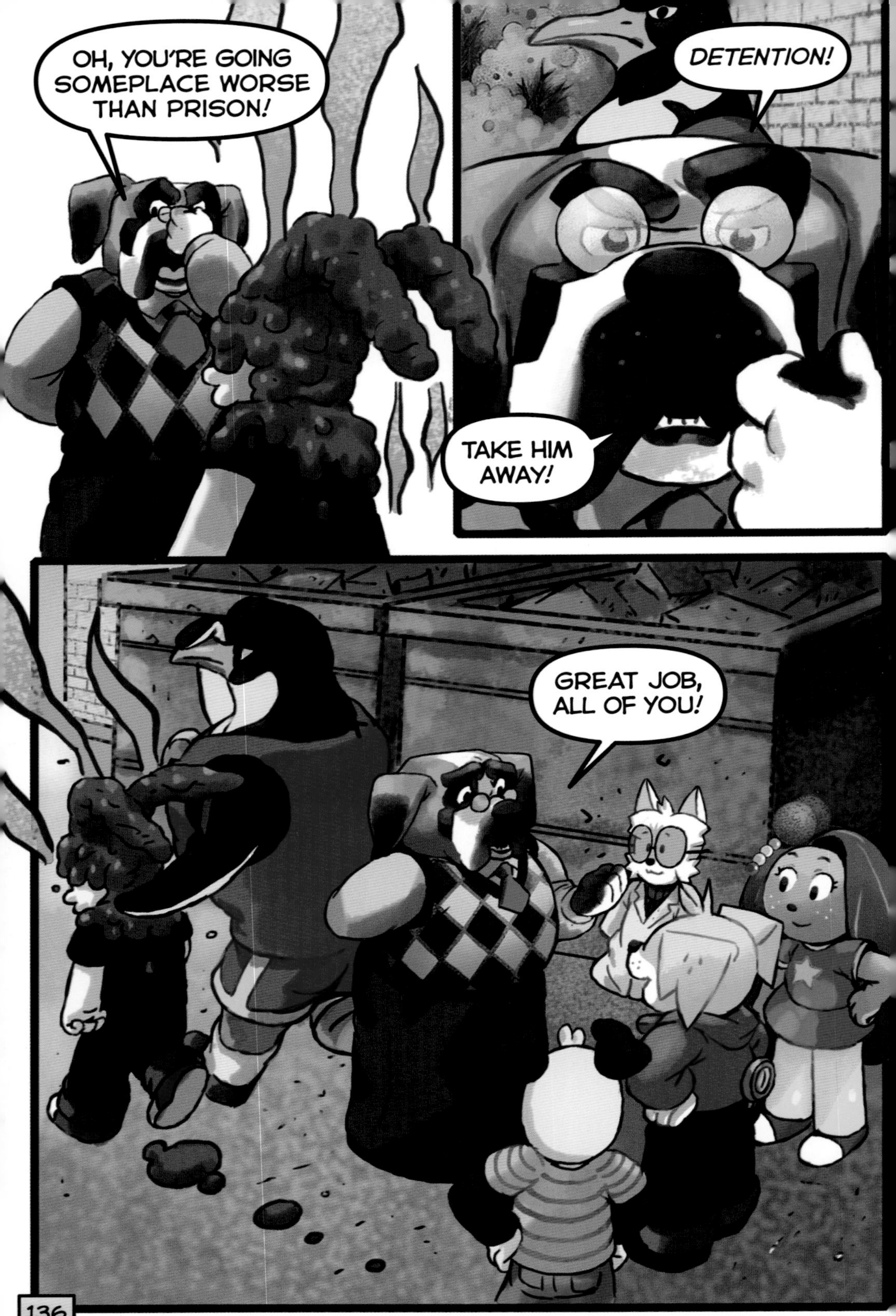
OH, YOU'RE GOING SOMEPLACE WORSE THAN PRISON!
DETENTION!
TAKE HIM AWAY!
GREAT JOB, ALL OF YOU!

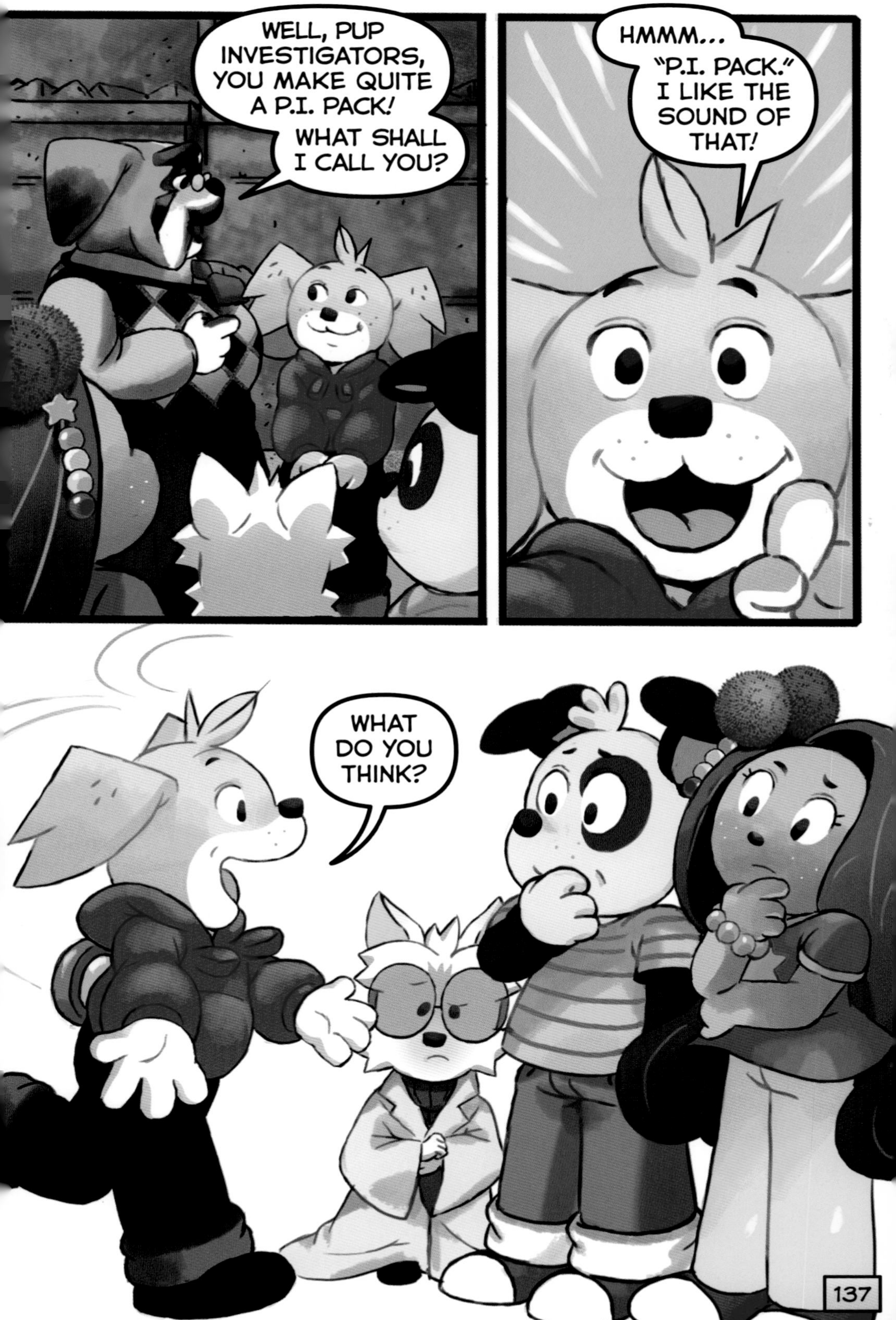
WELL, PUP INVESTIGATORS, YOU MAKE QUITE A P.I. PACK!
WHAT SHALL I CALL YOU?
HMMM...
"P.I. PACK." I LIKE THE SOUND OF THAT!
WHAT DO YOU THINK?

A NEW CASE AWAITS IN THE NEXT INSTALLMENT OF

Graphic Novel
PUP DETECTIVES
FEATURING...
THE TIGER'S EYE
WESTIE BARKER
ZIGGY FLUFFENSTUFF
MATTY MEOW
PAWSTON ELEMENTARY • P.I. Pack • #002
2

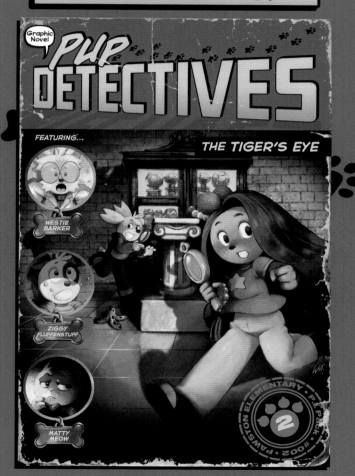

TURN THE PAGE FOR A SNEAK PEEK...

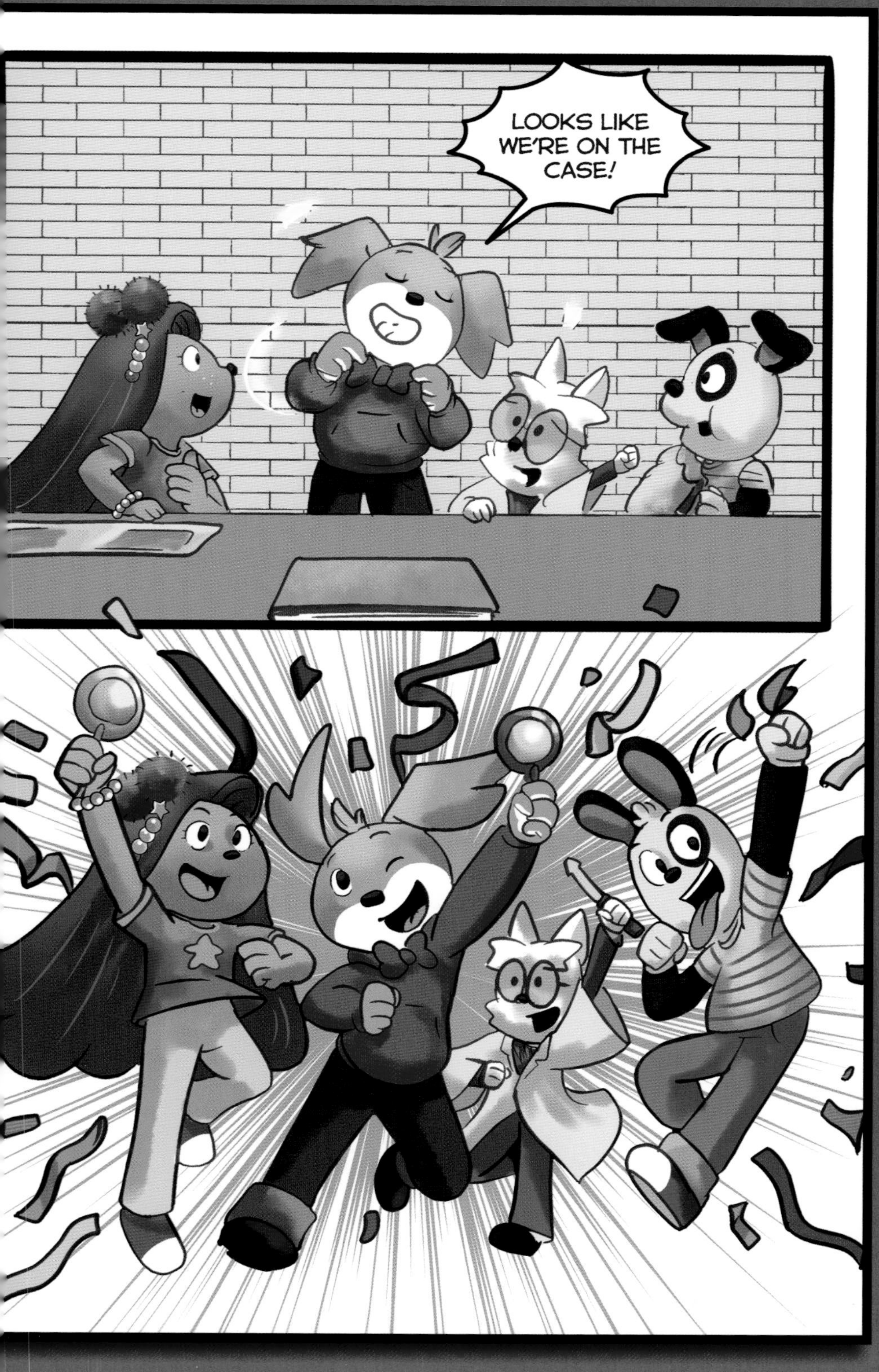
LOOKS LIKE WE'RE ON THE CASE!